lump

lump

a novel

nathan whitlock

RARE MACHINES

Publisher: Kwame Scott Fraser | Acquiring editor: Russell Smith
Cover designer: Laura Boyle
Cover image: Thomas Vogel

Library and Archives Canada Cataloguing in Publication

Title: Lump : a novel / Nathan Whitlock.
Names: Whitlock, Nathan, author.
Identifiers: Canadiana (print) 2022048581X | Canadiana (ebook) 20220485836 | ISBN
    9781459751286 (softcover) | ISBN 9781459751293 (PDF) | ISBN 9781459751309 (EPUB)
Subjects: LCGFT: Novels.
Classification: LCC PS8645.H566 L86 2023 | DDC C813/.6—dc23

We acknowledge the support of the Canada Council for the Arts and the Ontario Arts Council for our publishing program. We also acknowledge the financial support of the Government of Ontario, through the Ontario Book Publishing Tax Credit and Ontario Creates, and the Government of Canada.

Printed and bound in Canada.

Rare Machines, an imprint of Dundurn Press
1382 Queen Street East
Toronto, Ontario, Canada M4L 1C9
dundurn.com, @dundurnpress ✗ f ⊚

For Meaghan

A woman like that is not ashamed to die.
I have been her kind.

— Anne Sexton, "Her Kind"

You're doing your best and
it is absolutely and completely
good enough.

— Dr. Brianne Grogan, "Guided Meditation
for Pelvic Floor Relaxation"

CAT IS FINALLY HOME FROM A MORNING SPENT judging other moms at the park and being judged in return. The kids are no help at the front door, leaving her to drag the stroller up the steps to the porch, where she dodges a fallen Spider-Man and two clean diapers. She shoulders her way into the darkness of the house, hungry for a shower, horny for a nap. When she woke up that morning — summoned by the desperate cries of little Silas, loaded with pee but afraid to cross the hallway to the bathroom on his own — she wanted nothing more than to get everyone outside. Not just her own children, but every child on the street. Adults, too. She wanted to lead the whole neighbourhood out into fresh air and sunshine and over to the park. *Outside! Outside!* Now that she's back, she can't get inside quick enough.

Right away she can tell Donovan is not around. Her husband's presence changes the composition of the air; his skin throws off pheromones that make her bristle or swoon, depending on where things stand between them. There were times, early on, when all she wanted to do was fuck. Later, all she wanted was to fight. She's too tired for either now.

She sends him a text: *home all good*

No answer.

It's hot. Her favourite water bottle is gone, left behind in the park. With each outing, she and the kids leave debris in their wake. All families do; the playground fences display forgotten hats, sunglasses, swim trunks, and shoes. Even when she sees a tiny pair of forgotten underwear, with Superman punching his way through the crotch, Cat understands. It's difficult enough to herd an entire group of little people around unharmed, to stop them from falling backward off the steps or getting hit by careless drivers. You can only do so much.

Off come her Blundstone boots, on go the laceless runners she wears around the house, the ones covered with squiggles like thick veins where Silas went after them with a magic marker. Isabelle did the same thing to a pair of Cat's shoes when she was little, though her squiggles were much more careful and deliberate, the colours more varied. She'd been trying to make rainbows, which at the time she believed had the power to induce happiness in anyone who saw one. Isabelle wanted other people to see the shoes and be happy. Cat kept those rainbow shoes long enough for her daughter to be embarrassed by what she'd done. *Why do you still wear those?* Because they'd been drawn on by her little girl, her first-born. Because it is the imperative of all parents to revere creativity in their children. Because they're *art* now.

She pairs up a dozen small shoes scattered across the hall-way floor. The Velcro flaps on one pair hang loose — at three and a half, Silas is hard on shoes. Like something from a myth: The Boy Who Will Not Stop Running, going around the world in a day to bring back fresh olives from Egypt, fresh dates from Turkey, fresh iPhones from China. His sister was not so hard on shoes at that age. Each pair lasted until her wonderful little feet pushed past their borders. Now she wears only scaled-down versions of Converse All Stars. Black, and kept in near-perfect condition. Not a scuff.

The new *New Yorker* has come. On the cover feral cats wait in line for a food truck. She puzzles over the illustration for a while, thinking she has seen it before. There is a flyer from a real estate agent, offering to find buyers for their home. She often checks what houses on their street are being sold for, and is both embarrassed and proud at the results. She tells Donovan, but he doesn't care and doesn't understand why she pays at-tention. He tells her she sounds like her father when she does that. Ron, who spent his childhood in rented home after rented home, likes to brag that his house in Peterborough, the one Cat and her sister grew up in, is worth at least five times what he paid for it back in early '80s. Maybe six times. He made this exact same boast when he spoke at Cat and Donovan's wed-ding, though it was worth only three times as much back then.

Dropping her keys in the hallway drawer among all the foreign coins and expired membership cards, Cat finds a half-eaten Fig Newton, hard as a stone and chomped like a surf-board after a shark attack, every tooth mark visible.

· · ·

Isabelle is sitting on the floor of the living room, reading. It's a Professional Development day, which means all her teachers are busy developing professionally, though Cat never sees a change in their approach. Isabelle resents the break in routine and the fact that she has to wait out an extended weekend before she can once again be out of the house and away from her family.

"Why don't you call someone?" Cat asks her. "You can have a friend over."

"They're all *away*."

"Every single one of them?"

"Yes."

"That's an amazing coincidence."

Isabelle shrugs, not willing to admit she doesn't know what *coincidence* means.

"Why didn't you want to play with anyone at the park?"

"There wasn't anybody I know."

"That's not true, that DeeDee girl was here. You've played with her before. And that girl with the red hair."

"Spirit."

"Right. *Spirit*." So many kids with names more suited to horses.

"I don't *like* Spirit."

"What's wrong with Spirit now?"

Isabelle winces. "Spirit thinks she's an *actor*. She wants to be in charge of everything and tell everyone what to do."

"An actor? She's been in, like, *one* commercial. And that was years ago."

Isabelle looks up with the sudden hope that her mother might violate parental norms by trashing one of her classmates, but Cat catches herself. "That's still pretty cool, though," she says.

Disappointed, Isabelle goes back to her book. On the cover a young girl in a brown tunic holds a sword that glows red. Isabelle has explained the story to her mother in exhaustive detail — it's the third or fourth book of a series, so there are acres of plot to catch up on. Cat knows, for example, that the glow of the sword is connected somehow to the purity of the girl's heart. Red sword, good; blue sword, bad. No glow at all means you are in the zone of Nothing, a cross between a zombie and a ghost, with no soul. The whole thing sounds ridiculous in the usual preteen novel way, but it makes Cat wish there was such an indisputable way to demonstrate her own virtue. Her ruby-red glow of goodness would be obvious to others, and she could finally stop working so hard to prove that it's there.

Silas and his little cousin Jessica are wrestling on the couch. Silas climbs up the couch and flexes his arms like a bodybuilder, then dives face-first into the cushions, bouncing his cousin to the floor. The boy is all instinct. Isabelle asked questions from the moment she could speak; existence stymied her. Silas is troubled by nothing for very long. He accepts it all and plows forward.

"You're my perfect baby," Cat tells him when getting him out of the bath or getting him dressed. "You're my perfect Silas baby."

One time when she said it, he grabbed at her fingers and said, "I *not* perfeck."

His voice was calm and patient; he wanted her to understand.

When she told Donovan what Silas said, he immediately pulled out his phone to share the moment online. She watched him standing there, his thumbs poised, trying to come up with the exact right hashtag.

She checked later. He went with *#DadLife*.

Baby Jessica is her sister Claudia's little girl. She comes with bags of necessary things, jars and bottles and folded towels and extra outfits and comforters and diapers with pale green trees on the front. Cat watches her niece a couple of times a month, whenever her sister needs a break — a *mental health day*. But it's the girl who needs the break. Baby Jessica, not quite two years old, is already in swimming, Song Circle, storytime at the library, baby yoga, and something called Creative Play, which happens in the large, open front room of a hippie mom in Claudia's neighbourhood and involves parents lying on their backs with eyes closed while their babies climb over them like little dogs.

When Isabelle was a baby, Cat tried to do those kinds of things, too. She signed up for anything that looked enriching, that got her out of the house. Anything with the word *creative* in the name. She never lasted long. She couldn't maintain the smiling, earnest facial expression that was required. She didn't have access to the Encouraging Voice, which they were always being urged to use. She couldn't pretend that all she ever wanted to do was sit on the carpet with her baby and sing about wheels on the bus or robins in the rain, or that she didn't want desperately to be back at her job, surrounded by adults. The song that really bothered her was the one about Bingo, the dog with the disappearing name. The blank hiccup that gets bigger with each passing verse. You keep singing until the poor dog is entirely gone, clapped right out of existence. Cat preferred the one about monkeys jumping on the bed, and their mother who gets repeatedly scolded by the doctor.

"We try to avoid that one," she was told. It reinforces the idea that mothers must defer to medical authority, that they don't have the inherent wisdom to solve such a situation on their own. It's condescending and paternalistic.

Baby Jessica doesn't nap, which Cat finds sinister. Claudia says her wonderful baby started sleeping through the night as soon as she was weaned off the boob — though she says *breast*, not *boob*, believing they all ought to be past the point when anything to do with their bodies can be seen as shameful.

"I'm not *ashamed*," Cat tells her.

"Yes, you are," Claudia insists. "If you have to use all these cutesy nicknames, that's what that means. Does Silas still say *peepee* instead of *penis*?"

Yes. And Isabelle used to refer to her vagina as her *whizzo*, her own invention.

Baby Jessica says *'gina* the same way Donald Trump says *China*: hard and aggressive on the first syllable. Loud and proud. *This my 'gina.*

Cat calls Baby Jessica *The Only Baby Ever*. The only baby ever to take a step. The only baby ever to hug another child. For the baby's first Christmas, Claudia sent out a custom-made card with Jessica's globular face on the front, wreathed in bright gold. A singular cherub, the infant queen of the angels. The previous year's card was an ultrasound image of Baby Jessica inside the womb, Photoshopped to look like she was inside Santa's sack. The best gift of all.

"She knows we have two of our own, right?" Donovan asked Cat.

"Baby Jessica is of a different order," Cat told him. "She's The Only Baby Ever."

"Isabelle or Silas will hear you say that and repeat it in front of your sister."

"She'd take it as a compliment."

• • •

Cat checks her phone. A job search site she signed up for in a moment of panic has sent her its weekly roundup of employment opportunities she is under- or overqualified for. Her mother has sent her a link to a story about the incidence of West Nile virus in southern Ontario, and another about plants that naturally repel mosquitoes. Cat has told her repeatedly that mosquitoes are not a problem in Toronto the way they are in Peterborough — the air is too dirty, the blood all wrong.

An email reminder that she booked a spot in a CycleFit class flies in like a bird. Just thinking about it makes her tired, but she worries how another no-show will appear to the other women in the class, women who see their schedules and routines as divine law, who talk about their children and their spouses (male and female) like they are partners in a small, successful firm. Cat gets home from those classes exhausted from trying to not look frivolous. If, at the end of a session, she jokes that her ideal cool-down exercise involves lifting something in a glass with a long stem, her fellow cyclists-to-nowhere will move in on her.

Drinking alcohol can be so damaging after a workout, they tell her. If she wants, they can send her a list of restorative teas.

"Thank you!" she tells them, sweating, red as raw beef.

She fishes an extra-strength Tylenol out of the bottle in her bag, her third of the day — the bottle says four, max, so she still has some room left. She swallows the pill, washing it down with the chunky remains of a green smoothie she made for herself that morning. For months now she has been swallowing Tylenol like vitamin C. She refuses to Google the dangers of taking too much over too long a stretch of time, knowing that whatever information she finds will either be confusing or alarming. There is already enough to worry about. She has lost sleep over the appearance of new moles on her arms and back, her stomach is always upset, she is always tired, and the little lump on her right boob has gone from being a joke to a worry and back again so many times, she isn't even sure where it stands now — a joke they worry about, or a worry they joke about, like the kids?

There are new pains, too. Strange, sudden bolts of hard lightning that shoot up her spine and down her arms. There is a deep, lingering pain in her lower back, like someone drugged her in her sleep and inserted something there as a sick joke, a quarter or a bolt or a rusty bottle cap. She kneads at it with her fingers, trying to dissolve the pain. When she stretches her arms high above her head, she has to catch her breath, as if that movement puts a fold in her lungs.

Claudia finally convinced her to tell her doctor about the lump by bringing up the story of a woman from their old neighbourhood who, at the age of thirty-five and with a newborn baby, was found to be riddled with tumours and was dead within a year. Claudia barely knew the dead woman — she found out from something posted on Facebook — but speaks of her in a way that suggests the loss of a spiritual twin.

In her bag, next to the Tylenol bottle, is a slim box containing three unopened pregnancy tests, tiny magic wands with the power to see inside her, to detect new life. Her period is overdue by a few weeks. There is a question mark in her abdomen, a hollow space. All she has to do is pee on one of the little wands and the mystery is solved. But she fears this pee-magic. Twice already she has brought the tests with her into the bathroom and sat on the toilet, holding the box in her hand, willing herself to unseal the package.

She shifts around the contents of her bag to hide the box.

Telling her doctor about the lump sparked a series of tests Cat is certain will answer none of her questions. The problem, she's convinced, is *her* — her character, her existence — not any foreign or invading ailment. She is fundamentally wrong, lumpy to the core.

She texts Donovan again: *hot out*. This time, he replies right away with a picture of a fat, smiling sun sitting under an umbrella with something cold in its hand.

This means *Just Chillin'!*

She wonders where he is *just chillin'*, exactly. For years Donovan was the communications manager for a company that bought up and developed big chunks of unloved property around the city, turning scrapyards and empty lots and old factories into cold stacks of gleaming condos. Donovan helped shape the messages that transformed fat nests of new condo towers into visions of renewal, community-building, and organic growth, which soothed the rich hippies and dog walkers who inevitably try to prevent ground from being broken on any such project. He was good at it, and he got paid enough that they never had to live near any of the buildings his company built.

And then, out of nowhere, Donovan got laid off. A shock. But he said it was better that way. Now he could finally chart his *own* course, make some *real* money.

"Since when have you wanted to go out on your own?"

He dismissed the question. She'd gone freelance after Isabelle was born, after all. Now it was *his* turn to be set free.

He rented an office in a building on Dundas West, above a street-level space that had a new business in it almost every time Cat passed by. For a while it was a store that sold high-end party decorations — special mylar balloons and such. Then a pop-up gallery full of photographs of broken teeth. The last time she looked, it was a combination deli and café, with two small tables and stacks of blond cheese sweating behind glass.

Cat worried about the financial drain the office represented, but Donovan said there was no other option. Cat's "office" was the spare bedroom on the second floor, which was fine for what *she* did, he told her — she could throw together her websites from the back seat of the car if she had to. He needed more room.

"You haven't worked in an office in a while," he said. "So you're used to being home. Plus, I can't exactly meet with clients here. Not with kids' shit all over the place."

It would pay for itself, he assured her.

"We at least have to stop having Lena come," she said. Lena, who comes once a week to clean the house, was a gift from Donovan's parents, who paid her wages for the first few months after Silas was born. After they saw how Cat was struggling to keep up.

"Lena is fine. We'll be fine."

The clients did not appear. A few months later, the office was gone, taking most of Donovan's severance package with it.

Without a steady second income, health benefits, and the rest, and with Cat's income dependent on an irregular flow of freelance work, they are living in the shadow of a giant boulder balanced on a small stone at the top of a steep hill. One strong gust of wind and it might tip over and start to roll, crushing everything in its path. Every time the boulder creaks and shifts, Cat puts her palm against its cold skin to steady it. *Easy now. Stay. Please.*

Her phone chirps in her hand. A text from Claudia: *Hows baby J?*

Cat writes back: *thought you had her.*

She deletes this and starts over.

its fucking hot come get her now

She deletes this, too.

Cat knows that her sister has likely spent the past few hours wandering the aisles of some antique market, her brow in a thick furrow above her designer frames, as if she were a professional collector or curator, as opposed to someone who likes to highlight the clean, contemporary feel of her home by dotting it with impractical knick-knacks from the past.

Doing great everybody happy and tired.

She sends that one.

For lunch Cat makes the kids whole wheat wraps full of cream cheese and cucumber, with raisins and thin spears of carrot on the side. Baby Jessica gets yogourt and a wedge of pear with most of the skin cut away. She brings the unbreakable plates into the living room and sets one near each child, then waits like a zookeeper to see if they will notice. None of the kids thank her — she could slip out the door and run off without them saying anything. Not that she'd get very far. The sticky strands of maternal guilt and duty would twang and throw her back into the house, ready again to serve. Donovan clipped the umbilical cords on both of their children like a mayor cutting a ribbon, but she is still tied behind them. Had the drugs and the doctors allowed, she would've taken the little seafood clippers out of his hands and hacked away at the cords herself.

Before Cat became a mother, every day was like fancy Japanese paper that could be folded however she wanted. She could make a swan of her day, or a scorpion. It is miraculous, the idea that she spent decades living only for herself. How had she not awoken each morning laughing out loud at how easy it all was? Now, each hour is like a hard lump of dough that refuses to rise and has to be gnawed through and swallowed dry. She often tells herself: *I will miss this*, but is never convinced. She knows mothers of teenagers and grown-up children — her own mother included — who say they miss the park days, the sandbox days, the endless swing days, the snack-and-nap days.

"It's so *easy* when they're that small," they say.

Liars. Not *one* of them would trade places with her now. Always, out of the corner of her eye, Cat can see the swift-moving shadow of a hawk, the hawk that will swim down through the air and take her children up in its talons the instant she looks away. She knows of a little girl who, left alone for a minute, grabbed hold of the cord of a boiling electric kettle and pulled the whole thing down on herself in a furious, steaming cascade. She sees the girl sometimes at the pool, her skin red and pebbled as if erupting with shame — her mother's shame — as she floats in cool water.

She has to remind herself to be grateful that her kids are relatively easy to be around. Silas's friends from daycare are dirty and greedy. When they come over, they point at the TV and demand she turn it on. When they get hungry, they slap the fridge door like it's the flank of a stud horse, their eyes angry and impatient. *Give. Now. Bitch.*

She takes a moment to breathe deeply, the way every podcast and YouTube video on stress and relaxation tells her to do. Her thoughts fall in heavy clumps. The mortgage is due in a week. Donovan's parents helped them out the past two months, over Cat's objections. She will need to scare up new clients, which means she needs new clothes, job-type clothes. Especially bras — she has gotten out of the habit of providing her breasts with coverage and support. No one hires old-lady web designers who have exited the world of sex. Her hair needs attention from a professional. On her own she can manage only a shapeless bob that adds five dry years to her face. In a few months, she'll be thirty-nine years old. In the park she had to squint to read the empowering words about midwives on one mom's T-shirt. Age has finally found her. It is creeping in, breathing on her. She doesn't want a birthday party, especially not one with her sister, her brother-in-law, and a handful of friends (who are mostly Donovan's friends) getting day-drunk and making jokes about menopause.

"When is Dad home?" Isabelle asks.

"The usual time. Why?"

Her daughter doesn't reply, but Cat knows the answer. Mom is no fun. Mom can only offer protection and nourishment and order. Dad offers unpredictability and surprise. He's like another kid, lazy and silly and fun-seeking. Dad gets it.

Must be nice.

They should ask their father what he does, what his job is, exactly. They should ask why he sometimes forgets to shave or change his shirt for days at a time. They should ask why he comes home so tired that he sleeps through dinner on the couch.

They should ask why Mom hates Dad so much right now, why she is so angry all the time.

She wishes she could tell someone the whole stupid story.

The whole stupid story:

One fine day in mid-December, Donovan came home late and would not talk to her, would not even say hello to the kids. He went straight to bed. She found him asleep in his clothes on top of the blankets. He stank like cigarettes, which was unusual. He only smokes when he is stressed or drinking or both. The next day, everything was back to normal. *Some weird flu bug*, he said. He even apologized.

For a while there was nothing. He got up early each morning as usual, left the house, and was gone all day. When he came back in the evening, he said little about work beyond a few vague mumbles. Once in a while he would stay home, not leaving the bedroom until Cat got back from dropping the kids off. He said he was owed some lieu days — he had it all worked out with his boss.

But something had changed. He got fatter. He was sweating more. There was always a smell about him at night, booze and toothpaste. On evenings when he came home late and a little wobbly, he told her there was a birthday party for one of his co-workers, or they all went out to celebrate a new project.

He was sharp with her, too. He had no patience for anything, especially for questions about why he had no patience.

"I don't go after *you* when you're on the rag."

She laughed. "Don't say *on the rag*."

"Am I in trouble for everything I *say* now? I'm a fucking adult, Cat."

That went on for almost two months. Then she saw the credit card bills, the statements from their shared bank account. She brought it all into their bedroom, where he was lying on his back, looking at his phone. It was late, the kids were asleep. When she asked him about the bills and the account statements, he put down his phone and told her everything. He had no job. He'd been pretending the whole time. Every day he went to a coffee shop downtown, far from the house, to read magazines and use the free Wi-Fi. He'd been doing that for weeks and weeks.

"How ..." she began.

"What do you mean *how*?"

She dug around for the words.

"How did this even happen?"

He told her that back in December he'd been called into the conference room as soon as he got to the office. At one end of the long table was his manager and the head of human resources with papers and folders in front of them. Donovan said he asked, as a joke, if he were being fired. Neither of them laughed, and that's when he knew. He left the office less than fifteen minutes later, holding a letter that outlined the details of his severance package and instructed him not to discuss the terms of his departure with anyone other than his wife.

He did them one better: he didn't tell *her*, either.

Lying there on the bed, he laughed at his own joke. In an instant, all of the testiness and anger of the past couple of months was gone. It was if he were confessing to a bad hangover.

After leaving the office that day, he went straight to a bar and drank bourbon after bourbon, followed by beer after beer, then a few shots of something. He woke up the next day with his right arm hurting, and there was a scrape on the back of his hand.

Cat was in shock, only able to take in small parts of his story. Their lives had utterly changed, had been changed for months, and she'd had no idea. She kept waiting for him to say something more, to provide some other vital piece of information about what had happened that would explain why he had deceived her. He could've said anything: that he was scared, that he was certain the company would reconsider, that he'd been targeted for assassination. Anything would make more sense than that he'd simply decided to lie to her.

"Do your parents know?" Cat asked.

He looked puzzled. "Why would I tell them, of all people?"

"That's not an answer."

"No, they don't know. And don't tell them. Let *me* tell them."

She asked to see the letter, the one he'd been given on the day he got fired. It was still in his laptop bag — he hadn't bothered to hide it. It took him a minute even to remember that it was there, it meant so little to him. He gave it to her, then lay back on the bed and picked up his phone, as if the conversation had run its course.

The letter didn't tell her anything. It was signed by his manager, whom they'd had over for dinner and drinks a few times along with her partner, a tall woman who did photography.

Cat did not recognize anything of that woman in the formal language she found in the letter.

"Oh, there is another thing," he said, not looking up from his phone. "This is hilarious: they gave me all this information about counselling. Like, if I was feeling depressed or suicidal. They gave me a brochure, but I lost it. I was *so* tempted to say I was coming back with a loaded rifle. I guess you can't joke about that kind of thing anymore."

After that Cat spent a few nights sleeping in the back room that is also her office, more out of the belief that she ought to make *some* kind of show of resistance than out of genuine anger. When she realized that Donovan was not planning to protest this arrangement, she moved back into their shared room. She realized only much later that at no point did Donovan offer anything resembling an apology.

Donovan keeps telling her not to worry about money. If things get really bad, his parents will help them out. Cat sometimes wonders if it would be better to let the boulder roll and flatten them. The resulting destruction would at least be *theirs*.

Claudia comes into the house, eyes wide, eager to find her baby. She has on dark pants that end just below the knee and a white blouse that flows around her like a sail. The upper part of her face is hidden behind sunglasses. She almost falls over when she sees the little ones together on the couch, absorbed by a cartoon about dinosaurs taking dance lessons around the world.

"*Ohmygodhowadorable!*" she cries. All one word.

She moves in on her baby girl and blesses her with a kiss. Jessica's chubby face floats in the black pools of her mother's sunglasses.

"What did *you* do today?" Claudia asks.

Cat knows the question is for her. She is being asked for a debriefing — Claudia is particular about the kinds of situations her baby is exposed to. Everything her little girl does needs to be full of new sights and sounds and new experiences, everything needs to be rich with learning. Having the TV on in the afternoon is a worrying sign.

Cat gives her a rundown of their day together, careful to emphasize the opportunities for creativity and personal growth inherent in each activity.

"She went down a big slide at the park. And we watched people plant baby trees. It was very exciting."

"*Very* exciting," Claudia repeats.

Cat notes how immaculate her sister's hair looks today, the whole thing a perfect foam of expert blond dye and professional highlights. Cat and her mother have the same hair: mousy brown, and cut in a way that requires the least maintenance. A thoughtless flop of hair. Claudia, meanwhile, has been dying her hair straw-yellow and getting it professionally cut since she got her first job as a teenager.

The kids are content to keep watching their show — the dinosaurs are now stamping their heavy feet to the sound of bagpipes — so Cat and Claudia move into the kitchen. Claudia, removing her sunglasses, asks if Donovan is around. As if he might be hiding behind the coffee mugs or in the glass containers filled with dry pasta.

"I think he has a bunch of meetings."

Cat can't tell if her sister believes this. She was worried at first, after Donovan stopped working, that her sister would treat them like welfare cases. Instead, Claudia shows new respect for her brother-in-law. She has always loved that he is a rich kid and an only child. Now that he is jobless, she sees him as a kind of outlaw. She practically flirts with him when he's around.

"You want any coffee? Or water? There's some wine here."

"Water is fine. Oh, I have this for you."

From her oversize canvas bag, Claudia brings out a small cardboard box, tied with a red ribbon. Inside is a tiny bell attached to a brass arm to mount it on a wall. Claudia can't say enough about the bell: how adorable it is, how she fell in love with it as soon as she spotted it, how she would've bought it for herself, but decided it was the perfect gift for her sister.

"A bell," Cat says, trying to process the meaning of the object.

"Do you love it? Isn't it gorgeous?"

A small bell does not fill any obvious gap in her life, but Cat says she loves it, anyway. Its chime is pretty — not harsh and high, but surprisingly low and mellow, as if the tiny clapper is made of fresh butter. She is shocked by the price listed on the sticker inside.

"You're supposed to put it near the front door. For good luck."

"I need *that*."

Claudia decides she wouldn't mind a glass of white wine, after all. Cat pours herself one, too, though she isn't sure how it might mix with all the Tylenol in her system. Claudia sips at hers, then sits down at the kitchen table. She puts her hands in her hair to signal distress, though is careful not to disturb it.

She puts two fingers to her forehead and closes her eyes. Cat knows this means there are *things to talk about.*

"Everything okay?"

"It's fine, I'm just tired. It's been a long day, I guess. A long *week.*"

Claudia prefers to be drawn out. Cat waits. Finally, Claudia tells her that she and Dale are in one of those relationship cul-de-sacs where neither partner is willing to budge and everything is a fight. He is mad at her for who-knows-what. Money stuff.

"I'm tired of hearing about it. We're not poor."

She is mad at *him* for refusing to use some of his vacation time to go to Cuba with her. Dale is a project manager for a company that does engineering jobs around the world, and has to do a lot of flying around to visit project sites. He hates running around airports and hotels on his time off. Flying somewhere exotic feels too much like work. He'd rather stay home and putter. Lately, he's become obsessed with adding water features to their yard.

"You were in California not long ago, weren't you?" Cat asks.

"That was for a *wedding*, Cat. And we were only there for three days. Not exactly a vacation." Claudia cheers up suddenly. "Did I tell you about dipping my feet in the ocean? I've made this pledge: I want to dip my feet into every ocean on the planet. I've done two now."

"Terry Fox did that," Cat says. "Isabelle did a project on him. He dipped his leg in the Atlantic before he started his run."

"Which leg? The real one or the fake one?"

Cat has to admit she doesn't know for sure.

"Oh, I want to *go* somewhere!" Claudia yells, grabbing at the air. "I'm so *sick* of Toronto. I'm so sick of running around and sweating. I want to be on a long, white beach where no-body speaks English."

"Jessica would enjoy that, I bet."

Claudia makes a sour face. "Oh God, Cat — we wouldn't drag her all that way. That would be a *nightmare*. We'd be stuck in the hotel room every night. I don't want us to go all that way just to sit and watch movies on my laptop."

"So how …?" Cat starts to ask, but she already knows their parents will watch precious Baby Jessica. Just as they do at least one weekend a month. Just as they did when Dale and Claudia went to California. It angers her to see how much free babysit-ting her sister extracts from their parents, who are too nice to say no. Ron spends his retired days happily planning new ex-tensions for their house that never get built. He wants to build his wife a sunroom for her plants. And he wants a room for himself where he can read spy novels and doze without being in the way. Sue-Ann, their mom, is retired from her accounting job, but still works the odd shift at the used clothing store run by the church that she and her husband attend infrequently.

"Have you asked Mom and Dad if they can do it? A week's a long time."

Claudia finishes her wine. "What else are they doing? They never go anywhere. It'd be a vacation for them, too, being at our place."

"You should still ask them."

Claudia closes her eyes and holds her hands up in surrender. Then she smiles, reaches over, and gives the new bell a quick shake. *Ding!* Almost immediately, Silas comes running in to the kitchen, as if summoned. They laugh at his eager expression.

. . .

Cat helps her sister bundle the baby up. Claudia insists on packing the baby bag exactly as she had it, minus the diapers that have given their lives in the line of duty.

"We should have you over for a barbecue," Claudia says. "Dale likes to show off his new meat smoker."

"Absolutely," Cat says.

Outside she takes a moment to breathe as her sister walks around the car. She had planned to tell her about the late period and the packet of tests in her bag. She wants someone to tell her she is crazy to even *suspect* that she is pregnant, and she can always count on Claudia to let her know that she is crazy.

The passenger-side window whirs down and Claudia leans over. "You didn't say anything about me driving."

Claudia has zero confidence behind the wheel. Cat was in the car with her once when her sister stopped dead, unbuckled her seatbelt, and got out, refusing to drive another inch. She couldn't take the stress, she said. Cat shouted at her to get back in. They were blocking traffic.

"I'm impressed. Good for you."

"I know, right? Dale said I needed to try again or I'll never do it. So, now I'm doing it."

Cat wiggles her fingers at Baby Jessica, who stares back impassively, as if the window is a two-way mirror through which she cannot be seen. She has a small stack of board books next to her. She selects one called *I Can Do Anything I Want!* Cat waves at the departing car, which blows through a stop sign at the end of the street.

Back inside Silas is grumpy. He missed his nap. He wants more TV. Isabelle says she hates the dancing dinosaur show, forcing Cat to find a consensus cartoon.

"*Woof Rescue*?" Cat asks.

"*Woof Rescue!*" Silas shouts.

Isabelle rolls her eyes but does not object. If tale after tale of daring rescues performed by remarkable talking puppies is the best thing on offer, she'll take it. They're at least better than the nature shows Cat used to insist on. Kids don't want Sir David Attenborough narrating a scene of nervous zebras crossing a river spiked with crocodiles; they want a cartoon zebra who walks on its hind legs and speaks with the voice of a famous comedian.

"No touching the remote," Cat says as the show's theme starts up.

The air is thick and soupy. The wine she drank has gone sour inside her. There are tiny ropes pulling her down. She tries to think if she has eaten anything that day, and can only come up with a smoothie and some cheese popcorn. She is sore all up her left side, and tries to stretch it out, but moving in any unnatural way makes the little navigational instruments in her head start to whirl and blink. She tells the kids to make room for her on the couch.

In the episode a short bald man with a thick, brown moustache gets stuck down the deepest shaft of a gold mine. He isn't completely bald, Cat notices; there are three thick lines across his scalp, as if drawn there with a Sharpie. A combover, the universal symbol for self-delusion. Cat sinks into the couch. She wants more Tylenol. She has no idea when her husband will be home. Or if he will come home at all. Maybe this is the day he doesn't.

The man in the mine is talking to himself, telling himself that his plan was a good one. He'd thought of everything. What went wrong? The man is scared. As he walks down one tunnel, jabbering in fear, he passes a fully intact dinosaur skeleton embedded in the rock wall. He doesn't even notice it. A little joke. This man, too, will be lost down there, will starve and die and be absorbed by the earth. His skeleton will become embedded in the walls.

"You are pathetic," she tells the man.

I know! I know! I'm a piece of shit!

"They should leave you down there to die. You should suffocate, you should die of hunger."

Yes! I'm a horrible waste! I'm nothing!

Isabelle says something, but Cat isn't listening. She is focused on this awful man. She wants him to stop his fearful pacing, to tear off his clothes and roll naked in the mud until he is scratched and filthy. She wants him to shit on the floor and smear himself with it. Smear the walls around him. She wants those heroic talking dogs to be disgusted by what they find.

"They ought to tear you apart and eat you."

Oh, please!

She closes her eyes for a moment.

When she opens them again, the man is gone, the mine is gone. The brave dogs are in the Arctic now, wearing doggie parkas with the Woof Rescue symbol on the back and trying to reach a baby seal trapped on the ice. Isabelle looks as though she is asleep. Silas is drinking in every second of the drama.

"Woof," Cat says, and can hear her voice coming from far away.

Neither of the kids notice that she has spoken. She tries to stand. The house tilts. She just needs a minute. It is hot, and she is tired. She wants her water bottle. It fit her hand like something carved in wood. She can picture exactly where she left it: on a bench near the swings, pointing at the sky. She wishes she could unzip her skin and take it off. Unzip herself, tits to toes, and let her muscles, organs, everything fall out into a baggy, bloody pile. Just vomit herself onto the floor and lie there for a few minutes.

Fatigue hits her like a dust cloud. She puts her hand out to stabilize herself and misses the wall. Silas, for whom the world is a cartoon, laughs to see her stumble and drop to the ground.

II

LYING IN THE BED HE AND CAT THEORETICALLY
share, Donovan tries to remember his dream. He was outside,
it was dark. Was it raining? No, but the lights and the sky had
that gauzy look as if it were. He was walking down the street
away from his first apartment, toward St. Lawrence Market. He
could barely keep his balance, and every time he took a step
the ground warped beneath him. Like the earth was made of
gelatin. He was trying to find something or someone. A dog
barked in the distance, and he somehow knew the dog was
his, but also that it hated him and would attack him on sight.
Before it had the chance, he got lifted back into consciousness
by an unlit elevator.

When Donovan and Cat were first dating, he would tell her
his dreams the moment they woke up together. Every detail,

everything he could remember. It's something his previous girlfriends loved about him. Talking about dreams showed he wasn't afraid to be vulnerable, that he was not some thick dude who wanted to pummel them into the mattress, who only got sensitive during the sad parts of action movies or in the middle of being dumped. Donovan liked to lie beside these women and tell them about the strange nighttime performances he'd taken part in, trying his best to do justice to their impossible curls of logic. He never lied about his dreams, even when he had been dreaming about other women, different girlfriends, people he had a crush on. He omitted names, but that was it. He believed in honesty.

Then he would ask to hear about their dreams. That was the part that really got them. He *listened*.

Years later, after Cat got pregnant, she admitted she never liked to talk about her dreams. She hated it, actually, when people talked about theirs. She just didn't find them interesting. She wasn't trying to be mean; it was a fact.

He was angry. "Why didn't you say anything?"

She had no answer.

He still can't tell her about his dreams. Whenever he tries, she looks as bored as if he were showing her the contents of his wallet.

Donovan allows a fart to slip silently into the mattress. He pins the sheets down around him to prevent it from escaping — he had three or four dark beers the night before, plus some leftover curry, so who knows what evil his body might produce today? He gets up and goes out into the quiet of the hallway and then to the top of the stairs, where he dips his ear into the silence. He executes a quick patrol of the second-floor bedrooms. Isabelle and Silas are gone, but the sense of them is

still there, the buzz of them. If he were to yell out for hiders and
seekers, their ghosts would come running.

In the back bedroom, he stands and absorbs the idle hum
of her computer. She slept in here last night. The spare bed is
dishevelled where it once again accepted her as a guest in her
own home. He tries to remember what he did *this* time to make
her choose to sleep alone. Not that he did anything, necessarily.
His transgressions, as defined by her, are too plentiful to separate into distinct crimes. His very being is a crime.

"I like that mattress more," she tells him. "And sometimes
you're up late on your phone with Twitter or whatever, and I
just want to sleep. I'm with the kids all day."

See how she slips that last part in? About the kids? Little
pinpricks of accusation. Does she even know she's doing it?

The spare bed is a single, only big enough for one person,
but Cat sleeps right on the edge of the mattress. Once or twice
he has tried to climb in with her in the middle of the night,
thinking that maybe the two of them pressed together in that
small bed might lead to a hotel-style fuck, but no, each time she
angrily rejects his intrusion and sends him back to their room
to sleep. If he doesn't leave right away, she pins the blankets
around her to prevent him getting any closer.

Cat's book is on the floor, next to the bed. She has been
fighting her way through a fresh translation of *Anna Karenina*.
He keeps finding the book in odd locations — on top of the
fridge, on the edge of the sink in the upstairs bathroom, out in
the backyard. Her progress is slow.

They'd both read the novel before, back when they were
childless, in an older translation that is presumably less transparent than the new one — though how would they know?
They'd read it, each of them with their own used copy, over

a brutal Christmas holiday when all of Toronto was encased in grey ice. Donovan can't remember where the urge to read the book together came from. How did they end up with two copies? Did they buy them together? Was that the plan? He remembers them lying across each other with legs intertwined, each holding a blocky paperback under the light of a separate lamp. He remembers stroking her, undoing her bra, while making formal declarations of love in a thick Russian accent.

"*Fuck* me, Dmitrievich," she told him, as she emancipated his hard little serf.

He has trouble connecting the relationship he and Cat had back then with the one they have now. They are like the last living members of a financially bankrupt family of aristocrats who have ended up as caretakers for the mansion built in their name. They've been moved out of the central spot of their own lives — by the kids, obviously, but by something else, too, some other corrosive force that has eaten away at the ground beneath them. The worst part is that he can't say for sure that this bothers Cat. She might even prefer not being in the primary spot — the way she prefers sleeping in the guest room instead of her own. The way she refuses to pass anyone on the highway when she is driving, no matter how slow the car in front is going. She's always telling him how much houses on their street are going for, as if any of that means anything. As if they'd cheated, somehow, by getting this house.

"We *earned* this," he'll say.

"Maybe," she'll reply, not convinced.

. . .

Donovan isn't sure what he thinks about this house anymore. When they first moved in, he'd been so cramped up by living in apartments that this place felt infinite. Obviously, it was small compared to his parents' house, something Ruth and Don pointed out when they first came to see it. But Donovan didn't care. He'd loved it. After a while, though, your existence expands, the way traffic always eventually fills any new lanes added to a busy highway.

He misses his office, the one he rented. Those first few weeks in it were like a whole new life. It was exactly what he'd been hoping for. A space, a cave, a sandbox. So much creative work could have been done there. He knows Cat was right about letting it go, and by the time he finally did he could barely stand to be in there on his own, but all the same, for a while it had been *his*. It wasn't just an office, it was a doorway, a portal. He never got to find out what lay beyond. The stink and weight of boring reality pulled him back before he could step through.

The main floor of the house is as empty as the upstairs. Cat is off doing whatever. Something responsible, something that will bring in a bit of money, though not a lot. Not enough to be worth all the phone calls and emails and coffee meetings required to make it appear. Donovan makes himself an omelette. While the eggs bubble and congeal, he scratches at the underside of his scrotum like a thoughtful monkey and finishes a half-eaten piece of toast with almond butter. He finds a sheet of blue paper on the counter: the monthly newsletter from Silas's daycare, full of things like recent birthdays of children who aren't his and announcements of new staff in the kitchen whom he will never meet or think about again. Walking Wednesdays, when all the kids and staff go for a walk together around the block, have been such a success that they are thinking of starting Marching Mondays.

Well, *whoop-dee-fucking-doo*. What is he supposed to do with this information?

Donovan has never liked the fact that Silas goes to daycare instead of staying at home with a young nanny like most of their friends' kids. They can afford a nanny. Or they could, before — maybe not now. Cat insists their highly social boy has more fun with other kids his age. And she doesn't like the power imbalance when it comes to nannies.

"I don't want Isabelle and Silas to get spoiled."

He points out that *he* had a nanny as a kid. "I had a few, actually."

"I know."

He wonders if Cat allowed Isabelle to walk to school on her own that morning. Their daughter has been asking to for months. Most of her friends already do. Isabelle is constantly asking to be left behind when the rest of the family goes out together. It hurts him to hear these requests, to see her pulling away from the core of the family. Why is his little girl — his first-born child, his baby daughter — so intent on getting away from them all the time? Where does this darkness come from? He suspects, but never says, that it might have more to do with Cat than with him. Girls get weird with their mothers. Isabelle isn't exactly a daddy's girl — Donovan winces at the very *thought* of that phrase — but maybe they have an easier relationship. Because there is no competition, or something like that. If Isabelle is *really* upset about something, she might seek out her mother, but for most of her regular troubles, she cuddles up with Dad. She trusts him. He isn't sure she trusts her mother the same way.

Sometimes *he* doesn't, either.

Has it always been like this with Cat? They had fun, didn't they, way back when? They were light with each other in a way they can't seem to be anymore, when every step is weighted down with emotional clay.

She'd given him clues about how things would be. There was the time, early on, when they'd ridden bikes around High Park, and he'd blown right through a dense cloud of midges that assaulted his eyes and his face, and sent him into the ditch with a sore arm and a scraped knee. She'd laughed so hard she almost fell off her own bike. That night, having a drink together at a bar on College Street, still bruised from the fall, Donovan reached deep into his ear and drew out a dead midge.

Cat laughed so hard she said she might pee herself.

He sulked until she, grudgingly, asked how his knee was.

Donovan sees that his mother has called and makes a mental note to call her back later. He's hoping she'll invite them all over. He loves to bring the kids to Ruth and Don's house on the weekend, to let them enjoy the miracle of a big-screen TV, which Cat will not allow them to have in their house, and to sit and drink his father's bourbon on their generous deck. Cat rarely comes with them when he does, saying his parents would rather he come on his own. Sometimes she says they prefer *his* presence to that of their grandchildren.

"They never offer to take the kids," she points out.

Ruth and Don are not the babysitting type, Donovan tells her. That just isn't them. They're more into their own lives.

Cat doesn't accept that. *Her* parents are two hours away in Peterborough, and still manage to watch the kids for a night or two every once in a while.

"*My* parents don't have lives?"

Donovan doesn't dare answer, because he's not sure they do. Not the kinds of lives that count, anyway. Not the kinds that have dimensions and weight. Donovan's mother, after meeting Ron and Sue-Ann for the first time, called them *very sincere*. Coming from her, it was a devastating judgment, and one he has never forgotten. *Children* are sincere. Small animals are *filled* with sincerity. Cat's parents are part of the vast category of people who exist to keep things moving, who fulfill a function, perform a task: raise kids, build homes, drive cars, fix air conditioners. Once they retire, they scramble to fill their time with shopping and gardens and book clubs and grandchildren. His own parents are not like that; they are full-on human beings with three dimensions. Ruth and Don are never at a loss for things to do. For them, having a child was a kind of indulgence, not an obligation. Existence was a gift they offered, a privilege.

When Donovan finally told his parents about losing his job, they got angry — not with *him*, but with his former employers. The *idiots*. The *creeps*. Had there been any warnings? Had they calculated his severance correctly? Did he have the letter they gave him? How dare they? Their anger evaporated when he told them about his new venture and his new office. Both began to see him, not too far in the future, at the head of a boutique communications agency with a half-dozen employees and a select list of high-profile and high-paying clients. They pictured him profiled in the *Globe and Mail* or *Toronto Life* as part of the city's new power elite. In the photos he'd be slimmer and wearing a sharp suit — they are both bothered by Donovan's slide into neglect when it comes to his weight and his clothes, but are convinced his personal conscientiousness will return the moment his business begins to take off.

"You're better off without them, for sure," Don said. "Their loss."

Donovan agrees with this assessment. He still occasionally indulges in a fantasy that the two managers who'd spoken to him in the conference room that day — the ones who accused him of having behaved unprofessionally and who presented him with his fuck-off letter — will ask him back. They invite him to meet them at a bar near the office where they buy him a drink and tell him they made a mistake. It's not working out without him. He needs to come back. He's a linchpin for their whole operation.

What about Bianca? he asks. What about the woman who made the accusations against him? What about the destruction and unhappiness she brought to his life?

All that was a misunderstanding, they say. Bianca is prone to melodrama and exaggeration. *She* wants him back, too! In fact, they've already fired her!

Donovan is generous and forgiving. He waves away their apologies.

His managers were decent enough not to put anything in his severance letter about Bianca, about any of what happened between them. In the boardroom during that last meeting, they told him they'd convinced her not to make a formal complaint about him, but only by promising to let him go right away, with no notice. Despite what he'd done — his manager told him again how truly disappointed she was with his behaviour — they believed he was a good man, and that he'd respect Bianca's wishes, which were that he not have any contact with her again, in any form. Nothing.

"I could go through the whole list, but you get the idea. No contact of any kind."

He agreed to this, and has mostly stuck to it. The two times he texted her, a few weeks after it all happened, trying to apologize — those don't count. He sent her a third text, also an apology, but a sarcastic one that ended with him calling her a *lying bitch*. That one probably counts.

In the upstairs bathroom, he strips off his pajamas and steps into the shower. He has to remove Silas's toys from the bathtub after almost falling over a rubber duck.

The moment the hot water hits him, his mood improves. The water pressure in this old house is impressive. He loves to think about this hidden power, pushing up from the basement and through the walls. The force of it propels him all the way out of the shower, into a clean set of clothes, and out of the house. He has nothing planned for the day. Yet again, he is stealing something everyone else insists on paying for with their happiness.

He decides not to bother locking the front door behind him. This is *his* house, in *his* neighbourhood. Who would dare?

There is another fantasy he likes to linger on, one in which his old office building goes up in flames, trapping his former

co-workers on the sixth floor. Firefighters try to pierce the stair-
wells but can only get a couple of floors up. The smoke keeps
pushing them back like a hand. Only Bianca makes it down to
the sidewalk — scorched, disfigured, lungs full of ash and heat.

JUST BEFORE TEN O'CLOCK IN THE MORNING,
there is a soft thump on the front porch. A key clicks home,
the lock releases, and the door opens with a hiss. The house is
unsealed, and through the gap slips a young woman who looks
as though she is arriving home after a long journey. Her clothes
are all lightness and cotton. Her button-up shirt is the colour
of vanilla ice cream. Her white pants end just below her calf.
Nothing sticks to her; she is not sweating. She looks as though
she might be cool to the touch. She is carrying multiple canvas
bags.

   She is not smiling. This is not her home.

   The woman has the face of someone at least a decade
younger, the face of a teenager. This fact determines the nature and tone of most of her daily interactions with strangers.

Men tell her to smile, though they are rarely smiling themselves when they tell her this. Older women tell her sometimes, too. When she gets these requests, she will smile out of embarrassment or a wish to avoid trouble, though she can never figure out why this outward sign of happiness, so easily faked, is of such interest to people who don't know her, and who will likely never see her again.

Her hair, glossy and black as electrical tape, hangs straight and is parted in the middle. The cut — which she performs herself every month, standing naked in the shower of her small apartment — is a concession to efficiency. Long hair gets in the way and takes forever to dry. That makes it a dangerous hazard in this cold city for at least four months of the year. It was horrible, the first time she exited the grimy front doors of her Don Mills apartment building early on a February morning with long hair still damp from the shower. Right away she got hit with wind that had scraped its way down from northern Ontario. By the time she arrived at the useless non-enclosure of the bus stop, her hair was as stiff as dried sugar. Lena cut it short that very night. When she woke up the next morning, she'd forgotten what she'd done. She gasped and laughed when she saw herself in the mirror.

Her father, always emotional about small things, almost cried when she showed him her new hair in one of their video chats.

"You look Chinese!" her aunt shouted, entering the frame and nudging her father aside so she could properly judge Lena from the other side of the globe. For her, to look Chinese is the worst thing possible.

"How long are you staying there?" her father asks almost every time they speak.

Lena's cousin Patricia tells her to ignore these questions. Patricia arrived in this city a few years before Lena and helped connect her with the slippery cleaning agency that provided the work offer that allowed her to come in the first place — for a fee that represented most of what Lena had saved. It was Patricia who put her in touch with clients in need of a cleaner, the agency having disappeared from sight once the fee was paid, as expected.

Patricia tells her to be friendly with her family back home, but to take every word they say about her new life and throw it away.

"They're not here. They can go fuck off."

Lena has learned not to cringe when her cousin swears. Patricia has had a hard life. She is actually Lena's *second* cousin, but would be insulted if Lena ever called her that. Lena's family and Patricia's family never had much to do with each other when they were growing up. Lena's aunt says Patricia's mother and father are too loud, the family too wild. Her father died of a heart attack the same year Patricia came to Canada. She missed the funeral. Her mother takes every opportunity to link those two events, her husband's death and her daughter's departure. And now the mother is sick herself, which only strengthens her belief that Patricia's leaving put a fatal crack in the health of her family.

When Lena asks if she plans to go home to visit her mother, Patricia shakes her head. "Faking," she says, which is probably at least half true.

"You should still go."

"I would never get away."

That ends the conversation. Nothing scares Lena more than being left alone here.

. . .

This is the third house Lena has entered this morning. She has one more after this, and then she's done for the day. Four in one day is enough, though she knows cleaners who do five, even six. Those women probably conveniently overlook items on the lists left for them by the owners. Lena doesn't do that. She always completes her regular routine, plus anything extra on the list, the *if-you-have-time* requests, and then goes looking for other things that need her attention, things the owners have not thought of or noticed. *Oh, Lena, you're a godsend!* Which always sounds a little funny coming from these people who live in homes in which God is rarely made welcome.

When everything is inside, she pushes the door shut so quietly a guard dog in the prime of its life would not notice. She takes a moment to straighten the shoes scattered across the front hallway. She has barely ever seen either of the children. And yet, if something comes up with them, Lena will get a text early in the morning: *silas is throwing up. we need to cancel.* Or *isabelle is home with the flu.* As if they are mutual acquaintances.

Lena knows that the kind of people she works for tend to value discretion and quiet even when they are not home. It is her job to be a living ghost, and she is good at it. She can slip in and out of these homes without detection. She is an anti-poltergeist; she un-disturbs each home. It helps that she is naturally quiet, unlike Patricia, who has been spoken to dozens of times about the loud phone conversations she engages in while she works. Her cousin has lost a few clients because of it. She would lose more, Lena guesses, but for the fact that children tend to like her. She knows how to act funny and silly around them, and she always has good candy hidden in her pockets that she is willing to share. Lena knows that her cousin carries the candy — which she buys in bulk at Shopper's Drug Mart and at dollar stores, grabbing multiple bags the instant they go on sale — specifically so she can win the children over. Patricia never eats snacks of any kind. She is planning to marry a Canadian man, and knows she has to stay skinny to do so.

"*You* don't have to try," Patricia says to Lena, with both scorn and envy. "Your little-boy body. Who's going to marry you?"

Lena says she isn't interested in getting married.

"*Lesbian*," Patricia says, frowning. "Lesbian with a boy body."

Some Canadian men like that, her cousin tells her, but not the kind you want to marry. Not the kind who will get you a house with two bathrooms, a car, children.

Lena hates how small she is. When she undresses in the women's change room at the community pool, which she does every Sunday afternoon for the free Aquafit classes, she feels as though she is trespassing. The women she does the classes with are grey and thick and unpleasant like sullen pachyderms at the zoo. In the showers with them, with all that flesh, she is like a little kid. In her Bible study group, the other members of the group are all older, like at Aquafit. Two sisters from Trinidad, both elderly widows, are currently engaged in a contest to see which of them can survive the longest on nothing but baked goods and tea. And Timothy, who is also from Trinidad and looks even older than the twins, always wears a suit he appears to be drowning in. Ria, one of the widowed sisters, told Lena that Timothy is dying from a disease that is shrinking him. Anya, the other sister, told her he will not let the group pray for him — he doesn't want them wasting their prayers. They all do so anyway, during the coffee break, when he is in the bathroom. Timothy usually smirks at Lena when he comes back, as if he knows what they've been doing in his absence. As if he can hear their quiet prayers over the roar of the ceiling fan and the churn of the flush.

"When we getting married, *hm*?" he asks her.

The same question every week, with the same smirk. She blushes and smiles, hating him.

Timothy had a wife, the sisters tell her, but she left him long ago because of his drinking. He stopped drinking to get her back, and it almost worked, but then she got hit by a garbage truck that took a corner too wide and went up on the sidewalk. There are two adult sons who never speak to him. One sends him money every other month, though not a lot of money. He still doesn't drink. Ria and Anya tell her all this.

Lena smiles at Timothy's weekly marriage proposals out of politeness, because he is old and sick and because his wife was killed by a garbage truck, but she wants to tell him to shut up. She has stopped praying for him when the others do. She goes through the motions, she mutters the words, but her thoughts are unforgiving.

Lena pauses and listens. This is a trickier house than most. Neither of the adults in it have jobs that require them to be elsewhere, so she can never predict who will be around when she comes. Wives and mothers, when they first interview her, always ask which she prefers: to do her work when the house is empty or when they are home? Which will be easier for her?

She learned quickly that this is a trick question. It doesn't matter what *her* preference is, only that of the owners, the clients. So she says that she is fine either way, but that it would probably be easier for *them* if she did her work when they are not home. Always there is a look of relief — in the end, they prefer not to see her, except at first.

She goes into the kitchen and pulls the plastic wrap off a fat roll of paper towels. Then she does the same for a new pack of sponges. With the bottle of bleach-free cleaner she sprays both kitchen sinks. There is a small bell attached to the wall.

That's new, she thinks. She doesn't dare touch it, though she wants to.

Sometimes, early on, the wives and mothers do the thing that Patricia warned her they will do. They will make a big display of telling her she is going out for a while and will not be back for over an hour, and that Lena will be alone in the house during that time. They always make a point of emphasizing that last fact: *You're on your own for a while, hope that's okay.*

Then they leave.

And then — just as Patricia said would happen — they come back through the front door after less than ten minutes, chattering about having forgotten something or their appointment being cancelled. They always barrel into whatever room Lena is cleaning, trying to catch her out. They want to storm in just as the new girl is trying on jewellery or smoking a joint on the back porch or falling asleep on the couch.

"The first time, I'm almost having a poo," Patricia told her, laughing.

Lena giggled so hard her nose ran.

A lot of the wives and mothers grow so comfortable with Lena's presence they stop seeing her. They walk right past her,

humming to themselves or looking for something on their
phones, and don't even notice her standing there, adjusting
the pillows on the couch. Lena has stopped having a visual
existence independent of the people paying her. At first it was
just when she was working, but now it happens wherever she
goes. When she's in the change room at the pool, she's tempted
to strip everything off, her bathing suit and her cap, and walk
out past the men sitting in groups at the small tables and the
little kids chasing each other in circles. She wonders if anyone
would notice her, if even *one* of the people there would point
at her little breasts or her little bum and say: *That's a woman!*
Look at that!

At the top of one of her canvas bags is a receipt for various
cleaning items. Lena needs to leave it for the woman named
Cat so she will get reimbursed on her next cheque. She affixes
it to the fridge door with a magnet shaped like a stegosaurus.

"Anywhere else and it'll disappear," Cat told her.

The woman was smiling a little when she said it, but her
voice sounded sad. This is a house, she was saying, where lots
of things vanish without a trace. Not just receipts and keys and
coins, but feelings and people, too.

Cat is in hardly any of the photos attached to the fridge,
Lena notices. She spots her in one taken on a beach somewhere,
her face partly obscured by those of her children, who are both
smiling and wet and topless. She is there again in the photo of
a small group at what looks like an outdoor wedding. Everyone
is smiling and holding up glasses of champagne — everyone
except Cat, who is looking down into her empty glass.

There are no photos on the fridge of Cat and Donovan getting married. There are hardly any photos of the two of them alone together anywhere in the house. There is one in the living room of the two of them, much younger, together in some kind of boat, wearing lumpy life jackets. And there is one in their bedroom upstairs of the two of them at a party, both of them much younger, paying attention to whatever is happening just outside of the frame. Someone making a speech, maybe. Donovan looks thinner than he is now, and his hair is longer and wilder. He has his arm on Cat's shoulder — lightly, as if they are merely friends — and she is tilted toward the weight of it.

For a long time, Cat would not give Lena her own key to the front door, so Lena had to ring the bell and wait until she appeared there with a baby in her arms, or on her own and holding a finger to her lips. *Shhh, baby's sleeping.* Lena finally insisted on having her own key, after coming twice in a row to find no one home. It was the husband, Donovan, who gave her the key in the end.

"Keys to the kingdom."

She thanked him.

"Go with God," he said, smirking, his eyes on the cross around her neck.

In every photo Donovan is grinning, his smile confident. It is the same smile with which he greets her each time he sees her. She will unpack her things and start to work, and suddenly he will appear, often wearing pajama pants and a T-shirt. Or pajama pants and no shirt. He sometimes emerges from the bedroom or the bathroom just as she is passing the door. Twice, he came out of the bathroom still wet from a shower and wearing only a thin towel.

"Where are you from, exactly?" Donovan asked her early on. "Like, a village or a city?"

She told him, but kept the details vague. Patricia had warned her about these kinds of conversations. Most clients stop asking any questions after the first few visits. They show a lot of curiosity at first, then lose interest, often before you finish answering. Once you are established in the house, you are like an object. You just *are*. Any major life changes you might be going through should be kept to yourself, unless they are going to affect your work. Lena is okay with that.

Donovan doesn't do this. He listens, then asks more questions. Does she like it in Toronto? Where does she live — in an apartment or a house? On her own? Is that expensive? How many other clients does she have? Is cleaning houses a thing, or just a way to make money? Just the money, right? Does she have a lot of friends here? What kind of stuff does she do when she isn't working? The cross around her neck — is that a thing with her? Is she religious? That's cool. He's heard that a lot of women from her country are. Does she have someone here, or back home? Like, a boyfriend or whatever?

"I have a boyfriend here," she lied.

"Oh, nice. What's his name?"

Before her brain could come to her assistance, her mouth released a name, one she'd been seeing a lot on in the news: "Gord."

Donovan looked puzzled for a moment. "Gord? Your boyfriend's name is *Gord*?"

She nodded yes. He smiled like she'd walked into a trap.

Now when he sees her, he will ask her how *Gord* is doing, and she will have to say that he is fine, thank you.

Lena starts her routine. With her earbuds in, she thumbs through the various options on her phone until she finds her favourite, a French composer named Erik Satie, who wrote weird little tunes with names she never says out loud in case she pronounces them wrong. She sticks her phone into her pocket and climbs the stairs to the second floor of the house. Without thinking, she falls into step with the music. Each stair is a bar, and she is moving across the page with the unseen performer.

Music is the one indulgence Lena allows herself while she works. She is fine to tiptoe around all day and not speak, but she needs beautiful sounds in her ears. She needs to be reassured that there is a world beyond these living rooms and bathrooms and kitchens. In these dry homes, music is a hidden creek that sparkles and shines and flows endlessly through her. In some houses, she will arrive to the sound of old jazz — which she hates — or worse, things that sound as though they were being sung or chanted by tribespeople in some village that has yet to know a light bulb. Rhythmic, endless folk songs. Lena sometimes worries this primitive chanting has been put on for her benefit.

What she wants is the sound of a piano. A clean, black-and-white keyboard, all on its own. Bare hammers on tight, metal wires. No drums or guitars or chanting. Her piano at home was an upright, brown and chipped and further out of tune the higher up you went. She misses it. She misses spending hours trying to work out fingering, getting herself to the point where she could play without sheet music in front of her.

Patricia calls the kind of thing Lena likes *funeral music*. She says the tinkling of it gets in her ear like an insect. What *she* wants are tattooed rappers who can brag and dance, and women with artificially extended hair and bums that stick out like valentine hearts. Lena likes some of that, too. When she and Patricia are together, that music makes her laugh and feel a foot taller. It makes her forget she has to cut her own hair because of the cold. But when she is alone, when she walks quietly through these houses, wiping away stains and straightening pillows and scrubbing the insides of toilets, she wants the simple mechanics of a piano. The rappers and big-bum women would be too much. They would make her impatient, unable to face yet another wet bathroom or another child's bedroom that has been stirred and flung apart. The sound of a piano keeps her steady and focused. In her mind she steps on each key as it is played, tiptoeing from room to room.

One time, Donovan appeared behind her and startled her so much that she yelled without meaning to. She was in one of the kids' bedrooms, straightening sheets and picking up toys. Ravel was in her ears like syrup, and she had stopped for a moment in the centre of the room to let the sounds dribble down through her. She just stood there, her body filling with thick musical sugar, when suddenly he was at the door. She hadn't even realized he was home. His hair was a mess, like he'd just gotten up.

"Sorry," he said, laughing.

Without thinking, she apologized, too.

Another time he told her, out of nowhere, that he'd had a dream about her. He laughed at the look on her face.

"Don't worry, it wasn't anything *weird*. I think we were looking at cars. At a dealership, I mean. New cars. But, like, out in the country. Maybe Prince Edward County. It looked like Prince Edward County. Have you been out there? You should totally go. Anyways, we were buying a car together, just you and me. You know anything about cars?"

"Not really."

"Me neither, actually. Ha ha."

Then he offered her fruit from the wooden bowl in the kitchen.

Another time, he came up to her with his phone out, not saying anything. When she looked at what he was showing her, she laughed. It was a photo of a tall building covered in plants and flowers, with smooth, rounded balconies made of wood. The Rainbow Tree.

"This is in your city?" he asked.

She said it was, but that the building doesn't exist, at least not yet. Her father has sent her lots of proud pictures of it.

"I hope they build it," he said. "What a beauty. Imagine living there?"

Donovan sometimes apologizes for the state of the house. He always smiles when he does so, as if he's actually proud of the chaos his little family is capable of.

"Are we the worst you do?" he asks her.

"No, no."

His eyebrows go up. "Who's the worst? Like, the absolute filthiest?"

When she doesn't answer, he says, "Ah, *client confidentiality.* Got it. I'm sure you see some horrific shit."

He has asked her a few times about the cross around her neck. She told him it was a gift from her father when she left home, that it had belonged to her grandmother, who died the year before she left.

Donovan just nodded, his eyes still on the cross.

"The God thing, is that big with you?"

Lena shrugged, not knowing how to answer.

"But do you do the whole church thing? Singing, prayers? All that?"

She said she is in a Bible study group. And she goes to church.

"I haven't seen any miracles," she said, smiling. "Not yet."

Donovan looked at her, then laughed and declared the whole thing cool — her faith, religion, miracles. The whole deal. Cool.

"It's not my thing, but I respect it. For real. I'm into the idea of people just doing whatever it is, believing in whatever. As long as it makes you happy."

His sincerity took her aback. She thanked him.

"Amen," he said, smiling.

There is something else Lena insists on when she is cleaning a house. At some point early on in her routine, sometimes even while the owners are still around, she must steal something.

Nothing big like a ring or a phone or cash. Nothing that might be missed. Always something small and inessential, something whose absence creates the tiniest possible rip in the existence of the house's occupants. In one house it might be a fancy elastic for a young girl's hair. In another it might be a single apple, which she will eat as she walks back to the subway. Sometimes it's the dimes or quarters she finds on the floor or under the couch. But she has to take one thing from each home.

She does nothing with the things she steals, doesn't collect them or worship them or curse them or anything weird. Most of it she throws away. She leaves the coins on ledges outside the subway station for homeless men. But the act of removing things from the houses makes her feel as though she has taken at least one small bite out of her clients' lives. Scratched a mark on the wall.

From Cat and Donovan's house she has removed a blank postcard, a tiny bottle of hand sanitizer, some forks, a corkscrew, a few of the young boy's toy cars. She kept the corkscrew, which says *New Orleans* on the handle. She has yet to use it. When Patricia comes over with wine, the bottles she brings have screw caps.

Lena has visions of carrying the corkscrew with her when she travels back and forth from her clients' houses. She pictures herself holding it in her fist with the screw part out, and punching it into the chest of someone on the subway, pulling it so their heart pops out through their rib cage. It scares her a bit to think like this. The twistiness of the screw is what does it, she thinks, the metal curves round and round like a pig's tail. It's demonic. But she doesn't get rid of it.

Her cousin would give her shit if she knew. Not for the stealing itself — though Patricia says she has never taken anything that wasn't being thrown away — but for how small and useless the items she takes are. A pointless risk. If she is going to take something, she should take a phone charger or old jewellery she can get cash for. But that would make Lena a thief. Which she knows she is, sort of. But there has to be room for small acts of transgression. When she was little, she imagined God having small blind spots in his vision, places and times where his awareness is obscured. She still catches herself thinking that if she just stays very still and very quiet, his gaze will pass over her and somehow not fall upon the tiny sins in her heart.

Lena comes quietly along the upstairs hallway, passing a small, decorative wooden table that sits directly below the window. On it is a peace lily in a red pot, and next to that a nice little cactus in a coffee mug with the Chinese symbol for *patience* on the side. There is also a mug of cold, forgotten coffee and one of Silas's robot men, the kind that collapses into the shape of a red-and-black sports car. The robot man stands with his arms in the air as if trying to signal Lena, as if trying to warn her of something.

I see you, she thinks, and makes a mental note to clear and wipe the table.

In her ears the piano is doing a kind of funny stutter, as if the performer is just a child. Lena loves this part. You make your fingers like little jackhammers. The trick is to not hit the keys so hard that it sounds like noise, so people tell you to stop.

She decides to start in the bathroom. Everything else is easy once that task is done. The Satie piece comes to an end, the last chord decaying to nothing. She likes that, for a second or two after the music ends, she can hear the sound of the room it is being recorded in. She likes to picture the man or woman lifting their hands away from the keyboard and sitting for a moment in silence. She likes that better than live performances, where the end of a piece is inevitably followed by the sound of an unseen crowd applauding. As if clapping their hands together had anything to do with what they'd all just heard. The brief hum of a studio recording is more solemn, more like church. This is why Lena doesn't like the famous pianist named Glenn Gould, who lived in this very city. He plays everything like it is beneath his abilities, flying through each piece at a ridiculous speed, taking dark geniuses like Beethoven and Liszt and riding them around like a drunk man on a bike. Just because he can. Because his hands cannot fail him. Worst of all, he is never quiet. He mutters and hums and sings along while he plays.

Shut up, she thinks as she tries to listen. *Be humble.*

The door to the bathroom is open slightly. She pushes at it just as the next piece begins, a piece she once tried to learn to play, but could never perform with the right sense of lightness.

Her fingers twitch on the door as she pushes it, pressing invisible keys.

She takes one step into the room and stops.

Donovan is standing on the bare tile floor, completely naked. With one hand, he is leaning against the counter. With the other, he is pulling at his penis, which is red and erect and pointing at her. The pinkness of his body, in the blue gloom of the bathroom, shocks her more than anything. He is a raw chicken breast, come to life for the sole purpose of doing this awful thing. Donovan looks up at her, right into her eyes. He stares right at her without blinking. She breaks away from his gaze and looks at the floor. She takes a step back.

"Please," he says.

It is shocking to hear him over the music in her ears. He sounds calm, but with a wave of tension rising behind the word.

"Stay. *Please.*"

Something holds her in place. She is hovering over a dark pit, a ravine. On the other side is the rest of her day, the rest of her life. If she stays still, says nothing, she will find herself over there, and she can continue on. If, however, she says anything right now — voices an objection, yells out in anger, demands to know why — she will drop down into darkness and complication, from which she might never find her way back out.

Donovan's phone gulps and moans on the counter. She can't see what's playing on it.

"Please," he says again, less forcefully. His gaze falters. He makes a sound like he is being pushed, and a line of grey shoots from his hand, arcing out and away from him and hitting the counter and the floor. Two more smaller spurts follow. One fails to fully launch, and is left hanging from his knuckles.

"Oh *fuck*," he says.

She turns and walks quietly back down the stairs. Behind her, she hears his voice, faint but insistent: "*Thank you.*"

She closes the front door behind her, not bothering to lock it.

Walking back to the subway, she reaches into her pocket and pulls out a small cloth for cleaning glasses and a two-dollar coin, both taken from houses she visited before Cat and Donovan's. She throws them deep into a dark hedge. She aches to have the corkscrew in her fist.

IV

THROUGH AVA, ONE OF HER FORMER CO-WORKERS, Cat gets hired to redesign the website for a boutique yoga studio. The money attached is substantial — she gave a high estimate for the job, urged on by Ava, who told her the studio owner's dead husband came from an unimaginably rich family. The owner's own parents were diehard communists — or so she frequently tells the women who come to the studio — who raised their only daughter to hate the accumulation of wealth. *Her* wealth, since she married into it and inherited it and therefore did nothing to accumulate it other than outlive her rich husband, is presumably exempt from such blanket hatred. Ava has friends who've attended classes at the studio. Meredith is a character, they tell her. A local celebrity.

"So she's a rich person who pretends to hate rich people," Cat says.

"Honestly, I don't know if she's pretending."

Cat wonders why she is so judgmental, hearing this. She married into money, too, though she and Donovan had been together for months before she became aware of the glittering cloud of family wealth that lay behind his easy confidence. There is also a difference of scale. Donovan's family is rich in the sense of having more money than they need. They are aware of that fact and must work to maintain its current level. The family Meredith married into is apparently so wealthy as to have no concept of the word *need*. Cat sometimes meets such people at the overstuffed weddings of Donovan's cousins. They are another species altogether, who are probably surprised each day when an urgent pressure in their stomach and bowels compels them to sit on the toilet: *What, this again? Can't we hire someone?* They exist on a planet of wealth, where money is an inexhaustible natural resource, where individual fortunes can be boozed away or lost through stupid investments, but will inevitably be restored. They could waste every dollar they possess purchasing all the moons of Jupiter, and it would not affect their fundamental richness. One strategic marriage and the money comes back. Money never stays away for very long, and always seeks to return to its natural level.

The site Cat builds is a simple one, with few whistles or bells. Someone from the studio sends her detailed instructions. She has made so many with a similar structure, she barely thinks about it as she puts it together. Like how kids on YouTube complete Rubik's cubes in a matter of seconds while blindfolded. Soon enough after the deadline she gave herself to count as having hit it, she sends off an email with a link to the beta version of the new site, along with a friendly request for comments. An hour later, she gets a panicked call from the studio's owner, who demands the whole thing be taken down. She wants to know why the site has been presented — that is the word she uses: *presented*, as if the internet is a kind of dog show — without her permission.

"This is the first time I'm seeing it."

Cat explains that the new site is not yet truly live, that only the two of them can see it. She repeats her friendly request for comments and changes. Meredith says that Cat will need to come to the studio to show her in person how it all works. At that point she will tell her what needs to be changed, the implication being that the list is a long one.

"Come Thursday. Before ten."

Cat, accustomed to having clients forcibly claim parts of her week, says Thursday morning is fine.

But Thursday morning is not fine. Thursday morning is a devastating landslide. Thursday morning is a collapsing circus tent. There are multiple fights about breakfast and clothes and the brushing of teeth. Donovan sleeps through it all, as usual. It is already after nine when Cat finally pulls up in front of Isabelle's school. Her daughter gets the door open a few inches, then freezes. The air is filled with the sound of children yelling with excitement.

"Oh my God, Mom!"

Track and Field Day. The reminder slip is fastened to the fridge door by a magnet, forgotten. The bag with her shorts and running shoes is at home, too, waiting for Cat to do laundry.

Cat leaves Isabelle standing near the school entrance and promises to return right away with the bag. When she gets back, less than ten minutes later, Isabelle takes the canvas bag from Cat with almost no acknowledgement of her existence, and no thank-you. She's with two girls from her class, and flinches slightly when Cat says *goodbye* and *love you*. The girls give Isabelle a matching pair of sympathetic smiles. Some gross creature is bothering their friend, some useless old gargoyle who insists on playing the role of mother.

By the time they reach daycare, Silas is in a frenzy over being denied the fun day his big sister is enjoying. She finally has to leave him struggling in the arms of one of the cooing daycare workers while she walks quickly out of the building, fighting back tears of frustration and guilt.

At the gate she runs into Priscilla, one of the other moms. Priscilla's twins are in their double stroller. The three of them have stopped to follow the progress of a white moth. Priscilla never hurries. She almost always drops the twins off late, after the other kids have already had their snacks and are being prepped to go outside. The twins are as blond and pale as summer beer, though their mother is dark and Spanish-looking. Her partner is dark, too, suggesting the paleness of the twins was a conscious decision, an act of aesthetic will. Their family needed contrast.

"Sorry," Cat says, and tries to step around the wide stroller just as one of the twins reaches out to grab at her leg. She almost topples onto both of them.

Priscilla smiles at her from behind her sunglasses. "You look *hot*." Slurring the words. Priscilla has a habit of sending out waves of warm bisexual interest, whatever the context.

Cat laughs. "I don't know about *hot*."

In her client-meeting slacks and blouse, she looks more like someone performing a census count or canvassing door-to-door on behalf of a centrist political candidate. Priscilla is wearing jeans that are stylishly savaged at the knees and a thin blue button-up shirt with the top two buttons undone and the sleeves rolled to just below the elbow. The glow of morning sunshine lights her from behind. Cat can see she is not wearing a bra.

"I mean *hot*, like you're roasting," Priscilla says, fanning herself for effect and lifting a bottle of kombucha to her mouth. "You shouldn't run in weather like this. Take it slow."

One of the twins grabs at Cat again, and she has to stop herself from swatting the tiny hand away.

Driving east through the city is the usual grind. Cars cluster and accumulate at every intersection. Bike messengers death-wish their way in and out of her lane. Crowds cross slowly from corner to corner — Cat can swear she sees some people, having reached the opposite sidewalk, turn and start back across the street again. After getting stuck in a narrow traffic funnel created by an entire block of construction, she pulls into a hospital parking lot, gestures apologetically at the attendant, and texts Meredith to say she'll be late. She doesn't dare wait for a response.

The better part of an hour later, she makes it to the Beaches, right on the eastern edge of the city. The yoga studio is built out of a large coach house behind an even larger house. Cat passes the studio, slowing as she does to get a look, then parks half a block away, over the objections of her phone's navigation app. She tries to back the car into a small space behind a black SUV. To help her focus on the task, she turns off the radio, silencing the female host who, with infinite patience, is interviewing a man about the province's Catholic school system — Cat has not been listening closely enough to know if he is for or against. The space offers very little room for mistakes, so she twists herself around to get a better view. As she does, pain cuts through her shoulders and her neck. A taste like sour beer comes into her mouth, and her vision shivers. She takes four deep breaths. One of her hands looks whiter than the other. The air conditioning is on, but she is hot and cramped, and a fine sweat has broken out all over her skin.

At last her body rights itself, and she is able to unbuckle and climb out. Instantly, she can smell the lake, the trees, the dogs, the calm. She both loves and loathes this area. It is beautiful and quiet and close to the lake, but also white and precious and too far removed from the actual city. It reminds her of Peterborough, except everyone has money, and instead of hockey practice and trips to Walmart, people spend their weekends pushing strollers in and out of bookstores and coffee shops, or walking dogs by the water's edge. Months ago, having dinner and wine at the house of some friends, she fell into a rant about the place.

"Every woman out there looks like a fuck-bot. They all have toddlers with them, but they're as skinny as rakes. I bet they get C-sections so they don't get stretched out."

Donovan rolled his eyes. "Easy on the merlot, comrade."

"I'm not drunk, I'm just expressing my opinion."

She was very drunk.

"I'm not crazy about the place either," their friend Sean said, "but I guess I'm not sure why it bothers you so much."

Before she could answer, Donovan said, "She's showing off. You get her away from the kids, pour some wine in her, and she wants to burn everything down."

"Oh, fuck you."

The next day, hungover and smeared with shame, she sent apologetic emails to the other two couples. She refused to apologize to Donovan.

She has not told Donovan about passing out in front of the kids, though she knows that she should. It is something he ought to be aware of. At first she is unable to think of a way to make it happen. What words could she use, what is the best opportunity? Just come out and say it?

Oh, hey. I fell. Hard. For no reason.

Later, she is able to admit she was afraid his reaction would confirm that passing out in front of the kids in the middle of the afternoon like some drunk mom is a thing to be worried about. She's afraid this is Bad News, signalling a shift into new and darker life territory. Keeping this information from him, therefore, prevents such a shift from happening.

She could argue that she is merely conforming to the new pattern of dishonesty in their marriage. Isn't the concealment of important information how things work now? Should Isabelle and Silas get in on this? Her son could hide cash in the mattress of his bed. Her daughter could start a relationship with a married woman. All four of them could be at different corners of the house, holding lit cigarettes out windows so the smoke won't be detected.

When she fell that time in the living room, it took her a few moments, sprawled stupidly on the ground, to figure out what had happened, and when she did, she tried to pretend it was all a joke. Her vision was blurred around the edges, the living room floor was bowed in the middle. There was something hard beneath her foot. A crayon. Isabelle kept looking at her as if she were expecting more shocking things to occur — a bird to hit the front window and snap its neck, the TV to explode. She pointed past her mother to where a framed photo was barely hanging on to the wall. Her favourite: a black-and-white shot of Cat and Donovan on a long-ago canoe trip.

"Fix it, please."

"Mommy's okay, everything's okay."

"Fix the picture."

When Isabelle was young, younger than Silas is now, Cat told her the photo was taken while Mama and Dada were on a fun trip together in a place called Algonquin Park. "Gonkin!" Isabelle yelled happily, and so the photo was named for years, until Isabelle demanded they stop calling it that — she thought they were making fun of her. When she first showed Isabelle the photo, Cat pointed to herself and to Donovan, sitting there in the canoe, tired and stoned, and then to her own belly, hidden under the life jacket.

"We didn't know it yet, but you were right there."

She told her about the fish that moved around them in the water, quiet as cows. She told her about the moose Daddy saw, but Mommy didn't, because she was napping. How they stayed up late every night. She told her how the light from the sun would dissolve, leaving a vast hole above them through which you could see a thousand other galaxies and shooting stars that scratched the speckled blackness. Isabelle called them *shooting scars*.

They drank vodka every day of the trip, sipping it straight from the bottle as they paddled, or mixing it with orange juice in a Thermos and chugging it while they set up the tent. In the evenings they smoked weed until they felt as though they were wrapped in warm furs, and then body-surfed through shallow rapids under a sky showing its late-day scorch. Cat got so wasted one night that she told Donovan she hated him. She was so tired. Tired of paddling, tired of trees and rivers, tired of *him*. She called him every awful name she could think of, then stumbled into the woods until she came to a low, jagged cliff that dropped into the water. She nearly fell in trying to climb down, and got stuck on the rocks until Donovan found her. She let him tease her about it until they got back to the edge of the park a few days later, back to where they had parked the car.

"You called me a *faggot*," he said, chuckling. "Who says that?"

"Stop it," she finally said.

When they found out she was pregnant, he said it explained why she'd gotten so mad at him. Hormones.

A year later, on her first birthday as a new mother, he gave her the framed photo as a gift. Cat was in a sour mood. Isabelle had barely napped, and Donovan hadn't done anything to get the house ready, so she was forced to clean the place while carrying the baby in a sling. She wanted to know what the photo meant. Was it more teasing? Was it some kind of sick reminder that they'd been happy and free once? But he *was* still happy and free — the baby hadn't altered his life much at all. Somehow, they'd fallen into ancient, hated gender roles, as if they had gotten so far past them evolutionarily that they'd lost their instincts to avoid them.

Meredith's house dwarfs its neighbours. Ava told Cat that she lives alone in that huge place with a dog.

"*Don't* react to the dog."

"Is it big? Dangerous?"

"Not at all. Totally the opposite. You'll see."

Cat does. Moving toward her after she presses the doorbell — which, instead of a ring or a buzz, stirs heavy chimes deep within the house — is a living portrait of canine decay, a *memento mori* for all dogkind. It is small, with yellowish fur that is matted and greasy, erupting in thick hunks of doggy dreadlocks. It walks with small, painful steps, and, even through the glass of the door, Cat can see that it is at least partly blind. It doesn't bark at her, but waits on the other side, quietly trembling, to see if Death has finally arrived to release its poor soul.

After a minute or two, Cat stirs the chimes again. This time, there is more movement beyond the glass, and the door opens.

Cat guesses Meredith to be in her late sixties, though it is just as likely that she has been living in this house since it was first built, more than a century ago, and grew up among lumber barons and railway magnates. Her long, curly hair masses around her head like an angry red cloud. Its colour is intensely bright and thoroughly artificial, the shade of a crayon designed to represent a sunset. A white hoodie protects her thin bones like paper on a picture frame. Below it are tight yoga pants and fluorescent green running shoes. Her waist is as narrow as Isabelle's, maybe narrower. Only her face, angular and full of shadows, gives her age away. Her hollow cheeks make her look like something is pinching her, like she is forever getting a needle.

Instead of greeting Cat, Meredith speaks quietly to the dog, saying he is a good boy, yes, but why did he not tell her someone was waiting?

Cat introduces herself, and the older woman nods, willing to accept for the moment that the information she is being given is correct.

"This is Louis," Meredith says, gesturing toward the dog.

"Hello, Louis."

"*Louis Riel.*" She pronounces the name with an accent that sounds like it has been borrowed from a French waiter in a skit.

"Oh, okay! That's an interesting one."

"Because he's mixed breed and a little eccentric. Or *crazy*, if we're going to be totally honest about it. I guess you can't say things like that anymore — I don't actually believe in those terms. *Crazy, sane.* But he's my true love."

The dog does not react to any of the words being spoken about it, which makes Cat wonder if it is deaf, too. The smell of it. Like raw chicken left in the sun for a day, mixed with old bar carpets stored in buckets of standing water. She imagines stepping forward and kicking the poor thing to death, out of mercy, as it whines with gratitude: *Thank you, stranger. Thank you thank you thank you goodbye.*

"It's not as hot today," Meredith says, looking past Cat.

"It's hot enough for me," Cat says with forced brightness. "I'm sweating just walking from the car."

Meredith looks her up and down. "Are you pregnant?"

"Excuse me?"

"Sorry, is that a personal question?"

Cat laughs involuntarily. Meredith doesn't smile; she is waiting for an answer.

"No, I'm ... I have two children, though. Do I look pregnant?"

Meredith waves her question off. "I wasn't suggesting you were overweight. I don't believe in the concept of *overweight* or *fat.* Come in."

Stepping into the house, Cat is greeted by an enormous picture in the hallway: a framed painting of Louis in better times. In the painting the dog glows with youth and health, its fur is

clean, its eyes are clear, it is slightly chubby, and it sits at attention, delighted to be the subject of so much attention. Sitting
on the floor below the painting is the poor beast itself, shedding
health by the minute, its life ticking down. It is like the reverse
of that story, Cat thinks, the one about the vain man who keeps
a hidden portrait of himself that ages and decays for him while
he stays young and beautiful.

Or wait, the reverse of that story is just how life works.

"I was doing my breathing. In the music room. That's why
I didn't hear the door."

"Oh, okay!"

From somewhere deep in the house, she can hear cellos drawing out long, low notes while heavy bells are struck with soft hammers. It sounds like some great fallen leader is being laid to rest.

"I could go get a coffee and come back, if that's better."

Meredith shakes her head. "I have another group at eleven.
This morning I led the sunrise session, as I always do. I like to
have a few hours in between."

"Oh, for sure. This shouldn't take long."

Cat starts to pull her laptop from her bag, but Meredith
flinches and gestures for her to stop, as if she were about to
squat down and pee. She says they can talk in the studio itself.

"It's such a mess in here."

Cat looks around. The house is clean and immaculate, with
exactly the right number of visible books, flowers, and random
pottery creations.

"I have toys and clothes all over the place at my house," Cat
says brightly.

Meredith says nothing, and Cat tells herself not to bring
up the subject again. Some women without kids take even the
vaguest reference to motherhood as a passive-aggressive attack.

"The person who comes to clean my house is sick this week. And the person she recommended has not replied to my messages. It's very frustrating."

"I have the same thing happening," Cat says, relieved to have finally found some common ground. "Our … *person* has gone AWOL. No texts, no emails, nothing."

"You wonder what the hell they're thinking."

"Ours is pretty young. But I thought she was more responsible."

"Is she from here?"

"From Canada, you mean? The Philippines, I think. But she's been here for a while."

Meredith nods. "You don't want to say it, but sometimes I wonder if the problem is cultural."

She tells Cat to wait while she finds her glasses.

"I want to be able see this."

Alone for a moment, Cat touches her stomach. She's still a little thrown by the pregnancy question. Just over a year ago, she had a scare. She bloated up, her tummy got as firm as a new mattress, and her nerves were raw, just as if she were on the verge of a period that would not come. She waited in fear for the tide to rise inside her. About a week later, her body went back to normal. Cat has been waiting for the same bloat to return, for her belly to tense up in preparation. Some of her friends got pregnant again the moment they stopped breast-feeding their first babies. They wanted to be put back into bondage; they feared freedom. They wanted to burrow into permanent motherhood and be safe. She knows moms who asked for and ate the placenta. In a soup, usually, though Cat likes to picture them gobbling at the thing raw, their faces and arms slick with blood.

"What does it taste like?" she has asked them, disgusted and impressed.

"Like *life*," said one.

"Like *shit*," said another.

The pregnancy tests are still in her bag, and her period is still AWOL, just like her cleaning lady. Maybe they are off together somewhere, that young woman having somehow stolen an entire menstrual cycle from her.

Meredith leads them around the side of the house and up the wide driveway, which has been converted into a gently curving pathway of grey, rounded pebbles. Cat slips on the pebbles and puts a hand out. This would be a bad place to fall. The studio is low, flat, and as wide as a barn. The exterior is covered with tastefully stained wood. Cat can't see any windows. It could be an enormous sauna, or a place where dark experiments are being performed. Meredith tells her she rarely locks the door.

"I used to worry that maybe a homeless person might get in and sleep here or use the toilet. But that has never happened. Nobody even comes up the walkway. Just raccoons. And we have a fox running around the neighbourhood now. Have you heard about our fox? It's quite a celebrity. It ate one of my neighbour's cats, the poor thing. Ate it and left its tail on the back step. Imagine. That's why I keep poor Louis inside."

Cat does not suggest that being dragged away by a healthy fox might be the best outcome for the creature she has just met, one it would likely welcome.

Thank you thank you goodbye.

Inside, the studio is airy, spacious, and bright. The ceiling looks to be thirty or forty feet above them and has multiple skylights to let in the sun. Meredith walks around, turning on hidden pot lights that make the room brighter still. She presses a hidden panel in the wall, which clicks open to reveal a small stand on which is placed an iPad. She dabs at it with her index finger, and in a few moments, Cat hears again the sound of cellos — sprightly and non-mournful this time. The sound comes from everywhere and nowhere, as if the woman has woken the ghosts of the musicians to let them loose in the room.

"I had the audio system put in last year," Meredith says. "Excuse me." She walks across the room, slides open a door, and disappears. After a moment Cat can hear the sound of running water.

"Yo-Yo Ma," Cat says to no one.

This place is nothing like the YMCA gym, with its fluorescent-lit change rooms full of big ladies who shower until their skin is red and who display wild bushes like raw broccoli at a farmer's market. She allows herself to fantasize about living alone in all this silent space. She would put her bed *there*, her desk *there*. She would eat quiet meals alone in a spot painted by sunlight every morning. She would work in the far corner, with a deep, plush chair next to her desk, in which she could sit and wait for design ideas to swoop down and take her by surprise. When she is done working for the day, she would sit in that same chair with a healthy glass of red wine and a fat novel set in Victorian London or on a Russian country estate in the time of the Tsar. She would not own a TV. She would program the hidden iPad to wake her each morning with soft music. Satie or someone like that. Or that one Miles Davis album she likes. All alone. No Donovan. No kids.

Maybe the kids could visit on weekends.

Meredith reappears to announce that they need to hurry, as if Cat is the one who has been delaying the progress of their meeting. It takes Cat a while to locate an outlet in the smooth walls of the studio. She winces a little while crouching down with the power cord in her hand. Her shoulder is still bothering her, and she can sense the first, tentative approaches of a migraine. She hopes she can at least make it through this meeting without having to gobble Tylenol like a pill fiend.

The computer awakens, and the two women stand before it, with all that warm space at their backs.

"I tried to preserve as much of the feel of the old site as I could, while giving it an updated look and making the navigation a lot easier. The back-end stuff is simpler now, so you can do the updating yourself with no trouble."

Meredith shakes her head. "I won't go near any of that."

"You sure? It saves you having to pay me or whoever to do it."

Meredith shakes her head again. Cat might as well be suggesting that she re-shingle her own home, drill her own teeth.

"Okay, but just so you know, it's pretty simple. It's almost all drag-and-drop."

"That sounds like you're getting rid of a dead body."

Meredith has already told Cat more than once that she does not trust the internet, nor, by extension, people who can navigate it with ease, who know how to manipulate all that dark, digital magic. She doesn't like that there is no *intimacy* in computing, no physicality.

"Where are the photos of the space? I had all those photos taken."

It sounds like an accusation. Cat tries not to take it personally. In the air around them, the cellos have been replaced by the sound of an unidentifiable stringed instrument plucking hesitantly at a series of random notes that keep threatening to cohere into an actual melody without ever making the leap.

"All the photos are here. Click on *The Studio.*"

Meredith makes no move to touch the laptop, so Cat clicks the link herself, opening a page filled with carefully placed images of the very room they were standing in. The photos do not do the place justice.

"It should say *Space*," Meredith says. "*Studio* sounds too much like something you rent."

"But you allow rentals? I added a rates page."

"Anybody can rent the space when there aren't classes happening. No, not anybody. I won't allow politics in here. Or religious groups. I want that to be clear on the site: no politics or religion."

"Oh. You gave me a rate for *spiritual groups*. It was on the original list."

"That's right."

Cat looks at Meredith, who gives no sign of being troubled by this apparent contradiction.

"Well, the rate for spiritual groups is listed, and I can maybe add something about not wanting political groups."

"I can always tell them when they call. I don't want to scare anyone off."

"I'll leave it as it is, then, but change the title of the page to *The Space.*"

"Just *Space*. I don't like the definite article."

"And you don't like politics."

Meredith nods but does not smile. "None of that means anything. My mother and father were *very* political, but that was a different time. People are greedy. They do what they are going to do."

Cat is surprised by the cynicism of this statement, especially coming from someone who believes in the transformative
power of stretching. She has already begun to imagine how she
will tell her sister about all of this, about Meredith and Louis
and *Space*. Claudia will lap it up.

"I've had so many fights with the city," Meredith tells her.
"There are so many rules and regulations about what you can
do with your own property. It's my property!" She pauses, then
adds, in a more yoga-fied voice, "That is, if we truly *own* anything. I'm not sure we do."

Meredith asks Cat if the blue on the site is the actual colour,
the one she had requested.

"It doesn't look right."

Cat turns her laptop so she can see the screen. "That's the
colour. Same as before."

"Is it? It looks darker. I think it should be more blue. It
should be the same as before. I really want it to be the same."

Before Cat can ask how the exact same colour can be
made to be *more* the same, the outside door opens and another
woman walks in who looks to be in her forties. She is thin like
Meredith, with wild black hair that explodes from her head in
dark ringlets. Despite the heat, she is wearing a kind of indis-
criminately South American poncho. Below its fringed edges,
Cat can see a more standard pair of black yoga pants and running shoes. She isn't carrying a bag. The woman pauses for a
moment when she sees Cat and Meredith, then crosses the floor
away from them, toward the change room doors. She moves
with a sense of nervous tension, as if she is the neighbourhood
fox in human form, ready to dash if Meredith suddenly comes
at her with a rake. As she moves she stares at Cat with narrow
fox eyes.

With a vague smile on her face, Meredith watches the woman cross the room. It's the first smile Cat has seen since she arrived.

"Oh, here's Wendy. Wendy helps me with some of the groups. Good morning, Wendy!"

Wendy slows her pace but keeps moving toward the change room and safety.

"Wendy, this is …" Meredith pauses.

"Cat," Cat says, jumping in. "Short for *Catherine*. But just Cat."

"You must be the thousandth Catherine I know, and you're not even a Catherine. Wendy, we're going to be presenting a new website for the space, and *Cat* is helping us build it."

Meredith carefully enunciates each word. Cat wonders if Wendy is deaf. Or mentally challenged in some way.

Wendy finally stops crossing the floor, but does not approach.

"A website," she says quietly.

"Cat is a web designer. We've been looking at it. It's quite lovely."

Meredith gestures at the laptop, as if offering to let her eat it. Wendy takes a few steps toward them, until she is close enough that Cat can smell something coming off of her, something earthy but not unpleasant, like freshly churned soil.

"You designed this?" Wendy asks, looking at Cat with wide, sincere eyes.

"I mean, some of it is templated. And Meredith gave me a lot of direction — this is her baby. I've still got a few tweaks to make. But it's almost there."

"There are all those wonderful photos of the space that Jorge took. You can look through each of them. You should try it, Wendy. It's quite lovely to see."

Cat is relieved to hear this praise coming from Meredith, even if it leaves the other woman unmoved.

"I know someone who designs websites," Wendy says, staring at Cat.

"You do? You should've told me," Meredith says in a playfully scolding tone. "It would've saved me the search."

"Rebecca's daughter."

"Yes?"

"She designs them."

The music in the space has changed again; the lower keys of a piano are being pressed down in soft, dense clusters while a saxophone emits long, low notes and a drummer strokes the skins of his instrument with the palms of his hands. After collectively deciding they have lingered in this territory for long enough to constitute a tune, the musicians all choose a random note to hold on, then stop. In the silence before they start up again, Wendy speaks: "She's thirteen."

"Ah. Then it's probably best that I found Cat. Though teenagers can do some amazing things."

Throughout this exchange Cat notices that Wendy is trembling. Just slightly, barely noticeable at first, but the longer she stands there, the harder it is to miss. A very subtle tremor runs through her entire body, never growing in intensity, never diminishing.

"Will you be around for the one o'clock group, as well?" Meredith asks Wendy. "Don't forget there's no five o'clock today." She turns to Cat. "I'm taking Louis to my place up north. He loves it there. Just water and trees and the sounds of the birds. Absolute heaven. He practically leaps out the window of the car."

Cat decides that Meredith is speaking metaphorically. The dog she met would not survive a leap from a low ottoman onto a nest of down-filled pillows.

Without indicating how nice or how awful it is to meet Cat, Wendy turns to resume crossing the space and disappears into the change room. The hidden musicians respond to her abrupt departure by unleashing random notes in shorter, more urgent bursts.

As soon as Wendy is gone, Meredith tells Cat that her studio assistant has early stage Parkinson's.

"Oh, that's terrible," Cat says.

"It's not terrible, but it is unfair, unbelievably so. Such a cruel disease. She is only forty-five years old. She has been working hard to heal herself, with my help. I'm very proud of her. Her family and her doctor want her on all kinds of medication, as if that would help. She's finding her *own* way through it. Now, where do people register for the groups?"

It's a good site, Cat thinks. Not her best, but very functional and easy to navigate, and at the same time pretentious enough to match the atmosphere of the studio itself. People sign up for *groups* and *sessions* rather than *classes*. There is no mention of money or payment until people are at least a dozen clicks in and have committed, twice, to being part of a particular group. People who purchase memberships gain access to a section that is full of vegan recipes, stretching tips, inspirational sayings, and the like.

They also gain access to the Dream Sack, where members can input, anonymously, a short description of a recent dream they had that feels significant. When you are in the Sack, you are presented with the randomly selected dreams of others. Hit *Return* and another dream comes up. Anyone can read them, but only members can contribute their own.

I'm walking through a beautiful park when dogs with human faces run at me.

I'm looking through every book in the house, every page is cut with scissors.

I am on a boat that is sinking, I am screaming.

My father a talking baby.

The Dream Sack was the first thing Meredith demanded be preserved. It was part of the studio's old site, created nearly two decades ago, using one of the brutal coding languages of the time and hosted on the web equivalent of a party line. Meredith insisted that all the old dreams be moved to the new site, which meant Cat had to copy each one individually and transfer it to the new Sack.

One night during the laborious transfer process, after deciding the task would be made much easier with the help of wine, she drunkenly added a few dreams of her own, most featuring implausibly athletic sex between multiple partners, animal and human. There is one she is particularly proud of, in which an all-girl volleyball team has their way with a spying, lecherous leprechaun.

Cat wishes now, as Meredith stares hard at the screen, that she remembered to delete the dirtiest ones before preparing the demo.

"I apologize for asking if you were pregnant," Meredith says, not turning away from the laptop.

Cat is surprised to hear this subject come up again.

"I really didn't mean to suggest you look like you are. I would never do that, and you don't. I just felt it, somehow. I'm usually right. I've been thinking I should do a special for new mothers, actually. My friend Vanessa does an eight-week program for new mothers at her studio. She says she gets a lot of people signing up for it, though not all of them stick with it for the whole eight weeks. They're so tired."

Cat is strangely touched. "I think it sounds like a good idea," she says. "Even beyond the exercise part, it would be a good social thing for women who just had a baby. Like getting together for coffee."

"I don't allow people to bring coffee or food in here. Just water, and any medication they think they need."

"No, obviously. But it would still be good to see other people."

Meredith closes her eyes. "Were you lonely when you had yours? That's what I always heard from friends who have children: that it's very lonely when they're young."

"It can be. You're kind of on your own for the first part. Even if you have other people around helping, it's all on you."

"I really could not do it."

There isn't a trace of regret or sadness in Meredith's voice. She could've been talking about an exotic dish she had never tried, like pig snout or fried beetle.

"I wasn't sure I could, either," Cat says. "But I did it twice, for some reason."

She laughs. Meredith only opens her eyes to look at her.

"What about being bored? I can deal with a lot of things, but I really can't be bored."

"Sure. You get through it, though. It's not easy."

Meredith reaches out and touches Cat's arm. She leaves her hand there, lightly holding her elbow. The gesture is so unexpected that Cat has a perverse urge to confess everything to this woman. To tell her how, when she first became a mother, she would walk out in the sunshine, on her way to get something at the corner store, having forgotten for a moment about the baby asleep upstairs. She would always stop dead on the front steps, horrified at having almost walked out on her newborn, but tempted to keep going, to make a run for it. She wants to tell her how Donovan would come home in the evening, and she'd be happy to see him, but angry with him at the same time, because she could smell the outside world on him, on his clothes. He stank of life, while she — having spent the entire day around diapers and creams and soiled sleepers and hypoallergenic wipes — smelled like a hospital ward. When he took some time off to stay home with her, it was worse. She saw the look that came over his face as he became aware of what exactly constituted her daily life. And she could see how bored he got. How *dare* he be bored. He, at least, didn't have to have a tit ready at a moment's notice. He wasn't a slave to the small creature that had, only recently, torn through her crotch with the force of an angry rat. She would stare at her baby's face, waiting for a simple change of expression that would let her know there really was a human being in there somewhere, that she hadn't been cheated somehow.

A wave goes through her, and she staggers a little. The floor rises up beneath her and the taste of sour beer is in her mouth again. She wonders if Wendy has turned off the studio's air conditioning. She is damp all over with sweat.

"You're white," Meredith says, looking alarmed. "Are you sick?" She lets go of Cat's arm and takes a step back, just in case.

Cat shakes her head, and is embarrassed to discover she can't speak. Her throat tightens, and there is a noise in her head like a hundred tiny mallets striking thin metal bars, each resonating with a uniquely pitched *bong!*

It takes her a second to realize this sound is real, and all around her, playing through the studio's hidden speakers.

"I just ... *chair*," she says finally, in the voice of someone pulled out of rubble after days of no light or water.

"I don't keep any chairs in here. They would just be clutter — we always sit on the floor."

As if she'd been waiting for this exact information, Cat crumples where she stands. She can feel herself falling, and the thought goes through her head that she ought to do something to prevent it. Instead, she drops like a magic doll whose animating spell has suddenly been withdrawn.

When she opens her eyes a second or two later — she has no memory of actually hitting the floor — Cat feels no pain beyond a general ache that is evenly distributed throughout all parts of her body and head. She hasn't broken any bones. Or maybe her bones have dissolved. The floor of the studio is surprisingly soft. Something appears in her line of vision: a white towel. It looks soft and delicious; she wants to stuff it in her mouth. Wendy is standing a few feet away, watching her with an anxious expression.

Though she wants nothing more than to stay splayed out on the floor, Cat forces herself to sit up. Her head spins as she does so, and the movement sets off another wave of nausea. She gets herself to a sitting position, and can go no farther. All of her instincts tell her to laugh off what just happened, to make a joke about getting her sea legs or the terrible coffee she had on the way over, but she is suddenly afraid to speak for fear the growing storm in her stomach might erupt into actual vomit.

Meredith, as if overhearing her thoughts, quietly asks Wendy to bring some water.

"I won't ask you again if you're pregnant," she says to Cat, "but I will say you're doing a very good impression of someone who is. I've had a lot of mothers-to-be sit down hard on this floor. One day we'll have a baby delivered in here, I'm sure of it."

Cat laughs at the idea. Surely the mess of a live birth in this space would force Meredith to burn the place to the ground.

"I'm sorry. So embarrassing."

The older woman shakes her head. She lowers herself to the floor and sits cross-legged, facing Cat. When Wendy comes back with water in a clear glass bottle, she, too, sits on the floor. The three women form a triangle of support, and Cat feels as though she is back at one of the library song circles, except without children. The soft, metallic bonging is still going on around them. She pictures rows and rows of large teeth hanging from fishing wire and being struck by tiny hammers. The sound is strangely soothing. She could sleep right there. She makes noises about having to leave and looks around for her bag, but packing up her laptop is an impossibly complicated task.

Without saying anything, Meredith gets up and goes through a door in the corner of the studio. When she comes back, she is carrying a rolled-up mat, which she unfurls against the wall closest to Cat. Then she puts her hands on Cat's shoulders and urges her to lie back down. Though everything in her brain is telling her to refuse the offer and to flee this wooden paradise full of strange bonging noises, Cat allows herself to be eased to the ground. Her head is spinning, and there are shivers of pain running up through her body.

"Thank you," she says.

Meredith sits close to her. With both of the other women watching over her, Cat feels like a village elder finally dying off in her hundredth year. These women are here to ease her soul's passage to the sack of infinite dreams, to help it find her way out of the endless purgatory of the Beaches.

"Did you drive here?" Meredith asks. "I'm not asking because I want you to go," she adds, "but only because I'm worried about you driving like this."

I won't be driving like this, Cat thinks. *I'll be doing it sitting up, like a real person. Like a grown-up.*

"I'm parked down the street. I'll be okay."

They are all quiet again.

"I took the streetcar here yesterday," Wendy says, out of nowhere.

From Meredith's reaction to this news, it is as if the other woman announced she recently climbed to the roof and took flight.

"You did? That's *very* impressive. Good for you."

From her position on the mat, Cat looks between the two women for some explanation. Neither says anything at first. Then, slowly, Wendy explains that she had left her apartment early yesterday morning, feeling guilty about the idea of calling a cab, the way she usually does. And so, on a whim, she walked down to Queen Street and waited at the corner for a streetcar.

"*Wonderful,*" Meredith says.

"There was one coming, or I might not have waited."

She nearly got off again at the next stop, she says, but something made her stay.

Meredith gives a few quick claps, as much to celebrate Wendy's story as to make clear they have heard enough of it. Wendy's eyes are closed, and she is trembling slightly and breathing deeply, drawing in all of the new strength and knowledge with which her recent, momentous streetcar ride has provided her. Meredith is breathing deeply, too, but her eyes are on Cat. She says a word that Cat thinks, but can't be certain, is *bamboo*. Is the mat made of bamboo? The floor? Or is this word a kind of mantra she ought to fix her mind on as the rest of existence spins around her?

Bamboo. Bamboo. Bamboo.

Cat cannot deny the trill of relief that goes through her when she thinks of it.

Bamboo.

Around her wire brushes on cymbals and drums become the rustling of fat pandas as they move among succulent stalks, pulling them up by their roots and stripping them of their leaves with wise Asian teeth. The bamboo grows over top of her, blotting out the light and the sounds of the forest. A small group of pandas move closer.

"You're beautiful," she tells them. She adores their fat, furry folds, and is fascinated by their colouring. They look like living toys. Parents ought to fill their children's bedrooms with these rolling, snuffling creatures.

"I'm usually scared of bears," she says.

"We're not bears," the panda closest to her explains. "More like large raccoons."

He speaks with the voice of Sir David Attenborough.

"I don't mind raccoons," Cat says. She wants this animal to like her.

The panda stands on its hind legs, breaking stalks of delicate bamboo as it shifts position. It asks, in a voice that is no longer Attenborough's: "Is she okay?"

Cat opens her eyes. A woman holding a rolled-up yoga mat is standing a few feet away, looking down at her. The woman is not wearing any makeup, and her hair is pulled back in a harsh ponytail. Other women holding mats are moving through the studio. Most take little notice of Cat's presence or her odd position on the floor. They unfurl their mats and do some preliminary stretching. A few women stand behind their mats with eyes closed and heads lowered. Meredith is nowhere to be seen.

Wendy, standing nearby, speaks to the woman who asked about Cat. "She's not feeling well. She's a web designer."

Cat can't tell how long she has been asleep. Her phone tells her it was less than ten minutes, but it could easily have been an entire day.

The studio bathroom is a disappointment. Cat was expecting a dimly lit grotto where everything is curved and soft and sooth-ing, with no right angles. She expected koans written on the wall in calligraphy, a small pile of eucalyptus leaves instead of toilet paper, the whole thing fed by a hidden creek. Instead, it is functional and beige.

She settles herself on the toilet with the lid still down and opens her bag, looking for the pregnancy kit still hidden in there, waiting. Her hands are shaking a little, and she nearly drops the package twice as she pries it open and slides out one of the devices. Out of a sense of diligence, she reads the instruc-tions on the package. She is stalling, and she knows it. She is stalling for the same reason she allowed herself to go this many weeks without checking.

There is a quiet, hesitant knock on the door. Cat guesses it is someone coming to see if she has collapsed on the floor.

"I'll be out soon. I'm fine."

It takes her a minute or so to get everything ready and into
position, but finally she is able to drown the testing stick with
pee, setting in motion whatever reality is coming her way.
She settles back on the toilet and tries to remember the last
time she and Donovan had sex. It was a while ago, weeks and
weeks. Claudia and Dale were over, and Donovan made dinner for everyone. Mushroom burgers and grilled vegetables.
He was more animated and generous than usual, and Cat
remembers wondering how much this shift had to do with
the top her sister was wearing, which was sheer and sleeveless.
Every time Claudia put her hands behind her head, which she
did a lot, the mellow balls of her breasts were visible through
the absent sleeves. Claudia kept saying how wonderful it was
to be somewhere without Baby Jessica — they'd hired a sit-
ter — but how nervous-making, too. Each time she did so,
she put her hands in the air and crossed them behind her
head. Donovan brought out wine and insisted on refilling
their glasses over and over. Isabelle fell asleep in one of the
Muskoka chairs, and Silas dozed in his mother's lap while
Donovan explained some complicated and painful thing
he'd seen Jackie Chan do in a movie and why he believed
Chan to be up there with Charlie Chaplin and Buster Keaton.
Claudia's chin was on her chest. Cat reached over and finished
her sister's wine.

Later, in their bed, Donovan rolled over and began stroking
Cat's back. He smelled like grill smoke and mushrooms. Her
first instinct was to say no — she was sore and tired, and had
what felt like premenstrual cramps — but the earnestness and
humility of his stroking made her feel guilty, so she rolled over
to greet him. After the shudder went through him and he settled onto her stomach, sweaty and exhausted, she was tempted

to ask whom he thought might have been the best fuck: Jackie Chan, Charlie Chaplin, or Buster Keaton.

Cat flushes the toilet, washes her hands, and adjusts her clothes. Only when she is all settled does she reach for the pregnancy test, ready for it to tell her fate.

"Oh, for *fuck's* sake."

V

DONOVAN NEEDS NEW SHIRTS. HIS OLD ONES ARE growing tight on him, which makes it awkward whenever he meets people about potential work. At the coffee shop with two young guys looking for someone to handle the comms side of their tech start-up, he wore his pale blue shirt with the tiny star pattern, his favourite. His new belly pushed against its constraints. The whole time he worried the buttons would pop out and fly across the table.

"Those glasses are *wicked*," he said to one of the young men, who wore transparent plastic frames, and who smiled sympathetically at his attempt to sound young.

Donovan later heard back that they'd decided to hire a student intern to handle it all instead.

He heads downtown, opting for public transit, wishing Cat could see him making the financially responsible choice, something she believes him incapable of. The streetcar grinds forward slowly, packed to the doors, forcing him to stand. Some high school girls get on, and Donovan stands straighter. The girls stand together in the aisle, not holding on to anything, moving with the vehicle like weeds in deep water. Each of their skirts has been cinched and shortened, and he lingers on the sight of their smooth thighs. One of the girls, the quietest weed, wears a stylish medical mask. Her skirt is not cinched as high as the others. Her modesty draws him in. She reminds him a bit of Lena. Same hair, same eyes, same deferential dip of the head when spoken to. He tries not to stare.

The last time he saw Lena — that crazy, ridiculous moment in the bathroom — she had appeared in the doorway like a ghost. What had he been thinking? He was out of his mind. He can still feel the emotional plunge that happened the moment he came all over the floor. He was rocketing higher and higher, the sky getting darker and the universe opening up, and then, like the shuttle exploding just as its tip nudged the void of space, he blew apart. Scorched parts of him dropped slowly back down to earth, trailing foamy ribbons of smoke. Before it was even over, Lena disappeared. Like she'd never been there.

Seriously: what the *fuck* was he thinking?

He remembers waking up that morning, thinking he had the house to himself. As always when that happens, he chose to mark the occasion by jerking off. The first video he tried had a woman who looked a lot like one of the moms at Silas's daycare. A bonus. He liked that she appeared to be enjoying herself — he hates when he can detect boredom or distress. He also liked that the woman in the video was a little older than most, in her early thirties at least. When he goes browsing these sites now, he often looks for people who are closer to his own age. That is how Donovan knows he is not a monster. He never goes looking for kids. He doesn't go the other way, either. Never gets off watching some poor old lady gag on a cock the size of an arm.

That's the nice thing about online porn: you discover exactly where your line is, beyond which you will not venture.

Naked, he moved to the bathroom and propped his phone on the counter. In the video the woman in the glasses expressed her surprise and delight, mixed with a tiny bit of mock fear, at the size of the cock she was being presented with. The cock's unseen owner, who was holding the camera, replied in a deep voice, "Yeah, you *like* that."

Shut up, Donovan thought. *Don't ruin it. Be humble.*

He pulled his way into their rhythm, catching and surpassing them, until it felt as though he were performing for *them*, not the other way around. Clouds of bad feeling, of tension and stress, gathered in his stomach and in his ass, ready to break and dissipate. He was right on the verge.

And then Lena walked in, and the floor of reality fell away from him.

After she left he'd stood there for a moment or two, trying to catch his breath, unwilling to relinquish the unexpected boost of pleasure her presence had given him. It was like he was drunk. But he wasn't drunk, he was *broken* — only a broken person would act like that. He was in pieces, like one of the rock creatures in one of Silas's cartoons, made up of discrete boulders that roll and clack together as they walk, but never fuse or become solid.

· · ·

Donovan spent the next week or two in fear, waiting every day for Cat to get a call or a text, to hear her disbelieving voice turn to sadness and anger. For the yelling to start and his marriage to collapse. But the call never came. Lena, as quiet and modest as ever, simply erased herself from their lives. She bowed out. Good for her.

Was what he did enough to end a marriage, really? Other couples they knew had gone through worse and come out the other side. A mom at Isabelle's school had fucked the international student who'd been renting their basement apartment and confessed the whole thing to her husband after the student went back to South Korea. That happened in the spring, and by the following Christmas, both husband and wife were there together at the school holiday concert, taking photo after photo of their little boy dressed as a dreidel.

Later, to reward himself for finding two new shirts that fit him well, Donovan goes to see a movie. There is an afternoon showing of a documentary he's been wanting to see, about a reclusive puppeteer from a famous kids' show who went a little bonkers after the show ended and had come to see the puppets as real people. Donovan has been trying to get Cat to see it with him, but she won't, declaring it exploitation to film someone so obviously at the end of their rope. Donovan counters that if filmmakers are not allowed to exploit people, no one will ever make another documentary.

She asks if that would be the end of the world.

In the theatre he sits in the centre of an empty row, less and less sure that he won the argument. In the film the puppeteer, defeated and ragged, is interviewed in his dim kitchen, accompanied by a pigtailed girl puppet who sits on his knee and who frequently interjects with a cheeky comment. Donovan leaves the moment the credits begin, right after a note — sombre white letters against a black screen — saying the old puppeteer died while the film was being edited. He is pursued into the lobby by the end-credits music, a solo piano piece that sounds pretty and mournful at the same time. He uses an app on his phone to identify the composer and makes a note to download a pile of the guy's stuff when he gets home. It sounds like good thinking music.

He allows himself to be drawn south down Yonge by the fast-marching crowd. At one busy intersection, he dodges a sidewalk preacher shouting angry rhetorical questions into a megaphone. One of the preacher's minions holds out a brochure for him to take, and Donovan has it in his hand before he even has a chance to say no. *Get Satan Out of Your Life*, the brochure commands, as if the devil were an ex-lover who refuses to move on. At the next intersection, he hands the brochure to a woman wearing a pantsuit and pulling a briefcase on wheels, who takes it almost without looking at him.

He is killing time, the way he did during those grim weeks before he came clean to Cat about losing his job. Before he was able to shift out from under the weight of everything he was carrying, the shame and the embarrassment and the guilt, and let all of it drop to the ground. It's all out in the open now, everything he did. He's past it, that whole business, though he knows that Cat has not entirely let it go. He can always see it there, looming up behind her like a bodyguard, ready to move in if he takes one step out of line. Nothing is ever exculpatory when it comes to Cat, there is never a statute of limitations, and

no such thing as reform. All evidence is relevant, all past crimes
stay on the books.

For a while after Cat found out about him getting fired,
Donovan, at her urging, went to see a therapist. The therapist
told him there were studies that showed how losing a job can
affect the human brain in almost exactly the same way as getting divorced or surviving a serious accident. There is grief and
there is shame, she told him, however misplaced. There is a deep
sense of loss. And, of course, there is the shock of it all. The
weeks of wandering Donovan did, the feelings of uselessness
and lethargy, the lying to his loved ones — it was all a reaction
to this trauma. His reaction is very common, she told him. In
one sense what he'd done, in terms of keeping the truth from
Cat, was even admirable. Obviously, it wasn't the best course of
action, and had its own negative consequences, but there was at
least some part of him that was trying to protect her, trying to
have her believe that nothing had changed, nothing had been
lost. It was a healthy instinct, and totally understandable.

"I think that's right," he said. "That's exactly what I was
trying to do."

In the eight weeks he saw the therapist, they talked through
all of his hurts and anger. She helped him turn a big spotlight
on all the shitty things that had been done to him, all the assumptions people made about him just because his family had
money, because he'd been good at his job and got paid well,
and because he was a man.

He misses those sessions. It felt good to be listened to, even
if he was paying for the privilege. It had been nice, too — in

that small office, nearly a dozen floors up, with a glittering view of downtown — to sit and stare at this woman, younger than him by a few years, and slim in an unmistakably child-free way. She wore skirts that ended a few inches above the knee and held her thighs like a tight ribbon. Halfway through each session, she would move in her chair to tuck her legs beneath her, a sign that the conversation had reached a new stage, a signal of the shift between acts, a move toward deeper empathy and understanding. Donovan would watch carefully, hoping one knee would move an inch too far to the left or right, lighting up the darkness and offering a glimpse of underwear he guessed was immaculate and clean and colourful.

Once they completed this tour of his pain, Donovan knew instinctively that the next step would be to take a closer look at his own responsibility for all of it, to assess his own culpability in creating pain for others. He cancelled the next appointment and never went back. The same day, he took Cat and the kids to a pizza place on a very Italian stretch of St. Clair, a place with a brick oven in the back. Cat glowed like a rinsed plum through the entire meal and didn't once mention her work or her weird pains.

"Thank you," she said as they walked back to the car. "That was really nice. I feel like I ate a whole loaf of bread, but I don't care."

Donovan, who'd had three bottles of Birra Moretti with dinner and needed to pee, started tap dancing on the sidewalk, and would not stop until Cat laughed and Silas began to copy him. Even Isabelle smiled.

The air that night was alive with happiness. Everything was sweet. The food and beer in his belly. The faces of his children. The warmth and wetness of Cat a few hours later, as he slid into her, slowly and lovingly, while she held her breath and gripped his shoulders as if they were acrobats about to perform a stunt.

Donovan steps into a falafel shop just off Yonge and orders a falafel with extra hot sauce, plus a can of Diet Coke and a half-dozen samosas to offer the kids when he gets home. The man behind the counter calls Donovan *my friend*, and for a moment, he allows himself to believe that that is exactly what he is: a friend.

"Stay cool," he tells the man as he is leaving.

"I will, my friend."

He walks until he comes to a coffee shop with a couple of empty tables outside, puts the bag with the food on one of the tables, and decides to eat the falafel right there, in full view of everyone packed into the coffee shop. Unlike them, he is not stealing a few moments' rest and happiness at the end of a dull day before wedging himself into a hot streetcar or subway or GO train. He is living right now, he is alive and fully at home in this city. He smiles at the thought and bites into the falafel, drawing away strings of lettuce and bursting a deep vein of hummus that threatens to spill beyond the edges of his mouth.

He chokes.

Inside the coffee shop, her body coming into view like a rare tropical specimen in an aquarium, is Bianca, the same woman who got him fired. Her black hair is shorter, but still flows around her head like a special effect. She is wearing a tight blue button-up shirt with short sleeves and a white skirt that ends just below her knees. She is holding a tall takeout cup and is looking intently at her phone. She could be staring into the reflected glow of a seashell.

Donovan has seen this expression many times. He used to study it from across the office while Bianca replied to emails, assessed spreadsheets, or gave marketing copy a final proofread. There had been no better feeling than to walk up to her and watch that hard stare melt into a welcoming smile. For months he has been wanting fresh mental images of her, so he feeds on the sight of her. Then he panics and steps away, leaving behind the bag of samosas. He walks quickly back toward Yonge, where he can conceal himself underground. At the entrance to the subway, he changes his mind and summons an Uber to meet him at the next intersection. At no point does he look back.

Bianca locked her Instagram account right away after he got fired, leaving him with only one good photo of her. He emailed it to himself before deleting it off his phone, then stashed it in the drafts folder where Cat could not find it. In the photo Bianca is on the patio on the roof of their office building, where people go to smoke and vape. Everything is dusted with new, sugary snow. It's just her in the photo, leaning back on a railing and smiling. A model pose, performed self-consciously but convincingly. She is wearing a form-fitting black winter coat with a furry hood that explodes out around her head. Donovan used to tease her about that coat, about the geese that had been plucked to fill its interior, and the wolf that died to provide her with its warm fringe.

"You don't even ever put that hood up," he told her. "The wolf died for *nothing*."

"*Don't*," she replied with a purr. "You're making me feel bad."

How old is she again? Twenty-six? Twenty-seven? Young enough to be of the generation that wants never to feel bad, and yet always does. Another thing he teased her about. Everyone her age is pillowed with privilege, yet they have impossible levels of anxiety running through them, paralyzing them.

He and Bianca often went to the roof together. Even if it was raining, they'd stand out there and talk, sharing one of the communal office umbrellas. He liked the rainy days the best, because no one else would come out, and they'd have to stand close together. Close enough that she could smudge him with her smoke, and he would say again that he liked the smell, leaving it an open question as to whether he meant the cigarettes or her. She told him she had a boyfriend, but that it wasn't serious.

He mentally filed the *not serious* part away for later.

Donovan was careful never to mention Cat in front of Bianca, though obviously she knew he was married. The ring was a giveaway, for one thing. She understood the game they were playing, and never asked him about his wife. Sometimes she asked about his kids, but that was as close as she ever came to the subject of his particular domestic reality. He became adept at avoiding any mention of her.

It's something he wanted to say to Bianca after all the shit happened, after he got kicked to the curb: *You knew what we were doing! You understood the rules!*

Instead of going straight home, he has the driver drop him off at a bar on Bloor, a few blocks from his house. He settles onto a corner stool — the place is already busy, despite the relatively early hour — and orders something dark and sour. The TV behind the bar is playing *Back to the Future* with the sound off, as if picking up a signal from the distant cultural past. Marty McFly is meeting his own father as a teenager.

There's a new text waiting on his phone. It's from Bianca.

What the fuck your spying on me you creepy asshole

She saw him out there, cramming a stupid falafel into his stupid face. She saw him turn and run. He burps out of embarrassment and anger.

Bitch. Fucking *bitch*.

But she looked beautiful. As much as he wishes he could say otherwise, her beauty is an objective fact, as undeniable as arithmetic. Her large eyes *plus* her dark skin *plus* the brutal pink cut of her mouth *plus* the austere angle of her cheekbones *plus* the generous shape of her body. He can't even imagine what it would be like to walk around like that.

There is another text: *If I see you ever I will call the police im serious fuck you.*

He finishes his beer just as Marty wakes up in the darkness of the bedroom belonging to his teenage mother. The young woman tending bar asks Donovan if he wants another. He decides to cut himself off.

"Get home safe," she tells him.

He slips a ten-dollar bill under his glass. "Where we're going, we don't *need* roads," he says.

She gives him a puzzled look.

He points to where the movie is still playing behind her head, "Ancient history ..."

She raises an eyebrow at him, so in one quick move, he reaches forward and takes the tip back before she can grab it.

"Just a barrel of laughs here," he says and walks out.

VI

LENA BRINGS THE BASKET OF DIRTY LAUNDRY INTO the kitchen. She does most things in her kitchen because her living room is haunted by the sound of a neighbour's TV. The walls are too thin. In her bedroom she wears earplugs to block out the sounds of people fighting and having sex — usually one following the other, in random order. The one time she got desperate enough in her own loneliness to try listening in on the sounds of sex coming through her wall, she was forced to stop — naked, knees in the air — when she realized the noise she was hearing was a fight. Someone was getting hurt, not held.

She lifts a shirt from the basket, presses it against her nose, and sniffs hard: hamburgers, fries, grease. She grabs another shirt from the pile. Hamburgers, fries, grease. She'd been warned this would happen when she started working at

McDonald's. One of her new co-workers, a young man named Lakhwinder who asks every new female employee out, advised her never to bring her own clothes to work or they will end up stinking.

"Just come in your uniform. Nobody cares."

Then he asked her out.

Angry now, she picks up another shirt. Hamburgers, fries, grease.

She has tried wearing her uniform to work, but hates being on the bus in it with the older mothers, the high school kids, and especially the women her age — white and brown and black, their hair stacked up and their makeup on full-blast, young women whom no one would ever dare ask to work the deep fryer, or mop the floor behind the counter, or take heavy bags of garbage out to the enormous metal container that swallows up whatever you throw down its throat. The restaurant sweats garbage; the yellow bags fill up almost faster than they can be dragged out. Twice she has pulled bags of garbage out the back door of the restaurant, only to have them grabbed by men desperate for a meal. They yanked the bags out of her grip and dug through the plastic with dirty fingers, in search of cold fries and discarded chicken nuggets. One sucked clean an open packet of ketchup.

She finally finds a shirt that doesn't stink, one of her nicer ones. She bought it at a clearance sale and got an unexpected extra discount when the young woman at the counter found a small flaw along its bottom hem, an area of less than a centimetre square where the white of the shirt is oddly translucent, from grease or melted wax.

"You want to pick another one, or do you want me to add the discount?"

The woman at the counter was younger than Lena, but had more authority, more confidence. Her skin was many shades darker. Her hair required more work and more chemicals. She had the power to judge goods to be imperfect and to add discounts at will. Lena took the shirt, and the discount, and went home feeling imperfect. She uses the little cardboard tag that came with the shirt as a bookmark. Right now, it is waiting for her in the middle of *Psalms*.

The first time men grabbed garbage bags from her, she tried to stop them by promising to bring them actual food. The second time, she stepped back inside and summoned the security guard to come deal with it. She'd been there long enough for all her self-pity to have been converted into contempt — the same contempt everyone else who works there feels for the desperate, crumpled souls who stumble through the doors, day and night. There is one man who comes into the restaurant wearing a bright red wig. Everyone calls him Ronald, because of the company's clown mascot. Ronald comes in smiling every time, but inevitably starts yelling at whoever is trying to complete his order. Alan, the security guard, moves quickly beside him, tells him to calm down, and instructs him to take his food outside. He does it so smoothly that Ronald obeys, as if Alan's voice is coming from inside his head.

"You should at least take that wig," Lena tells the guard.

Alan, rubbing sanitizer into his hands, tells her everyone deserves dignity and respect.

"If that wig is what he needs to get through the day, I'm not going to take it away from him."

Later, Lena submits an anonymous complaint against Alan, saying he is endangering the restaurant's customers and workers through inaction. She feels a little guilty when he is replaced, but is happy to see the new guard block Ronald at the door.

For a while now, Lena has been feeling as though the city she lives in is sliding into some kind of animal state. Or maybe it has always been like that. On the bus, she has to make herself as small as possible as high school boys fight around her. And she tries not to see, as she crosses the patch of green that separates her building from two others just like it, the young couples clutching at each other on the picnic tables, their pants down past their thighs. One morning, coming out of the elevator onto the ground floor of her building, she watches as a thick-shouldered older man tries to push open the front door from the outside. He is carrying plastic bags filled with something heavy. She is about to help him, but his impatience strikes first. He makes a sound like a creature tangled in ropes, then kicks at the glass of the door, shattering it. For a week the door has cardboard instead of glass.

A young woman from Lena's building, a Korean teenager who lives with her mother and grandmother, tells her that someone recently got attacked in the laundry room. Lena says she hasn't heard anything about that. *Of course* she hasn't heard, the young woman says, it was kept quiet. The guy who did it is the nephew of the building superintendent, and the woman who was attacked doesn't want to make a thing of it. She wasn't raped, just grabbed a little. She's frightened, and doesn't want to lose her apartment. Her mother and grandmother told her to be quiet about it.

It is only later that Lena realizes the Korean girl was talking about herself.

Lena never returned to Cat and Donovan's house. Never collected her final cheque. Cat sent her messages that she ignored. Eventually, they stopped coming. She told her other housecleaning clients that she had the flu and would be unable to come for a few days. The days stretched into weeks. A few of the clients, friends and neighbours of Cat's, fired her outright. Another hinted that perhaps a change was needed. Her remaining two, both of them messier than the others, but also at their cottages a lot in the summer and therefore less in need of someone to come in and clean just then, wished her well and said she could take time off if she needed it. Lena doesn't like abandoning those people, but in the end, there was no point going all the way downtown for just two houses, and she wasn't likely to get more clients any time soon, not with how things had ended with the others, and not in the middle of the summer.

Finally, with an eye on her dwindling savings, and conscious of the fact that a government worker could check in on her at any moment to confirm that she was still working hard and earning, as per the solemn promise she made when she arrived, she spent most of a weekend updating her resumé. The McDonald's assistant manager who hired her looked quickly at her address, then asked if she was legally allowed to work in Canada.

"I am," she said, and offered to show him documentation to prove it.

He shook his head, preferring plausible deniability, and asked if she preferred mornings or nights.

"I am okay with both," she told him, shifting her arms in case there was visible sweat beneath them. She was embarrassed at how nervous she was talking to this man who was maybe only a couple of years older than her and wearing a headset with a little microphone that dangled in front of his mouth like a thin worm.

He told her, with obvious impatience, that *everybody* says they are fine with both, but it is never true. So, which was it, really: mornings or nights?

"We need people for mornings more," he added.

"I can do mornings. I like them."

Other than for work, Lena almost never leaves her apartment. One of the fry cooks, a nineteen-year-old boy named Gary who looks Japanese but says he's Italian, provides her with small baggies of weed and edibles. She gives away the weed — smoking makes her feel like she is choking to death — but gobbles the edibles on her days off and sits at her kitchen window, from which she can stare down at the endless flow of the 401, and beyond that the random stacks of buildings that march all the way south through the city to Lake Ontario. There are no curtains on any of her windows, except on the one in the bedroom, which is covered to keep out the sun, not other people's eyes. She is fourteen floors up — who's going to look in? No one is trying to catch an illicit glimpse of Indian families eating dinner or Nigerian cab drivers rinsing their clothes in kitchen sinks or overburdened Haitian ladies watching TV.

She likes to put music on, as loud as she dares, and listen for hours as she stares out the window. Lately, she can't stand the sound of a piano. Too brittle, too thin. She gets impatient for it to do something, to go somewhere interesting or unexpected or fun. The sound of a piano leaves too much room for her own thoughts. So she listens to Lil Tigger, a favourite of Patricia's. Lil Tigger's all about anger and lust. She will not allow your mind to drift away. You are there for her, and her alone. Shut up and listen, bitch, Lil Tigger tells her, and so Lena does. She likes that Lil Tigger was once a stripper, but is now rich and famous, so nobody cares what she used to do. She is beyond shame. She also wears a cross twice as big as Lena's and is ordained as a minister. Lena often sees this quote from Lil Tigger: "Jesus don't fuck with people who have their face in a Bible. He's after the ones with their face in a pussy."

Sometimes Lena connects her laptop to one of the building's unprotected Wi-Fi streams so she can sneak her way to videos of naked brown bodies glistening and flexing as they twist around each other. There is too much focus on crotches and asses, she thinks. She gets her darkest thrills from the faces. From the bit lips and closed eyes and looks of extreme surprise. She can only enjoy it if she thinks the people in the videos are enjoying it, too. Too many look miserable or drunk. She browses and browses until she finds a pair who look like they genuinely enjoy climbing all over each other. She bites her lip without realizing it, her hand in her jeans.

She has even started skipping Bible study meetings, which would've been unthinkable even a few months ago. Patricia could never understand Lena's excitement about the Bible group, and refused every invitation to join it. God had more important things to worry about, and so did she.

"Everyone is so old," she said. "Why do you waste time with this, with these people? You have no friends. Except me."

But Lena remembers the way she felt when she first joined: exhilarated from all those hours swimming so close to the Word, along with others who were just as eager to find a source of almost unbearable heat and light that could shine out and burn away all the dark and dampness of their lives. She used to walk for a long time after those meetings, not wanting to have that feeling of exhilaration dissipate. Eventually, she would relent, her feet being too sore to continue, and she would wait for the next coming bus. By then the glow inside would be smaller and more compact, small enough to carry more comfortably, a smoldering patch of moss or wood shavings that can be used to light a fire whenever she needed.

Lately, she's been getting that same feeling from the edibles.

One night, running late, Lena shows up to Bible study still in her work uniform. A few people think it's a joke. Ria and Anya, the Trinidadian sisters, say the smell makes them sick. Timothy just licks his lips. She goes to get changed and finds all the cookies and coffee and juice on a table just outside the room, waiting for the break. She quickly scoops up the crinkly packages of cookies and stuffs them into her bag. She has to fight to stop giggling. At break time she acts just as shocked as anyone at the theft, though she worries a little when someone mentions security cameras. On the way home, she eats a few of the cookies, then gives the rest away to a group of kids smoking in front of a darkened computer store.

The only other place Lena goes is the Rabba's grocery store a few blocks from her building, where she buys tea, carrots, pineapple juice, and samosas, or just wanders slowly up and down each aisle of the store, scanning the packages of instant noodles, jars of peanut butter, bottles of dish detergent and bleach, and pre-packaged sandwiches and falafel balls in the bright deli section. She will usually gobble a few edibles on the way, and through the glaze of the weed in her system, the store's items are like magical, colourful beads and trinkets. She picks things up, amused by their packaging, then puts them back. She wanders the aisles like a lost bird.

She talks to Javed, who is slightly older than her, and has been working there since he was little — his father owns the store. Javed is tall and skinny and likes to wear golf shirts, even in the winter. After his father had a stroke a few years ago and had to let go of the day-to-day operations, Javed took over. Javed never questions Lena's presence in the store, never demands she buy something. Sometimes, if it is not busy, he will call her out. He calls her Fry Girl, because of where she works. Somehow, it never sounds like an insult coming from him. More of a recognition of shared labour, of being two people stuck doing a job that isn't glamorous or fun.

Lena likes telling Javed about the wild people she encounters at the restaurant. He likes to hear about the shouters and the nuts, the ones who come in and start yelling at the top of their lungs, or who go from table to table, singing off-key or mumbling to themselves until the security guard walks them back outside. The same thing happens in the store: crazies come in; crazies go out.

One time, Lena is in the middle of telling him about a man in a fluorescent green jacket who came into the restaurant yelling about Michael Jackson being a pervert, when the same exact man walks into the store, wearing the same green jacket and everything. He doesn't yell — he looks half asleep, and there is a new rip on the arm of his jacket. He picks up a Monster Energy drink and two hard-boiled eggs, paying for them with new-looking cash. Javed takes the man's money and executes a clumsy moonwalk to the cash register. Lena almost falls apart trying not to laugh. The man in the jacket doesn't notice.

"But Michael Jackson *was* a pervert," Javed says, a little sadly, after the man leaves.

Patricia texts her, asking to come over. Lena is embarrassed at how happy this makes her, and how relieved.

She writes back: *of course*

She hasn't seen her cousin in weeks. Patricia got angry when she heard that Lena had quit cleaning. Lena didn't tell her anything else, only that she'd stopped, and right away Patricia yelled at her. She yelled at her over the phone a few more times, then stopped calling. As the silence stretched on, Lena caught herself wondering if she should stay in this country after all. In the video calls with her parents, her father makes clear she is welcome to come back any time. They would make room for her.

She never says yes or no.

Patricia arrives an hour or so later carrying — surprise! — two bottles of bubbly white wine with golden labels. It's her mother's birthday, Patricia says, and they should celebrate. Lena apologizes for not having guessed at the occasion.

Patricia shrugs. "I only remembered when we're talking on the phone."

She gives Lena a warm hug, which melts her. Lena finds two small juice glasses in the cupboard above the sink while Patricia lays one of the bottles on its side in the freezer, snug between a rack of shrinking ice cubes and five packs of frozen mixed vegetables. She pokes at the vegetables. "These are the best kind," she says.

"You can have one to take home if you want," Lena says.

The wine is cool and bright in Lena's mouth and in her stomach. The alcohol brightens her mood. She drinks the first glass too fast and gets the hiccups, which makes Patricia laugh and call her a child. She unplugs Lena's phone and replaces it with her own. "Almost gone," she says, meaning her battery's charge. The surface of Patricia's phone is traversed with long cracks like lightning bolts. After a few moments of scrolling, she finds a song that is slow and silky, sung by a man with a thick Jamaican accent. It's one Lena has never heard before, and she loves it instantly. The sound of it fuses with the wine in her stomach and makes her happy and restless.

"Who is this?" she asks.

Patricia tells her it's someone new, someone who grew up not far from her neighbourhood. Lena is amazed at the idea of someone being from here. She is careful to sip slowly at her second glass of the bubbly wine.

"They have me on a breakfast shift tomorrow. I have to be there at six."

"I can't believe you work at that place."

"I know!" Lena says, laughing. It's the biggest joke in the world, her job. In the end, despite what he'd said, the assistant manager put her on both mornings and nights, dropping her all over the schedule at random. She doesn't complain. It's the only unpredictable thing about the job. Even the crazies who come in, shouting and swearing, have become part of a routine. She tells her cousin about the young mothers who feed their babies french fries — little babies who can barely sit up, faces smeared with ketchup. Patricia shakes her head and warns Lena not to eat any of the food or she'll get addicted to it. And if that happens? No man.

"It's garbage food."

Lena takes a sip and says she doesn't like the taste, anyway. Too salty. Only the new people eat it. Pretty soon you get sick of it.

"You only started. You're new people," Patricia says.

"I'm not, really." She has already seen three employees leave and get replaced in the weeks she's been there. The person with the most seniority is the assistant manager, who has been there less than two years.

"I would be out of there the first day," Patricia says, taking a long, leisurely sip.

Pouring them both more wine, Patricia tells Lena about the man she is seeing, a roofing contractor who lives in Barrie. They kept encountering each other in the neighbourhoods where they were both working — her to clean houses, him to work on the roofs — and he finally asked her out to a club. He lives with his ex-wife and two very young children: a girl and a boy. The whole thing with the ex-wife and the two kids is not permanent and not a problem, Patricia insists. Toby — his name is Toby — is looking for his own place, closer to Toronto.

"It's not easy. Toby needs a place to park his truck."

Lena giggles involuntarily. Something about a man named Toby looking for somewhere to park his truck strikes her as funny. She says she is happy for Patricia, which she is. They clink glasses, and Patricia admits she doesn't like the name *Toby*. It sounds like the name of a teddy bear or a dog. But she has heard worse. She hates the name *Brad*.

"Or *Gord*," Lena says, laughing. "Or *Donovan*."

"Isn't that the name of someone? One of your houses?"

Lena admits that it is — or was. After a moment she adds that it is because of that particular house that she isn't cleaning anymore. She is shocked at how easily the information comes out. The warm gold in her belly is making her feel invincible. It is stupid to be upset about a man like that.

"What happened?"

"It wasn't good."

"Tell me. You have to."

And so, Lena does. The whole stupid story.

Lena tells Patricia about coming into the house, starting her day, going upstairs, and finding Donovan in the bathroom, doing what he was doing. She tells how he did not stop when she saw him, how he just kept on going until it was over, and how she left right away and never went back.

When she is done, Patricia asks Lena to tell her again how Donovan looked, standing there naked, playing with himself like a monkey. She wants details. Is it big, his thing? She guesses not. Is he fat?

Lena's face gets hot.

"That's why you quit?" Patricia asks her. "You're so stupid! It's nothing, nothing!"

She lists off all the things that have happened to *her* while cleaning. One man grabbed her from behind and pulled her against him — she could feel his penis in his shorts. He'd been drinking; she could smell it on him. She just laughed at him. He was playing around. It was a joke. He never did it again. Meanwhile, she got a hundred-dollar bonus on her next cheque. There is another man who always walks around in front of her in little underwear, as if she's not supposed to notice. She has had to clean around clients changing in front of her, looking at porn, having a poo.

Lena insists that what happened to her is worse. Donovan actually did something *to* her. Or *at* her, anyway.

"Did he touch you?"

Lena has to admit that he didn't. In fact, right after he finished, he thanked her, she says.

"He said *thank you*?"

Patricia slaps the table between them in exasperation and tells Lena how, the first month she was in Canada, someone did the same thing to her in a parking lot. This man was sitting in his car, his pants open, but you couldn't see it until you were right beside the door. He called her over to ask her something, to ask directions, and when she came to the window, he was all ready to go. It was over almost before she even realized.

"And no *thank you*," Patricia says, her voice full of sarcasm. "No nothing."

Has no one ever done that to her before?

Lena doesn't say anything. *Of course* it has happened before. Back home, when she was about ten or eleven, one of her brother's friends did the same thing. Tricked her into watching.

She called him a pig, so he got embarrassed and begged her not to tell anyone. And here, guys are always grabbing themselves on the bus and giving her a look. Holding themselves through their track pants. Letting her know that it's for *her*, if she wants. Or even if she doesn't.

But none of that was the same as what Donovan did, in her mind. All those people know what they are doing is wrong, that it's dirty. Even the ones on the bus. They're trying to make her feel nervous, to upset her. Donovan wasn't trying to upset her. It didn't feel as though what he did had anything to do with her, really. She was just there to watch, to be a pair of eyes. She could've been anyone. Watching him do that was merely one of the many tasks she had to complete while she was in the house. When it was over, she was supposed to have gone and made the beds, emptied the garbage, wiped down the shower curtains. And he would forget she was even there.

That's what his *thank you* meant: *thank you, now go back to being nothing.*

They sip at the wine, though less greedily now, trying to get back the warm feeling it had been giving them. Patricia talks about her sort-of boyfriend Toby. He has a tattoo on his left arm of a basketball scratched by dinosaur claws. She says he got mad at her once when she asked what dinosaurs have to do with basketball. She asked him to buy her a Raptors jersey, a sexy one, and he did. It's a really nice one, very expensive.

Lena thinks this is hilarious — her cousin doesn't even like basketball.

"Why aren't you wearing it now?"

"I only wear it when I'm with Toby."

Lena is sitting on the floor. Her bum is asleep, but she likes being down there. It makes her feel like a grown-up and like a kid at the same time. Like she's claiming her apartment by sitting there, in a way she has never done in all the time she's lived there. And she likes that her cousin looks so relaxed.

Patricia sits back to put her feet up on another chair. She talks about the call with her mother.

"She has a new man — some man from the post office who delivers her packages. She buys all her things from Amazon. Every day: Amazon! Amazon! Amazon! Anyway, my brother is in love with a Korean girl, and my mother thinks the girl is pregnant. He cut his hair short. Remember Damián's hair? So long."

Lena smiles. "Longer than mine. Are they getting married?"

Patricia doesn't answer. For a while she is quiet, and Lena starts to think she is angry with her — did she say something stupid?

"They pay you?" Patricia asks finally.

"I get paid every two weeks."

"No. The man in the bathroom — did he pay you after?"

"I don't want to deal with him ever."

"But did they pay you?"

"No."

Patricia nods like a detective closing a case.

"Where was the woman?"

Lena says she wasn't there that particular day. "She sent me a text."

Patricia sits up and lets her feet drop to the floor. "After, she did?"

Lena nods. The woman named Cat messaged her a day or two later, wanting to know why she had not finished cleaning the house, and if everything was okay.

"Cat? That's her *name*? Cat? Like a cat?"

Patricia holds her hands up in an approximation of two feline paws. Lena giggles, says yes, and finishes the wine in her glass. The whole trouble with Donovan in the bathroom seems so stupid now, like nothing she needs to worry about. She got away from them, she has a new job — that's all that matters.

"She sent me a *lot* of texts."

When Lena didn't reply to Cat, and didn't show up the following week, the texts became impatient, then angry. Lena had wanted to reply with the whole story.

"Don't say anything. Don't get into that."

"I know. She's so angry. She'd go crazy if she knew. Do you think she knows?"

"Show me the texts."

Lena goes through her phone, then holds it out to Patricia to read: *I don't know what happened here but it's unacceptable.*

"How does she know you're not sick?"

"I think she talked to the other people, the other clients I had." Her cousin *tsk*s.

She finds another text for Patricia to read: *Obviously we will not be hiring you again and we can't provide a reference*

Patricia shrugs. What did Lena expect? Lena scrolls to find another one: *Lena — You made a commitment and did not honour it. I am very disappointed. I hope this does not affect your immigration status.* That's the last text she got. After she reads it, Patricia is quiet.

"Why does she say *immigration*?" Lena asks. "This isn't anything with immigration. I'm still working. I changed my permit. Why does she say that?"

Patricia shakes her head and says only, "Such a bitch." She stands up and goes to retrieve the second bottle in the freezer.

"*Bitch*," she says again as she refills her glass. She checks to see that her phone is still charging, and finds an angry hip-hop song by two men, one white and one Black.

Lena does a kind of shimmy on the floor and holds out her empty glass for a refill. For the first time in weeks, she can absorb and release joy. "Let's go out," she says. "Let's go somewhere." She is play-acting — she has no idea where they would go.

Patricia is still chewing on Cat's angry texts. She reads through the messages again.

"She can't do that. Not after him doing all that to you. And not even pay you."

Lena keeps moving, though she knows that something has shifted in the room, and that this unwelcome topic will not be banished. She is grabbing at happiness while she can, trying to stuff the joy down while it is being cleared away.

When she looks up, her cousin is holding her phone out to her, insisting she take it.

"Here's what you say," Patricia tells her.

VII

THE PLAN IS FOR CLAUDIA TO COME WITH CAT TO
the doctor, but Baby Jessica has woken up with a dry summer
cough that cuts her throat like a saw. The little girl thinks she
swallowed a bug, and is inconsolable. Cat knows the delusions
of sick children, when pain or a fever brings weird ideas that
can't be reasoned away.

The other problem is that Claudia has stopped driving
again. The last time she was behind the wheel had been a disaster; the sun, firing down the valley between two tall buildings,
got in her eyes and made her drift onto streetcar tracks. There
was a narrow miss: one of the hippo-like vehicles dinged its bell
at her. She panicked and turned the wrong way down a narrow
street that was closed off for a buskers' festival. A woman on
stilts hidden by long striped pants yelled at her to turn around.

She almost ran over a ponytailed juggler, who banged on the hood of the car with a fat bowling pin, one of five he'd been keeping in the air as if by magic just a few seconds earlier. The other four lay on the pavement around him.

"He called me a *cunt*," she tells Cat over the phone. "I think he was from New Zealand."

Cat says she's fine to go on her own. She knows her sister doesn't want to sit in a doctor's office full of sick people all morning, anyway, and she doesn't want to feel responsible for entertaining anyone. Neither of them mention Donovan. There is a tacit agreement to keep him out of the loop. In the end it's like hiding a credit card from a dog: you don't have to work hard to conceal something that isn't being searched for. "Follow up to what?" he asked when Cat mentioned the doctor's appointment. "Were you there already?"

"I told you. I had some tests. Couple of weeks ago."

"You did?"

No, I was joking. Get it? It's funny to lie about that kind of thing.

She waited for him to ask what the tests were for and to offer to come with her. She had excuses ready, though she was tempted to let him come and find out about the baby just like that, sitting there like an idiot in the little examination room with her. He said only that his ankle had been bothering him, and that he ought to make an appointment to see the doctor, too.

She has to tell someone about the results of the pregnancy test, so she tells her sister, whom she knows will react to the news with every emotion in the extreme, will fling the information in the air over and over like a killer whale toying with a seal, but will not pass it on. Claudia harasses and abuses every secret she takes possession of, but she doesn't snitch.

As expected, Claudia screams in her ear. She calls her crazy and laughs. Then she screams again and says the whole thing is incredible.

"I don't know if I could ever have another baby. I really don't know if I could do it," Claudia says when she finally calms down.

"I don't know if I can, either."

"How do people do it? I'm so focused on Jessica. Dale didn't want a nanny. Did I tell you what he told me?"

"Yes."

"He said babies always end up calling the nanny *Mama*. That's what happened to all our friends who hired one. At this point, I don't know — maybe that's a fair trade-off."

Claudia does not ask if Cat is thinking about *not* having the baby. For her that doesn't appear on the menu of options. It's Cat who raises the possibility.

"I need to think it through. I'm a little old for this."

"What? You're not old — not *that* old. God, don't even say that."

Claudia tells her about the sister of a friend of hers who, after three painful miscarriages, decided that she was not prepared to be a mother after all, and went in for an abortion before her body could flush away the fourth one. Like robbing her own house before the thieves can break in again. She did it with the full support of her husband.

"I couldn't even speak when I heard," Claudia says. "Can you imagine doing something like that? After trying for so long? And there's so many people who can't have one?"

"Isn't it better, though, if you know you don't want to have a kid, to figure that out before? It's not like they can't try again someday, if they change their minds."

"Are you kidding? No, they can't. How can you even *say* that?"

Cat asks her sister when she became pro-life.

It's not that, Claudia insists. "Okay, imagine they decide they want a baby after all, later on. The baby comes, they're holding it and kissing it and watching it sleep and everything. Wouldn't you be thinking the whole time about how you've already killed a baby exactly like that? What if the baby has Down's or something? My God, I couldn't do it. It's so crazy. You *can't* tell Mom and Dad."

"I know. I'm not stupid."

"You have to tell them at some point, but oh my God, don't say anything now. They're stressed already. They're coming to watch Jessica this weekend. If you tell them, they'll be nuts the whole time. I don't want them cancelling."

Claudia asks her if she feels pregnant already.

"Honestly, I'm not sure."

She tells her sister about the whole episode at the yoga studio. About the dog, the house, and about fainting like a goat. Claudia immediately wants to hear more about the rich owner.

"She has this thing," Cat says, careful not to use Meredith's name in case her sister runs out to sign up for a session. "You know when you meet someone for the first time, you do all these things automatically, like say *hi* and shake hands or whatever? You're nice to people, just because that's what you're supposed to do. Like a default setting."

"Such a waste of time. So fake."

"Anyways, this woman doesn't do that. She just snaps her fingers and says, *Skip all that. Here's what I want.*"

Claudia lets out a small gasp of pleasure. "Okay, she's my hero now."

"Her studio — I don't even think it's for money. She doesn't need it. You should see this place."

Claudia agrees that she should. She asks how the owner reacted to Cat passing out in front of her.

"It was almost like she was expecting it."

"So she's a witch. A really rich one. A rich witch."

Cat laughs and admits that this is a strong possibility.

"I'm sorry I can't come with you," Claudia says.

"It's okay."

"Call me as soon as you're done."

Cat says she will, and then, in reply to an expression of concern that hasn't been offered, she adds, "It'll be fine."

"As *soon* as you're done."

Cat wants to get to the clinic early. Instead, she is tripped up and delayed at every turn. In a fit of enthusiasm about the strength of his arms, Silas sweeps his glass of milk and dish of apple slices off the breakfast table. Cat moans like a wounded cow at the sight of milk dripping from the counter, the cupboard doors, the framed photo of lavender sprigs on the wall. She barks at Isabelle to get Silas dressed while she wipes everything down. The milk mixes with dark rings from coffee cups, as if the two substances, milk and coffee, are always trying to find each other. In the shadowy gap between the stove and the kitchen counter, she finds a single piece of toast stuck to the floor, hard as bark.

Without help she can't keep up.

It's a hard thing for her to admit. Especially after that little bitch abandoned them without a fucking word. Right when they needed her the most. Cat spent a week with her head full of evil fantasies about causing the young woman to be sent back to her own country. She spent the following week feeling guilty about them. Should she at least find out if the girl is okay? Should she ask someone, someone official?

Donovan said no way. It was none of their business. Lena took off on them, so they should forget about her. She did the same thing to all the other people whose houses she was cleaning.

"We'll probably never hear from her again," he said.

Instead, after weeks and weeks of silence, Cat got a text from Lena saying she wanted to meet and to explain why she left. The text said she doesn't want to do it over the phone or in an email.

Someone obviously helped her write the text — the tone was formal, with no spelling mistakes. It was as though she was using a template called *Letter to an Employer You Fucked Over but Want to Get a Reference From*.

"That's what this is about," Donovan said right away when she showed him. "For *sure* that's what it's about. Just delete it." He followed her into the bathroom. "You want me to delete it? I'm serious: block her number."

Cat grows less and less certain. She thinks about the quiet young woman who came to their house each week; she can't picture her as a schemer.

Lena sends another text, asking again to meet. *Please*, it ends. *I wont bug you again.*

Cat lets that one sit in her phone, too.

And then, typing quickly, Cat gives her a day and time. She sends the message almost before realizing she has done it. Her body hums with a strange excitement, like she has agreed to an affair. She picked a time when she knew the house would be empty. Donovan would be at his parents' house for the day.

She has to admit that she is curious.

Right away, her phone buzzes. A message from Lena: *Yes. Thank you. I will come.*

"Fuck," Cat says out loud.

How awful does she look when she finally gets to the doctor's office? She decides, as she sprints away from the parked car, not to clean herself up. She will walk in there just as she is, an honest mess. Maybe it will help.

There are lots of people there ahead of her. On the carpeted floor of the waiting room, a young girl in braids sniffs messily as she plays on the floor with a dollhouse. Most of the other patients, elderly Portuguese women in multiple layers of clothing despite the day's heat, sit holding their bags and glaring at the clinic secretary, astonished at how little urgency there is around making their lives better, or more bearable, or even just longer — which is what they've gotten dressed up and come all this way for. The elderly men are more sanguine; they doze on the hard chairs.

Cat picks up a months-old copy of *Toronto Life* with a cover story about a fortysomething couple, both doctors, who became addicted to painkillers and had to declare bankruptcy. There are multiple photos of the two of them looking glum but well-dressed in various rooms of their beautiful Leaside home, which they've been able to cling to with the help of their parents and some other wealthy relatives. Cat likes how they have bookshelves built right into the walls — she has always wanted that. The couple has no children, which she cannot help but feel gives them an unfair advantage when it comes to keeping their place tidy, painkillers or no painkillers.

She checks her voice mail. There is a new message from Meredith, which does not surprise her at all. Meredith calls almost every other day, always about some trivial thing she wants added to or subtracted from the website. The calls are friendly but firm, never displaying the slightest curiosity about Cat or making any reference to her having fallen in front of her the first time they met.

In the message Meredith says that she has been thinking more and more about the idea of starting a prenatal yoga class. Talking to an actual mother would be a huge help, so could she please call her back?

Cat is intrigued by the idea of doing something to help women in those last months of pregnancy. She knows that time well, when a mother-to-be is no longer told she has the sexy glow of fertility, the excitement and congratulatory hugs have vanished, and everyone begins to step away from the grunting, sweating, cranky, flatulent beast they once considered a friend. She could easily become one of those women herself again, and soon. All she has to do is nothing — to make no decision is to make a decision.

She calls back right away.

"Hello? Yes?"

The sound of impatience in Meredith's voice makes Cat wonder if she'd somehow misunderstood the message. As quickly as she can, she explains that she got the voice mail, and thinks the prenatal class is a great idea.

"Good." As if this were the only question she wanted answered.

Cat babbles about having friends who've done similar classes and that, based on what they'd told her, she could offer some suggestions on how to make it work.

"Good."

A nurse comes into the waiting area and calls someone's name. One of the Portuguese women lifts herself painfully from her chair.

"Who is that shouting?"

"Oh, I'm at the doctor's. I have an appointment in a bit."

Meredith makes a noise that communicates both disinterest and disapproval. "Don't let them make things worse."

"Pardon?"

She can hear Meredith take a deep breath.

"In my experience doctors don't really have time to make you *better*, whatever that means. All they are looking for is for something they can suppress with drugs. Most of the time, the things we think are *wrong* with our bodies, quote-unquote, are the things that need to be brought to the surface and seen for what they are. That's what makes things worse."

"Oh, my doctor's good. I've had some bad ones, but mine is good."

"That's called Stockholm Syndrome. Listen, I have a session starting soon. Call me tonight after six, please."

"Okay."

"And make sure your doctor actually *sees* you."

"I have an appointment."

"That's not what I mean."

She hangs up.

Right away, Cat texts Claudia the bare details of the call. She adds two exclamation points after "Stockholm Syndrome."

Claudia replies: *she sounds amazing.* Then sends another text: *Excited?*

About what? Cat writes back, just to be a pain.

She can't tell if she's excited or not. There is a war is going on inside her; her brain has become the comment section to an online news story, with anonymous voices chiming in on all sides and accusing the others of bad faith. Cat was certain, the instant she felt Silas's tiny, miraculous body fall out of her, that she would never again lie naked in a delivery room, never again lie there helpless while a team of doctors peeled her open and pulled the precious fruit out from within. That first day, Cat hardly had the strength to hold him. He'd been so eager to get out into the world that he trampled his mother in his haste.

"A beautiful girl, and now a beautiful boy," Donovan's mother said in the hospital, as she held Silas. "Wouldn't it be wonderful to have another little girl?" she added, nuzzling the baby boy's soft head.

Cat watched her mother-in-law sway back and forth with Silas in her arms, and in her confusion — they had given her something for the pain — she thought Ruth was stealing the baby. She reached out to take him back.

"Oh, one more minute," Ruth said. "You need to rest."

Rest, rest. Then start all over again.

She wonders if she is already showing. Everything is sped up, the baby expanding like an air mattress. She repeatedly catches herself stroking her belly, as if trying to encourage the minute glow of life within her. A smooth narcotic is moving through her system, making her feel as though this new reality might actually be welcome. Babies quickly become the answer to every question, the endpoint of every scenario. So much would be once again taken out of her hands and decided for her. All she has to do is to lay back into this new reality, allow it to envelop her with its new goals and new needs, drown her in a new identity.

Cat doesn't recognize her name the first time it is called. She sees the nurse staring straight at her, repeating the name that even her mother and father have stopped using.

"Catherine Joseph?"

"Oh, sorry," Cat says finally, and grabs at her bag.

She follows the nurse past reception, back to where the soothing music of the waiting room fades away and the light is brighter. She is shown into a small room with two chairs and a desk with a computer that looks brand new. The last time she was here, Dr. Kennedy sat across from her and asked for an update. After telling her what was going on, emphasizing the pains she'd been having, she allowed Dr. Kennedy to press all over her body with her fingers and ask her to breathe in and out while she did so. With a tiny light, the doctor stared deep into Cat's eyes as if searching for guilt.

It will all be obvious now; the secret is out. They will have found evidence of the baby in her blood or her pee. The ladies in the basement clinic, who hum along to the radio and talk to each other as they jab at people's arms — they will have found out by now. The man who did the biopsy on her breast — merely as a precaution, Dr. Kennedy told her — even *he* would know.

The door slides open. Cat smiles, expecting Dr. Kennedy. Instead, a young man in a white coat slips into the room, staring down at the contents of a file folder. He pauses for a

moment when he sees her sitting there, as if he'd been expecting to find an empty room.

"Are you here to see me?" Cat asks, and gives her full name.
To be helpful and to save time, she even says *Catherine.*

"Okay," he says. "I'm Dr. Toro."

"Toro?"

He gives a half smile and says, "Right, like the bull." It is
clearly a joke he has had to make many times before, and she is
embarrassed at having compelled him to.

"I'm *Cat.* Like the pet."

"The pet," Dr. Toro says, looking puzzled.

She guesses he is around thirty. No more than that. His
hair is curly, thick, and black — a little like Donovan's, but
tamer and more deliberate. His beard is also cared for, and
uniform in colour and length. There is something about his
face that surprises her, and keeps surprising her the more she
looks at it, the more she takes it in. His eyes are large and round
and dark. They look like an expensive dessert. Candied figs in
heavy cream. His skin is slightly dark, the colour of unbleached
paper.

"Is Dr. Kennedy sick?"

Again, he looks puzzled. "Um, *Dr. Kennedy,* yes. No. She's ...
at a conference, I think. I'm seeing her patients today. Let me
just ..."

He goes back to silently reading through her file. She notices that when he reads, he bites down on his bottom lip. Cat
suddenly realizes what it is about his face that she noticed: he
is beautiful. She had not been expecting beauty. She wants to
see him smile again. She wants to ask where he is from, where
his parents are from. She can't think of a way of doing so without sounding at least a little bit racist. Claudia would not be

so careful. She would immediately begin to pull words and phrases from the small mental basket of Spanish she has woven for herself in preparation for trips to Mexico and Cuba. In response, Dr. Toro would laugh indulgently and correct her pronunciation, even as he compliments her on her accent. Within minutes, he'd be telling her about the rich man he is seeing — Cat is convinced he is gay — the heir to a grocery store chain or the son of a famous Canadian folk singer.

Cat wonders if he will ask her to strip down for an examination. She wishes she'd chosen a better bra that morning. The one she has on is dun-coloured and distressed.

"You were here a few weeks ago."

"That's right." Her smile gets broader and yet more coy. She's waiting for the announcement she knows is coming. "A lot has happened since then."

She nearly winks at him.

"Has it?"

"I'm feeling okay right now, though."

"It says you had a fainting spell."

Cat's smile falters a little. "I did, yes."

"Were you hurt?"

She says no, and tells him she didn't exactly fall over, but sort of slid to the floor. She wants him to understand that no harm could've come to the baby inside her.

"Where did this happen?"

"The first time, in my living room. The second time at a yoga studio."

"Yoga? You were doing yoga?"

"No, I was doing this website ... I do yoga, but not there."

Dr. Toro gives her another beautiful, puzzled frown. She is having trouble making any of the details link together.

She tries to take command of the conversation. "I did a test," she announces firmly.

"A test?"

"At the studio, after I fell. Not on the ground, obviously — in the bathroom."

He shakes his head. "The bathroom. What test?"

"Oh! A pregnancy test. I've done two more since. So, there you go."

There it is: the news is out. She expects him to smile, to congratulate her. To put away his files and embrace her. They will talk and laugh about the initial awkwardness of the appointment, of their meeting. He'll ask her to have coffee with him during his break, and while they are sitting close together, he'll tell her that he and his partner are trying to adopt a baby, but that it is hard, even for two people with status and money. He'll come close to crying, and she *will* cry at the absolute unfairness of it. Here are two beautiful people who want a baby but can't have one. And here *she* is, awful and racist and ugly and old, with a baby in her belly that she's not sure she even wants.

Instead, Dr. Toro only nods and keeps reading her files.

"Yes, it says you are at least a month and a half along. Maybe more. Have you been feeling nauseous? Has there been anything unusual, any bleeding?"

"I'm pregnant. Is *that* unusual?"

"Not at all," he says without smiling.

He closes up the files in his hand. Then he pulls the other chair close to her and sits on the edge of it, their knees almost touching. He crouches slightly, so his head is lower than hers, as if waiting to be petted.

"Are you feeling pain right now?"

Cat searches herself. "It's okay today, mostly. Just the usual aches and pains."

"What is *the usual*? Can you describe them?"

Cat reaches up to touch the thin muscle suspended between her neck and her left shoulder. "A little tender here, I guess," she says. "I have to be careful when I turn my head."

Dr. Toro reaches out to touch the muscle, surprising Cat. She flinches and draws back involuntarily before his fingers make contact. He stops, his arm frozen in the air.

"I'm sorry — is it okay if I check it? I won't press hard. If you'd rather I didn't, I won't."

"Oh God, sorry. Of course. I just wasn't expecting ... it's fine."

He keeps his arm there for another moment, then brings it more slowly to the side of her neck. He does not respect personal space the way Dr. Kennedy does. Dr. Kennedy never moves close to her without telling Cat she is doing so, without giving her a chance to object.

Dr. Toro pushes back in his chair and opens her files again, as if suddenly growing bored of her situation and wanting to get some paperwork done. He skims over the top few pages again, makes a note on one of them.

"Are you feeling dizzy or sick to your stomach?"

"Not right now."

"But sometimes you do."

"Yes."

"Any trouble with your vision? You see everything okay?"

Cat looks over his shoulder at a poster on the wall: an exploded view of a human body, with the muscles and nerves drawn in. She focuses on the pelvis, which appears sharp enough to her. "I think so. No trouble."

"Appetite?"

"Mostly okay. Not great in the morning, but I usually don't eat breakfast, anyway."

"Any falls in the past few months?" Before she can answer, he smiles and says, "I guess I don't need to ask that one."

"I guess not. Ha ha!" She laughs louder than she means to.

He closes the files again and sits forward, his hands pinned between his knees.

"So, we have some big decisions to make. I know this must be a very difficult time. What did Dr. Kennedy explain to you about your options?"

Cat has a sudden fear that she has shifted out of time, that she has somehow skipped over the past five minutes of conversation.

"I don't ... I'm sorry, my *options*?"

He shifts back in his seat, relaxed now.

"Well, the most urgent thing is to do more testing and likely an MRI, but that's not our decision, and not our department. They'll schedule all that wherever you go. I'm guessing Princess Margaret, but I don't want to say for sure. We don't decide that here. It could be Sunnybrook."

"Sunnybrook," she repeats stupidly. Sunnybrook Hospital is in the northeast corner of the city, where the buildings all seem to be sliding into a ravine. She'd been there only a couple of times in her life, accompanying her friend Laura, whose mother had to get a lump removed.

"Or Princess Margaret. They are both excellent hospitals. Like I said, we don't make that decision here. Especially since there are other factors. Obviously, the biggest consideration in any of this right now is your health, but we also have to make a decision about ..."

He pauses, smiles at her with infuriating mildness, and pats lightly at his belly with one hand.

"That makes a big difference in how we proceed. It doesn't make anything impossible, but it's definitely an important consideration."

In her confusion Cat nearly imitates his actions and pats her own tummy. She looks at the files; something in there has betrayed her. She is being libelled, shamed, mocked by the impenetrable sentences and numbers they contain. She wants to grab them and fling them at the wall.

"Can I just figure something out? I'm pregnant."

"Yes, but most of the tests we need to do are not invasive, so there's no risk there. And then, look, if it comes to the point of chemotherapy and radiation, which I am guessing it will — and maybe this is something you need to go away and think about, maybe talk to your partner, your family — but with all of that there is obviously a whole question about your options with regard to a pregnancy under these circumstances."

"What is happening here? What is this about? Why are you talking like this?"

The anger in her voice catches Dr. Toro off guard, and he looks up, surprised. "I'm sorry, I know this is not easy."

"What the *fuck*?" It feels good to swear at him. "I'm here because I'm fucking *pregnant* again, and now you are talking to me about chemotherapy. Is that even in my file?"

Cat looks closer at his face. All his beauty is gone now. He looks like a sickly, overbred puppy, a useless and fragile creature who might die from the slightest germ.

"Catherine, I'm …"

"It's fucking *Cat*. Can you even get my name right? Why is Dr. Kennedy not telling me this? No, I *don't* know what my options are, because I don't know what is going on. Nobody has told me anything."

She stands up quickly. She isn't sure what she plans to do — walk out, scream for help, fling something heavy through the doors. Dr. Toro doesn't try to stop her. Her head begins to swim and she is suddenly afraid to blink, in case closing her eyes for even a split second is enough to destabilize the ground beneath her feet. Her stomach swings free, and she has a moment where she cannot decide which would be worse: throwing up all over herself while standing there, or dropping to the ground yet again. She chooses a third option: sitting down. She goes back down hard on the chair.

"I'm very sorry," Dr. Toro says.

She wants her mother. Or Claudia. Or even Donovan. She thinks about Isabelle, about Silas — she should be with them, and they should be with her. Everything beyond the frosted door of the examination room has gone quiet, as if they all know what is happening.

She has a crazy thought: she wishes Meredith were there. Meredith would not be thrown by any of this. She'd sort it all out and be back in time for her afternoon session. Cat yearns for that kind of certainty, to have it in the room with her.

Dr. Toro dips his head again — this time, more like a dog that has been shamed — and moves his chair closer.

"Has no one spoken to you before about this?"

She looks at him, afraid to say anything in case she breaks out in a childish wail.

"Okay," he says.

Cat knows that this pause, this brief moment of silence, is a hinge in her existence. Whatever he is about to say will change her. There will be the Cat who existed before he spoke, and the one who exists after.

He selects a few pages from her files and holds them out so she can see. One of them has multiple blocks of text highlighted in yellow.

"Here's what we are looking at," he begins.

Finally, he brings out the word she has been fearing: *cancer*. It has a hissing quality to it, like acid eating through steel. Dr. Toro says that as far as they know, the tumour in her right breast is growing. But, he says again, nothing is definitive, more tests are needed. There are some concerns about her left breast, as well. Experts will have to weigh in. The most important thing is to know if the cancer has spread. If it's all in one spot, the treatment is much simpler. If it has begun to scatter, things get a little trickier. Not impossible, just trickier.

"Will I be able to keep ..." Cat begins, then catches herself reaching for her chest. With everything else going on, with her life collapsing in on her, her first thought is for her stupid little boobs.

"I really can't say, it's too early to determine anything. No matter what happens, no matter where you are, you will have some difficult choices. After the tests we'll know more, but I can already say this will not be easy. Is your partner with you today?" he asks, then looks quickly at her files. "Silas? No, sorry, that's your son. Donovan? Is Donovan here today? We prefer that people not leave on their own when they've been given news like this."

Again, she has fallen out of time.

"That's it? I have to go?"

Dr. Toro smiles sympathetically. "No, of course not. I just wanted to make sure you have someone with you today."

I won't be leaving alone, she thinks. She has *two* companions now, both of them growing relentlessly within her. Both eating her from the inside. The urge she has been fighting for a few minutes finally overwhelms her, and she begins to cry. Bubbles of grief keep breaking inside her, and she shakes with each silent sob. She tries to tense her body, to clamp down on this sadness and stop it from escaping.

The nurse slides the door open halfway and leans through the crack to whisper to Dr. Toro that he is needed in another room. He looks both relieved and uncomfortable.

He wants to get away from me, Cat thinks. *He wants to get as far from this sick old woman as possible.*

"It's okay," she says.

"Are you sure? I'll just be a few minutes if you want to talk some more."

He is already half out of the chair when he says this.

Cat is alone. She arrived at the clinic in the hopes of shedding doctors for a while, but here she is, on the verge of acquiring more — more than she can guess. Whole teams. Even now, they are coming to pin her down and separate her body from herself again. She thinks bitterly of the fantasies she had only moments earlier about stripping down before her doctor, and the worries she'd had about her bra. There is *no* chance he would've seen her breasts as erotic things, even if she had. They are diseased bags of flesh, toxic appendages that ought to be sliced away from her as soon as possible and thrown away. She could stand naked in front of the horniest teenage boy and he would see only a body that is slowly and silently collapsing upon itself. She could stick two fingers inside herself and part her vagina, hold it open like a greedy mouth, give the dirty little boy a good close-up look.

Gross. That's where dead babies come from.

She looks around her for her phone, but it is not in any of the usual places — on the chair beside her or in her purse. Maybe it is the first thing to be taken away, to be confiscated.

Her files are still on the desk. She can see the yellow highlights from where she is sitting. She reaches over, takes the top few pages, and starts reading. The confidence of their assertions strikes her as insulting and condescending. They know what's wrong with her, but for the sake of argument and for the sake of absolute accuracy, they say possible and suspected. Her breasts are presumed innocent.

A few pages almost slip from her grasp. She grabs them before they can fall to the ground. She takes the top one and looks again at the highlighted phrases.

And then, without thinking, she tears the page from top to bottom.

It comes apart surprisingly easy, and makes little sound — even her files are flimsy and weak. She drops the two halves. They float silently to the floor and lay themselves down flat.

Curious to see if she can repeat the trick, she picks up the next page on the pile and tears that one, too. It is destroyed just as easily, and she feels wicked joy bloom within her. She begins to rip page after page, slowly and quietly, until she has destroyed all of the paper in her hands. She reaches for more, and continues to rip. She can see, from the dates at the top and the few words she allows herself to read, that she is ripping in reverse chronological order, destroying her past selves.

She rips apart the last of the papers. Now they have nothing on her. Now they will have to actually look at her if they want to see what's wrong.

The floor around her is covered with misshapen pieces. A large paper dragon has been shedding its scales. On the desk there are a few boring office supplies: a stapler, some paper clips, pens. She snaps the pens and drops them on the floor, too. She opens the jaws of the staplers, pinches out the squared row of tiny teeth, and breaks the contraption at its main hinge. The paper clips she can't do much with except bend into inconvenient shapes. All of this she drops into the bright yellow bin labelled for hazardous waste. There are blue-and-white boxes on the shelves above the desk filled with rubber gloves, swabs, dressings, and the like. She rips open each box and does as much damage as she can before dropping those into the yellow bin. There are empty, sterile vials there, too, and things like syringes missing their stingers. She ruins every one of them, breathing hard as she does.

Cat pulls at the device for looking into ears, the one with the intense light that comes from a short, pointed beak. She pulls at it until it snaps away from the wall. Then she grabs at the other instruments, tugging at them until they give way and snap their cords. She draws all of the antibacterial wipes out of the tub on the wall, tugging and tugging until the tub shifts in place from lack of ballast. Everything goes into the bin, which is starting to look too full. The examination table contains shallow drawers she'd never noticed before, all of them filled with more packages of swabs and gloves and such. She can't fit much more into the hazardous waste bin, so she contents herself with opening each package and disordering everything inside, desterilizing it all and rendering it useless. Then she mashes it all down and recloses the drawers.

When she straightens back up, she realizes how tired she is, and wants to stretch out on the examination table and sleep. Nothing would feel better. But the urge to destroy has not yet dimmed. The computer screen is showing the name of the clinic. She reaches around behind the humming monitor and pulls free the cords plugged into its back. The screen goes dark and the hum is silenced.

A buzzing comes from somewhere. Cat worries her destruction has set off some kind of alarm, that she was being filmed the whole time. Right now, there may be police coming down the hallway to retrieve her, already wearing rubber gloves in case she tries to bite their hands as they wrestle her out of the room. The buzzing stops, and for a few seconds the room is silent. Then the buzzing begins again, and Cat realizes it is her phone. Standing on the shredded remains of her files, she digs through her bag.

The number showing is Silas's daycare.

Oh God. Something has happened. The whole time she's been here, acting like a lunatic, her little boy has been lying injured, desperate to see his mother's face, to be held by her.

"Yes? Hello?"

"Hello, Ms. Joseph? Is this Silas's mommy?"

"Is everything okay?"

The woman at the other end chuckles and tells Cat not to worry: everything is fine, fine. The kids are outside in the playground right now. Silas is a wonderful little guy. Very friendly. Big personality. They all love him there. He makes friends easily. His big sister kept to herself a little more. She was a real *thinker*, you know? Both good kids.

Cat cannot say anything in reply. She is fighting back tears. She has betrayed these good kids, lost them.

The woman finally tells her the reason for her call: they have started planning an end-of-summer party for all the kids, and they need parent volunteers. They already have a few lined up, but are hoping to get some new faces to come out, parents who don't often volunteer at daycare events. Can't always be the same people helping out. That's just not fair.

"It would mean a lot. I know little Silas would *love* it."

Cat has a wild thought: were she somehow given the power to transfer the entirety of her condition to someone else, an enemy or a stranger, she would do so without hesitation. This nice woman on the phone would die within months.

"Ms. Joseph?"

"Um, sure, yes. Volunteer, sure."

"That's great news, Ms. Joseph."

"Not me, my husband. Partner. Donovan. Silas's dad. He will be happy to do it. Put him down. Donovan Greene."

Cat ends the call without saying another word. She feels dirty, her hands smell like antibacterial wipes, so she goes to the sink in the corner of the room and rinses them under hot water. She dries them with a few coarse paper towels and leaves the room without turning off the water.

VIII

LENA AND PATRICIA RISE UP FROM THE CONCRETE
coolness of the subway — side by side, staring straight ahead,
a pair of deadly assassins. At the top of the escalator, where
the grilled stairs get swallowed over and over again by the
floor, they step forward onto the plate that hides the machinery. Patricia's heels clack on the metal. Lena's soft shoes
are silent.

The two women come out at an auxiliary exit where there
are no ticket agents or people, just a floor-to-ceiling turnstile
like a set of giant metal teeth set on its side and glass doors that
open onto a side street. Beyond the doors is a small church that
has been converted into condos with reverent windows. Lena
pauses to let Patricia go first through the turnstile — an echo
of the fear she felt when she'd first encountered one of these

structures, years ago. Back then she was afraid that she would get trapped by its unforgiving mechanical tongs.

Outside, Patricia stands with her big sunglasses reflecting sky and storefronts. Three skinny girls in school uniforms are on the sidewalk, standing close together and facing each other. They could be smoking in a high wind, but instead are protecting the glow of new gossip, of minor teen scandal.

The two women fast-walk across Bloor, then turn down a residential street. Right away the stores and crowds of people melt away and they are alone on a narrow sidewalk being reclaimed by nature. Some of the tiny yards have signs poking out of them that say *Please Slow Down*, which reminds Lena of a word she saw posted on fridge doors in the kitchens she cleaned or written on the front of beautiful, slim notebooks left on tables in front hallways and next to the beds she made: *mindfulness*. She was disappointed when she finally learned what it actually means, which is little more than what the lawn signs say. Be aware of your thoughts, pause to reflect. Like the act of prayer, but stripped of meaning and significance, empty of love and fear and hope. At the community centre, there are flyers advertising workshops purporting to help people cultivate this mysterious invisible force. If prayer is a phone call, as one of her first Bible teachers told her, then *mindfulness* must be the equivalent of making a pretend phone with your fingers and holding it up to your head. What message is being sent? Who is supposed to receive it? Who will tell you you've gone astray when you are listening only to yourself?

She silently indicates the turn they need to make, which brings them to a narrow side street. Then one more turn, and they are on the street they've been aiming for, the one that contains Cat and Donovan's house.

. . .

They'd talked about what to do. Pacing around Lena's kitchen, Patricia outlined all kinds of possible scenarios. Confronting both of them at once. Tricking Donovan into doing it again, what he did in the bathroom. Smashing a window. She worked herself up into such a rage that Lena could barely understand her. Only twenty minutes earlier she'd laughed the whole thing off as ridiculous. Lena has seen her cousin do this many times — ignore or dismiss some incident, some act of injustice, only to suddenly explode with fury.

Patricia kept pacing the kitchen.

"Tell his children. Tell the boy and girl what their nasty father is about."

"I don't even *know* the boy and girl," Lena said.

The outrageousness of the suggestions calmed her down a little and made her think the whole thing might not be as bad as she thought. It was just something that happened, or at least something she can't do anything to fix. She was at least happy and relieved to have finally told someone. She hadn't told anyone else what happened. She certainly never told anyone at Bible study. They would urge her to forgive Donovan, to pray for him, to endure and be patient. She doesn't want to do any of that.

One thing she does want: she wants Cat to know. That's important. Somehow, that quiet, slippery lady needs to be told. Whatever Cat does with the information, Lena doesn't care — she just wants to be rid of it, to pass it on like a bag full of stolen goods. In the houses she's cleaned, Lena has discovered so many things in places where a wife or a husband would not look. Empty bottles behind the washing machine. An angry

mechanical penis in the basement bathroom that only the husband ever uses. Another in a daughter's mattress. A cache of
brand-new girl's underwear in a house with no daughters. Lena
got tired of carrying things like that around with her. She was
tired of being a beast of burden, loaded down with people's
secrets.

"I want to tell her," she said to Patricia.

Her cousin called her stupid.

"Who cares about her? She probably knows."

"I want to tell her what happened."

Patricia said no. It was pointless and would only cause
trouble. She had narrowed down the options to the only one
that made any sense.

"We get the money, and that's it."

Finally, Lena agreed. Just the money.

When Lena points out the house that is their destination,
Patricia nods and marches quickly up the front walk. Lena follows her, trying not to look like she is being led. She does not
look up at the house. She's strangely embarrassed at how big
it is — all this for one small family — as if she were somehow
responsible for that fact. They step up onto the porch, with
its warped wooden slats, then Patricia moves aside to let Lena
ring the bell. There is no button. She has to turn the little brass
crank in the centre of the door, which grinds against a hidden
bell on the other side. The first time she turns it, she does so
cautiously, only allowing a few quiet dings to sound.

Lena is anxious. She has been trying to slow down on the
edibles that she has been stuffing herself with for weeks. Today,

for this trip, she has not allowed herself to chew even half of one. She wants to be clear.

"So, her name is Cat, and she has a cat right there?" Patricia asks, sneering and pointing at the glass cat.

Lena looks up at the decoration, at its feline arrogance, the proud tail, the arched back. She tries to armour herself with Patricia-like contempt. She grabs at the crank again and twists it hard, twice in a row.

"What time did she say?" Patricia asks.

Lena tells her again. The house is silent.

"We should go," Lena says. She knows from experience that, at this time of day, if you stand on one of these porches for too long, curtains will start to move and faces will appear in the windows of other houses.

Patricia, indignant, can barely stand still. "I have to *pee*, Lena."

"Here?"

"She won't let me?"

Lena stares at her cousin.

"She has to," Patricia says.

There is a quiet click behind the door, and it starts to open. Patricia moves instinctively away from the movement, but Lena stays in place. She suddenly has a thought: what if it's another cleaner, her replacement? Should she warn her?

Or what if it is Donovan? What if the very man they have come all this way to accuse of being nasty is behind the door? He wouldn't be angry; he wouldn't tell them to leave. He'd make a joke that knocks every weapon out of their hands.

The door opens, and Lena almost gasps.

Instead of Donovan or a new cleaning lady, it is the mother, the woman, standing there in an oversize T-shirt and yoga pants. Her hair is tangled, her eyes are red, her face is blotchy. She's been crying. There are islands of sweat on her clothes. She looks broken, and has shrunk. Lena had always pictured her clients as towering over her. It is her default perspective: being small, she assumes the rest of the world is enormous. Now she sees that this woman is not much taller than her.

"Okay?" Cat says. It's more of a question than a greeting. She coughs a little. Lena smells alcohol on her breath.

"This is my cousin," Lena says.

Cat nods at Patricia. "I thought you were my sister for a second. Same sunglasses." She reaches up to her own face to indicate the place where sunglasses go. She looks like someone who has just emerged from a long stretch of involuntary confinement. She smiles unhappily, then looks back at Lena. "Did you ever meet my sister?"

Lena remembers an aggressive woman coming to visit Cat once, carrying a baby. The woman walked by her without saying hello and asked her to retrieve a bag from her car in a tone that did not make it sound like a request.

"I'm sorry for this," Lena says, and immediately Patricia hisses again. This visit is not about apologies. "We didn't know if you were home."

"I didn't hear the bell. I was lying down."

Patricia gives a small snort. Another rich white woman who sleeps all day while her husband works. She is vibrating with contempt, though it is mixed with a small amount of fear. Even so reduced and shabby, Cat is nonetheless a homeowner. They are on *her* territory. She has powers they can't contend with.

Lena reminds Cat that she said she could come today. She looks baffled, as if she is still deep inside a dream.

"I did?"

"You texted me."

Cat stares at her blankly, then shuts her eyes. "Ah, fuck. Okay."

Hearing Cat swear makes Patricia smile for the first time since the door opened.

"I have to go back inside. I need to get some water. I've been at the doctor's office all morning."

"I'm sorry," Lena says, ignoring the look Patricia gives her.

Nothing about this encounter is going right.

Cat steps back into the house. Neither Lena nor Patricia move. Before she disappears into the kitchen, Cat shouts back at them to close the door. She doesn't specify which side of the door she wants them on when it closes, so they both step into the darkness of the hallway. Lena can see Patricia looking around, assessing the inside of the house. She is looking for flaws, cracks. Lena only notices that the hallway is relatively clean. The shoes are arranged and the wall is not ghosted with handprints. Perhaps they *have* hired someone. She looks away from the stairs leading up to the second floor.

After a few moments, Cat comes back, carrying a pint glass of water in one hand and a pill in the other. She holds the pill, which is red and bulky, with the tips of her fingers. Patricia and Lena watch her swallow the pill and the water as if that is what they have come to do, to witness this.

"I don't know why you are here, but I've just gotten back from the doctor's." Cat's face creases again, then recovers. "I'm dealing with a lot right now; I've had some bad news and don't really need anything else added to the pile. Okay?"

Patricia jumps in: "You owe her money." She is still wearing her sunglasses.

Cat looks at Patricia and then at Lena.

"For real? *That's* why you're here?"

Lena does not reply.

"You take off and stop responding to messages, then just show up to tell me I owe you money? You didn't even *do* anything the last time you were here. You took off."

Patricia makes a sound that is both a gasp and a laugh.

"Excuse me?"

"I'm not looking for money," Lena says.

"Okay, so now it's *not* about money. I'm supposed to guess? I'm sorry, I think maybe you should both leave. Okay?"

The anger has already slipped out of her, as if she can't keep her hands around it. A quiver keeps invading her voice before she can get all the words out.

"What is the bad news?" Patricia asks.

Lena and Cat both look at her, amazed.

"What?"

"You said bad news. From your doctor. What bad news?"

"I don't … is that even your business?"

"I'm sorry," Lena says again.

"Okay, good, fine. Thank you. Apology accepted. *Please.*"

The last word comes out almost as a squeak.

Lena looks at the carved wooden bowl sitting on the drawers next to her. Dozens of times she went through that bowl, separating out things that looked urgent or important, returning toys and tools to their proper homes, recycling junk mail, disposing of random pills that had somehow gotten into the mix. She wishes she could flip it right now, spilling everything out onto the floor.

"Are you pregnant?" Patricia asks.

Cat's eyes widen, and she takes a small step back. Lena waits for her to come at them, hissing and scratching. Instead, she says only "This is fucking …"

"Was that the bad news? A baby?"

Lena wants to grab her cousin and push her out through the door, but Patricia has crossed her arms. She will not be moved.

"That is none of your business, oh my fucking God."

Lena sees her cousin's smile, then looks back at Cat, suddenly understanding. This woman has been infected by the very man they have come there to expose and denounce. He got to her before they could and laid claim to her in the most vile and disgusting way. She can no longer picture Donovan as a husband or father, or even as a man. Just a nasty monkey with his penis out. He stabbed at her with that stupid little thing and poisoned her. And now she's standing here almost crying in front of them, as if it were somebody else's fault.

"I'm sorry," Lena says again, her tone firm and forgiving. She knows already that she will have to pray for this woman, and does not resent it. She has prayed for worse. Finally understanding the gravity of the situation, she is calm. They are in the realm of health and sickness, life and death, good and evil, a place where no amount of mindfulness can help.

"Look," Cat finally says, with a voice drained of life. "If we owe you money, I'll figure it out and send you a cheque, okay?"

Lena shakes her head. "It's okay. I don't want any money."

Patricia shifts in the hallway, clearly wanting to object to this, but senses that Lena is in control of the situation. She takes off her sunglasses.

"I'm happy for you," Lena says. "Every baby is a miracle."

A visible shudder of sadness goes through Cat. "Oh my fucking God ..." she says, choking on a bitter laugh. She puts her arm over her eyes, as if shielding them from a bright light.

"I know this is a bad time and I'm sorry," Lena says, "but I need to tell you something."

Patricia looks like she is about to stop her, but Lena makes it clear she will not yield.

Cat's anger returns. "Jesus Christ, *what*?"

"Your husband," Lena says.

Feeling new strength, almost as though someone is speaking through her, Lena talks about the last time she was in that house. About Donovan standing there in the bathroom, naked, defiling their marriage. Cat slowly lowers her arms, and her mouth is pulled tight. She looks to Patricia, who meets her with a firm stare that confirms every detail.

When Lena is done, she apologizes again for bothering Cat at a bad time, then turns to go. Without a word, Patricia opens the front door and steps through it.

"Thank you," Lena says. "God bless you."

She turns and moves through the door for what she is certain will be the last time, and closes it behind her, not looking back at the woman she has left crumbling in the front hallway of her own home. Above her the small stained-glass cat twirls and swings.

They are more than a block away before Patricia says anything.

"You're so *mean*!" She sounds impressed.

Both of them laugh all the way back to the subway station.

IX

DONOVAN WORKS HIS WAY THROUGH A BOWL OF butter chicken and fries at a new place on Ossington that specializes in odd and unexpected versions of pub fare. This particular combination of meat and starch is his favourite. The heaviness of it is almost magical; it fills his belly with warmth and crowds out all worries. He bites down on a dripping french fry and imagines himself as a little kid, home sick from school with a rotten cold or the flu, lying on the couch in the TV room, while yet another thick blanket is spread over him like sauce by a nanny who lets him get away with intentionally mispronouncing her name.

He is supposed to be having dinner with his mother and father at the seafood place on Avenue Road that all three of them like. He had been looking forward to it. Depending on how the evening went, he might've even stayed over in his old room, in his old bed, which he preferred to either of the guest bedrooms. Cat wouldn't mind. Or maybe she would, a little, but she might also be relieved to have him far away from her. She's getting hard to read. All he sees when he looks at her is *no*. But Ruth and Don are at a party for a friend of theirs who has self-published a book about John Abbott, who was briefly prime minister more than a century ago, and of whom this friend is apparently a direct descendant. Because Donovan can't think of anything more boring, he is back in his own neighbourhood, eating alone.

Donovan notices, when the young bartender walks by, that she is not wearing a bra. She's wearing a T-shirt with the sleeves cut away, and he can see her breasts through the gaps. He likes that she doesn't care. Good for her.

At the recommendation of the bartender, he tries a beer called Garrison Creek, named after the hidden river that flows beneath the neighbourhood and surges up in the spring, flooding the bottom of Christie Pits Park and dampening a few dozen unlucky basements. At first it tastes like a mistake: too bitter and too earthy. But something compels him to order it again, and by the time he is halfway through the second, he is a convert. Each sip is thick with meaning. The creek is a force that has been buried and built over, but cannot be entirely subdued. It can still make its presence known and fuck things up.

Just like me, he thinks.

Donovan has decided to take action. A few days ago, he sat with his parents on the terrace that looks down over their swooping backyard and told them he had changed his mind about his old job. He wants to go to war with his former bosses. Not to be reinstated — he has no interest in working there again — but to be more fairly compensated, and to secure an official apology for wrongful dismissal.

He can't leave things with Bianca seeing him run and then threatening him. This has to end in a victory of some kind.

Ruth was delighted with his decision, but his father asked if it is maybe too late. The whole thing happened nearly a year ago; he'd accepted the severance package and presumably spent most of it. Wouldn't it be smarter to just focus on his own business now? He'd be burning a very big bridge, one he may not wish to cross again, but which will send up flames that will be seen from miles away. That's the thing, Donovan told them. It's all about perception. Doing nothing has made him look guilty. He'd assumed that the smartest, most strategic move was to accept his old boss's judgment, however mistaken, and get on with his life. But that judgment itself is messing up his plans. His business is struggling, very much because he went along with their decision. He chose peace, and now he's paying for it.

As he was leaving the house, Ruth caught him in the front hall to tell him he has their full support.

"I'm going to tell your father to get Andy to call you," she said.

Andy is a friend of Don's. A lawyer friend. A very well-known and expensive lawyer friend. The kind of lawyer who knows things about powerful people that will die with him.

"I don't think I can *afford* Andy right now."

Ruth made a gesture that told him not to worry about the money. They would pay.

It was the exact gesture he was hoping to see — he mimicked it in the car on the drive back.

. . .

As he sits at the bar, his phone buzzes. It's Andy. Donovan almost chokes.

The lawyer doesn't bother with small talk. "Two kinds of people file wrongful dismissal suits," he tells Donovan. "Young women who think every bad thing that ever happens to them is proof of sexism, and rich guys who think they've earned the right to be pigs. The old guys — I have a lot of friends like that, God bless them. Some of my colleagues call them *roofers*, because they let you put a new roof on your house *and* your cottage. That's a joke."

Donovan loves people like Andy, these older men who've done everything, seen everything. They've become immune to every poison, can tell you exactly which ones are fatal, and which can be sipped with only minimal side effects. They are creatures of the world, in a way that Donovan thought he never wanted to be.

"What about people who are actually wrongfully dismissed?" Donovan asks.

"Yeah, it happens."

Andy asks for every detail. Donovan is eager to give them all, but first asks for assurance that nothing he says will get back to his parents.

"You mean, am I going to go chat with Don and Ruth about privileged attorney-client information? No, I don't plan to do that, Donovan. They're paying the bills for this, so I have to keep them updated on where things are at in a general way, but this part is confidential. I can't tell anyone what you tell me, unless you say you're going to kill someone or blow something up. Are you planning to kill anyone?"

Donovan laughs again. "Not planning any mass shootings."

The two young men sitting next to him at the bar, deep in a conversation about the ethics of using computer technology to de-age actors in movies, look at him quickly, then go back to their argument. Donovan gets off his stool and moves to a quieter part of the room.

"There's this woman, Bianca," he begins. "She's the one who brought the whole complaint against me. The whole situation is stupid, except for the fact that I lost my job because of it. It's completely fucked up and unfair, the way this happened."

There is a pause. Silence at the other end.

"Are you done?" Andy asks him, clearly annoyed.

"Sorry?"

"Do you feel better now you got that out of your system? Donovan, I'm sure it all feels stupid and complicated and whatever it is you said, but if you want this to go anywhere, you need to take it seriously, and you need to tell me exactly what happened. You and this Bianca person, this was an affair?"

"No! Not at all!"

They chatted, maybe they flirted a little, but it never went beyond that.

"Well, obviously it did, or she thought it did, or we wouldn't be here."

"That was a stupid mistake. And everything went to shit because of it."

"You're drifting again. Just tell me what happened. Leave out the editorial context."

Donovan looks around to make sure no one can hear, then tells Andy the whole stupid story.

• • •

The whole stupid story:

It was the office Christmas party. His co-workers, who knew perfectly well how to have actual fun in other contexts and other locations, allowed themselves to be herded into a big office boardroom every year like prisoners, where they ate cold samosas and drank wine, beer, and sparkling water out of plastic cups, while the Phil Spector Christmas album played on a loop. Donovan always tried to make the best of it, and would slowly circle the room, trying to keep a series of fires lit. His bosses did not do this, the people who fired him did not do this. Instead, they stood as stiff as teachers at a school dance.

At the last party, last December, it was exactly as he expected, exactly as he feared. They were all crammed in there, backs to the wall, holding plastic cups, with whatever sixties girl group galloping through "Jingle Bells" for the third or fourth time. The interns stood in a protective knot in the corner, looking scared shitless. Donovan forced them to do a toast with him: "To paid work and benefits." They all laughed and loosened up.

After making a few rounds of the room, Donovan met Bianca at the drinks table. It was a spontaneous meeting. Here they both were, refilling their cups. He was already humming a little from the beer. He was wearing his blue shirt with the stars, and he felt invincible. For once he didn't even mind the music.

"Phil Spector," Andy says, interrupting him. "I had a friend who worked on that trial. Were there rumours of something?"

"About Phil Spector?"

The lawyer chuckles hard enough to lose himself in a cough. "About *you*, about you. You and this Bianca. Phil Spector, that's good … But were there rumours about you two?"

"I don't think so. We got along and would hang out sometimes. That's it."

"You'd *hang out*."

Donovan flinches a little at getting called out on one of the sustaining myths he has told himself about the situation with Bianca. It's as if he showed the man a cardboard refrigerator box and called it a time machine.

"Whatever — we'd talk. We were friendly. That's it."

What he doesn't tell Andy: Everyone else in the office was boring in comparison. The place was mostly filled with pleasant drones who lived an hour outside of the city. No one else wore dresses that fit them like gift wrapping. No one had skin that was brushed and oiled to perfection. No one had breasts as big as babies.

"Before this party, there was nothing. No actual complaints made. You didn't get a warning of any kind, formal or informal."

"Nothing. It was all the party."

"This is important — you need to be one hundred percent clear — there was nothing whatsoever communicated to you before this party that related to your relationship with this girl."

This *girl*. Donovan smiles at how easily Andy says it. He is employing fantasy language in order to make himself understood. He's playing along. Bianca's a *girl*, and Donovan's a *boy*. Two silly kids having a fling.

"Nothing."

. . .

In the boardroom, with the overhead lights dimmed, Bianca's face was glowing. She was wearing a white dress, and her skin looked even darker against the brightness of the material. The raw fact of her beauty lodged in Donovan's mind, and he could not shake it. The dress was sleeveless — he wanted to reach out and touch her bare arms with just the tips of his fingers. Just a touch. It seemed criminal not to.

And so he did. While she was taking a sip of wine, he reached over and pressed very lightly against the side of her arm, up near her shoulder.

"Just checking — I wanted to make sure it was real."

The joke made no sense, but Bianca laughed. Someone from her department came up to ask her a question, barely acknowledging Donovan, and he slipped away with his beer to make another few rounds. He chatted a bit with the head designer — a comfortable-sweater-and-baby-fat kind of older gay guy. They talked about some Dolly Parton Christmas thing he and his partner watch every year on Christmas Eve. Nobody could accuse Donovan of focusing on Bianca, though the whole time he was moving, he stayed aware of her location in the room. He tracked her from the food table to the corner where a few HR people were sitting and eating cake, then to a group of young women from her part of the office, who began to dance in a tight circle on the other side of the boardroom table. He watched the white dress hold her and move with her as she danced.

"Hold on," Andy says. "You touched her shoulder? This was what got you fired?"

"No, she knew it was a joke."

"How do you know that?"

"Because she did the same thing."

As he passed the dancing group, Bianca reached out to touch *his* shoulder. He stopped, pretending to lose his balance. She laughed and turned to face him, still dancing. Now she wasn't merely dancing with her friends and enjoying the music, she was dancing for *him*. She looked him in the eyes while she did so, and he fought to maintain eye contact, to not let his gaze linger down and feed on the delicious things her body was doing under that dress.

At the moment when he sensed this private dance was about to go on too long, Donovan asked her if she felt like a smoke. Her eyes, which had been half closed, suddenly brightened up. "I do," she said.

"Let me just grab another beer and I'll go out with you. I might even have one, too."

Donovan asked the other women in the group if they wanted to come, too. A bluff, an alibi. They said no.

"So, your idea to leave the party."

"She said yes right away."

"But you suggested it."

"Okay, yes. My idea."

. . .

Out on the rooftop patio, it was cold and dark. They'd forgotten to flick the switch at the bottom of the stairs. Donovan offered, as nonchalantly as he could, to go back in and turn them on. As he'd hoped, Bianca said not to bother. There was enough light coming from other buildings around them that they could see what they were doing.

"I prefer it like this, actually," Donovan said. "It's too bright inside."

"Why do they think we can have fun with every light on? What do they think we're going to do?"

"*Hands where we can see them, people.*"

She laughed. "Oh my God, exactly."

He could only see her in silhouette. Delicate white flames of breath and cigarette smoke kept flaring up around her head and hair. The hum of downtown traffic was soothing. He felt he was right in the zone where the alcohol in his system was firing him up, boosting him, drawing happiness out of the air.

Bianca's face suddenly bloomed with light as she looked at her phone with the hand not holding her cigarette.

"It's colder out here than I thought," he said.

She didn't reply, except to wrap herself tighter with her coat, which she had not bothered to zip up.

For no particular reason, Donovan started telling her about the long winter weekend he spent with some friends in a provincial park, sleeping inside a yurt. There were five guys in there, all friends of Donovan's from university. It was the last thing they all did together as a group, before kids and jobs and life scattered them. Everyone slept in wooden bunks around the edge of the structure, equidistant from the big wood stove in the centre, which someone had to keep feeding all day and night, or else they'd freeze.

In the dark he saw her silhouette give an exaggerated shiver, and he stepped closer.

"It was great. I came home stinking and filthy, but I loved it, and I've wanted to go back ever since. Would you go?"

She turned to face him, laughing with surprise at how close he'd gotten.

"Oh my God! Stay in a ... what is it?"

"A yurt." He was staring at the dark shape of her face.

"What did you *do* all day?"

Donovan said they mostly went out on long trips on snowshoes, which he had never tried before.

"And we slept — everyone took naps all the time because we were exhausted from the snowshoes and staying up all night to feed the fire. And we smoked weed."

"I bet," Bianca said.

He took another step.

"How much do you bet?"

"What?"

"Let's bet on something. How much money do you have on you?"

His head was spinning from the smell of her, the look of her, the sound of her — even the sound of her winter coat, rustling against itself in the close darkness. He wanted to get closer. "How much money?" he asked again, and slid his bare hands into her open coat, right at the level of her stomach. He felt her warmth, the curve of her midsection, her dress, and wanted to cry out. He wanted to stand and hold her. He pretended to pat her down, searching for money. He patted against her sharp hips and the upper slope of her ass.

"Yikes!" she said, laughing, and tried to step away from him.

He moved with her, keeping his hands within the bliss and warmth of her jacket. "What are you hiding in there?" he asked.

"And then it all got weird and she got mad," Donovan tells Andy, suddenly embarrassed. "But it was just a stupid misunderstanding. We were both drunk. I don't know — I overstepped, but it's not like I went *after* her."

"Okay listen, Donovan, I don't care if this all sounds dirty and awful and stupid, but you need to tell me *exactly* what happened, right where you are both on the roof, and you start putting your hands in her coat. Already that's enough for a legitimate dismissal, so know that. You made physical contact without her express consent, so some doors have closed. But I still need to know every detail. Tell me everything. Trust me, this isn't how I get my jollies."

In the darkness Donovan held her. His left hand moved up to her shoulder blades, while his right moved down. He pulled her closer, until she was up against him. He shifted so that he was partly inside the jacket, too, like a bear invading a tent. He gave a slight push with his right hand so that her hips butted up against his, and his erection, which had come into being almost spontaneously, rolled over her pelvic bone.

"Oh, okay, ease up, time out," she said in a hurry.

He didn't stop. He moved in to kiss her. As he did, his right hand slid around so that it was cupping her left breast, which was firm and unbound by any bra. He gave a slight pinch to what he was sure was a nipple, and her wriggling body became as rigid as a plank. She pushed at him hard and broke free.

"Donovan, what the fuck ..."

"It's okay," he said, and tried to close the distance between them again.

She took a reflexive step backward and nearly slipped on the accumulated salt beneath their feet. He stopped, but held out his hands in the darkness, inviting her to return them to their state of warmth.

"It's okay," he said again. "Careful."

"I'm going back in."

In one movement she closed her coat tight and tried to step around him. Seeing her coat close was almost painful to Donovan, and he let out a whimper. Then he made what he still considers his only real mistake of the entire encounter: he moved to block her way. As he did so, he thrust his arms around her to keep her in place. She shouted his name, sharp and loud — too loud, he thought, for the situation and for the small space they were inhabiting. As a reflex he put one hand over her mouth. He intended to do it gently, almost as a parody of someone trying to silence another person, but in the dark and with her struggling to get past him, he brought his open palm against her lips too hard, pressing against them and mashing them. She made a noise of protest and bit down on the meat of his hand.

"Mother*fuck*!" he shouted.

"Asshole!"

She stepped around him, ran to the door, and slammed it behind her.

"Ow," he said, alone in the dark.

There was a vicious throb where she'd bit him. In the darkness he couldn't tell if she'd broken the skin. He decided to rejoin the party as if nothing happened, but when he got back inside, the music was off and people were packing up. Bianca was already gone. Nobody mentioned her. The older designer offered him a ride back to his neighbourhood, but Donovan declined. On the cab ride home, he sent her an apologetic message that she did not respond to.

The following Monday, he got called into the boardroom.

Within a few minutes, it was all over.

Andy is quiet for a while. Donovan worries he might be staring at the wall of his office, wondering how a grown-up child of one of his friends could possibly have gotten this far in life without having already become entangled in some kind of legal trouble, given what an utterly naive and fucking brainless dipshit he is.

"Tell me again," he finally says.

"Which part?"

"The whole thing. From when you're *doing your rounds*, as you called it. Start there and tell me everything again."

Once again, Donovan provides a minute-by-minute account of that stupid night. Andy asks for clarification on a few points of chronology, and tells Donovan to email him a list of names of every person who was present in the boardroom during the party, interns included. He is silent when Donovan gets to the part about putting his hands in her coat. He takes a long, deep breath when Donovan talks about mashing his hand — totally without meaning to, swear to God — over Bianca's mouth, and her biting him. When he is done, Andy asks him to go over, yet again, the part about going outside for a smoke.

"You have to be very clear about who said what, and in what order."

Donovan lays it all out a third time. His newfound sense of hope drains away as he relates how he followed her up the narrow staircase, how cold it was out there, how they looked at the lights from the tall condo buildings around them.

"The next week, when they called you in and gave you the termination letter, did you say anything? Did you object to it?"

"I don't think I did," Donovan admits. He has never been able to understand why he was so passive in that final meeting. He didn't express shock, he didn't tell them to fuck themselves or demand a hearing of some kind, an investigation. He sat there like a dumbass, like a kid in the principal's office, completely silent, then took the letter away with him when he exited the building as requested.

"Should I have said something when they fired me?"

He says the word *fired* very quietly, in case anyone is listening.

"It might've helped to object, maybe. It wouldn't have changed what happened, but it might've helped with this."

Andy tells Donovan that a legal action like the one he is planning to bring is always tricky. There is an obvious gender dimension to the whole thing. And a racial dimension, too — is that right? Didn't he say that this Bianca is Black or something?

Donovan confirms that yes, she is technically a woman of colour. Maybe mixed race? They'd never talked about it.

"That counts, believe me," Andy says.

Something awful is coming, something that has been lurking just beyond Donovan's awareness for the better part of a year, but which he has roused and angered by merely *thinking* about taking legal action. A light is coming on inside him, illuminating all the mess and ruin he has piled up in there. His therapist tried hard to get him to turn on that light, and he refused, or was always able to move it so that it only shone on the things he wanted her to see, wanted himself to see. But someone like Andy is not so easily tricked. He will want the whole place lit up like a crime scene. He'll post work lights, bring in crews. In hats and boots and holding drills and shovels, they'll start to reveal exactly the heaving mess that Donovan has been trying to conceal. They will disturb whatever creature lives down there, and it will rise up, dripping and glistening, teeth bared and claws out.

"The way you've described it, there is no evidence of a pattern," Andy says. "It was one isolated, very stupid mistake."

"Yes."

"But one stupid mistake is still stupid. The fact that you and this Bianca were friendly right up until that moment, the fact that she did not complain about you in any way or express any resistance to your friendship before then — that's not definitive, but it can help. But I want to be very, very clear: the whole thing with grabbing her, putting your hand …"

"I fucked up," Donovan says.

"Fucking right you did."

Donovan laughs with surprise.

"Look," Andy says. "I'm trying to be one hundred percent honest here, as a favour to Don. Calls or messages or showing up at someone's door — none of that is good, but it can be argued away. The fact that you touched her, actually stopped her from leaving, and she had to *bite* you to get free …"

"I was joking!"

"Sorry, but it doesn't matter a whole lot what *you* think. I know that sounds harsh, but it really doesn't."

"It's my word against hers, you mean."

Andy chuckles. "No. Not at all. *Your* word is pretty much useless. Sorry. I'm just telling you the truth here."

"So, it's pointless?"

"Not pointless. Just difficult. People do stupid things. Men do stupid things. Women do, too, though that's not something we're supposed to talk about anymore. Point is, you shouldn't have to suffer forever for a stupid mistake."

Donovan pushes himself farther into the corner of the bar, so he won't be overheard.

"One more thing," he says. "It's tricky, I know, but ... if we go through with this, and we have to make all these details clear about what happened, can it be kept confidential?"

"Don't know what you mean. Like, from the media?"

He sounds amused.

"No, I mean, is there a way we can do this where other people outside the main part of it, the interested parties or whatever, don't see any of the details?"

"Like who?"

"Like my family? My wife?"

There is a pause.

"You don't want your wife finding out you were flirting with a co-worker. More to the point, you don't want your wife to know that you put your hands on this co-worker's body and forcibly tried to stop her from leaving."

He closes his eyes. "Yes."

"Donovan, the most likely result in all of this is that all of the details of the case will be kept confidential between the various parties. As far as what your wife knows, or will find out,

I'm guessing she's an intelligent woman — Don said she does computer stuff or something, which takes more brains than I've got, anyway. But if she's smart, she'll probably start to wonder what this whole case is about. And then you'll have to decide what to tell her and what not to tell her. But that decision will be yours. Understand?"

"I do, thank you."

Andy ends by telling him to send the letter of termination, his original work contract, and any correspondence between himself and Bianca — any email they exchanged, any text message, any Valentine's card.

"That never happened," Donovan says. "No cards."

"It would make things easier if it did, actually."

Back at the bar, the two earnest young men are gushing about a new Korean horror movie. A song comes on that sounds like it was recorded, first take, on an iPhone. Donovan tries to appreciate the aggressive clatter of it. His butter chicken is cold, so he orders another Garrison Creek while waiting for it to be warmed up.

His phone buzzes: Isabelle's school. School ended more than two hours ago. He wipes his face with a napkin and answers, assuming it's one of the place's frumpy, asexual secretaries chasing down some forgotten fee or library book.

Instead, it's Isabelle. She sounds angry and frightened.

"Dad! Where are you? You have to come pick me up!"

"What's going on, Iz? Where's your mom? Where are *you*?"

He hears an adult voice in the background, and then the sound of the phone being passed over. A woman comes on, her voice stern and mature.

"Hello, is this Isabelle's father?"

The woman introduces herself as Ms. Fortune. She runs the drama program at the school. Ms. Fortune explains that the after-school play rehearsal ended a while ago, and that she has been waiting there with Isabelle ever since. All students are supposed to be picked up by five thirty, sharp. They are the last people at the school. The school is doing a version of *The Wizard of Oz*. Isabelle is playing Glinda, the good witch, though she wanted to be the Wicked Witch of the West. She wanted to arrive in a puff of scary smoke, making everyone scream. She wanted to creep around the stage, hissing and spitting venom and pointing a crooked, accusatory finger at her schoolmates.

"She's okay to walk home on her own," Donovan tells the woman. "She has my permission."

Ms. Fortune takes in an impatient breath. Students *cannot* go home on their own after rehearsal, she says. This was made clear in all the communication sent home regarding the play rehearsal schedule. Someone in Isabelle's house — perhaps it was her mother? — signed and returned a letter agreeing to those exact terms.

"Is someone coming to pick her up?"

"Can I talk to Isabelle again?"

"I'll put Isabelle on again in one moment, but I need to know that someone is on the way. I can't leave until all the students have been picked up."

So, this is about you, Donovan thinks. He assures her that he will come, and when Isabelle comes back on the phone, the girl is more subdued.

"Dad?"

"Tell your teacher I'm coming in a cab. Maybe ten minutes, 'kay?"

"Okay," his daughter replies without emotion, and he hears her turn away from the phone to pass the message on. Before there can be any objection to this plan, he hangs up and asks the bartender for the bill.

He texts Cat: *where are you? Isabelle still at school im picking her up*

Before leaving he sends her another message: *not cool*

In the cab, angry at himself for not taking a much-needed piss before leaving the bar, Donovan wonders if he should tell Isabelle she can no longer be part of the play. He needs to do something to re-establish his authority, to remind these people of the fearful power he can wield if he so chooses.

His phone buzzes again.

"Yes, I'm on my way. I already *told* you that," he says before Isabelle can wail at him, and before Ms. Fortune can start in again on his responsibilities as a parent and whatever commitments he and Cat have made.

"Um, hello? Is this Silas's daddy?"

It's Maria, the director of Silas's daycare. She tells him that Silas has not yet been picked up. Is someone on their way?

Donovan's head swims a little. He wonders if this is to be his fate: to get a call every few minutes, telling him that yet another child is standing alone somewhere, waiting to be picked up.

"I'm sorry. I'm not sure what happened. This wasn't my day to pick him up."

Which is technically true, since it's *never* his day.

Instead of accepting his apology and explanation, Maria explains that the daycare imposes extra fees for late pickups, fees that are calculated by the minute, and that grow incrementally every five minutes. She estimates that the late fee for today is currently around $125, and growing.

"Motherfuck!" Donovan shouts and hangs up.

He is about to tell the cab driver to go to the daycare first, but they have already turned onto the street with Isabelle's school. Fine. *Fuck it*. Fine him a thousand dollars. Two thousand. And they can keep their fucking pointless newsletters and food drives and Christmas concerts. Fuck all of that. He is done pretending to care.

As the cab comes to a stop in front of the school, the driver chuckles and says, "*Scary*."

Donovan looks out and sees his daughter standing outside the main doors, wearing a tall white witch's hat and staring at her feet, looking as though she wants to tunnel and crawl beneath the grass and the roots of the trees and be smothered down there in the dark. Beside her stands Ms. Fortune, her arms crossed. She is tall and thin, with glasses and curly black hair that is pulled back behind her head. Isabelle begins to walk toward the cab without looking up, her face hidden by the broad brim of the witch's hat. Ms. Fortune does not change her posture or expression in any way.

"No one happy to see you," says the driver, grinning openly.

Donovan is tempted to tell him to drive him home, away from all this unfair judgment. Instead, he jumps out and runs around the cab to open the door for his daughter. She pulls her hat off. Her hair is stuck to her forehead. "What happened?" she shouts, her voice halfway between alarm and anger.

"It's okay. Your mother must have forgot, but everything's fine."

She says nothing in response and climbs into the car. He wants to get in the cab and be gone before Ms. Fortune can say anything, but she is already there, arms still crossed. He gives her a neutral smile that is not returned.

"Sorry about this," he says, smiling. "Not sure what happened. Her mom was supposed to pick her up."

Ms. Fortune is about to reply, then catches the smell of beer on his breath, and her expression darkens. "It *can't* happen again," she says. "Otherwise, Isabelle will not be able to participate any further in the production."

"It'll be fine. We'll make it work." He has decided for sure to tell Isabelle she can't be in the play. In his pocket he can feel his phone buzzing again.

"Next rehearsal is Thursday after school. Pick up is at five thirty. I prefer if parents are already here waiting when we are done."

"Well, *obviously*," he says. "Because nobody has anything more important to do. A school play by a bunch of kids is obviously the only thing happening in the world right now. How can we possibly be late?"

Taken aback, Ms. Fortune says nothing in response. Before she can recover, Donovan moves around to the other side of the cab and climbs in. "Fly, fly, my pretties!" he shouts at the driver, but Isabelle does not laugh.

He answers his phone. It is Maria from the daycare, as expected. He tells her that he's in a cab, and that they are on their way. She says she assumed he'd be coming to the daycare straight away when she first called.

"Well then you assumed wrong." He hangs up.

The driver looks at him in the rearview mirror.

"How do you like that one?" Donovan asks him, smiling.

Still no text from Cat, and the ones he has sent her have not been read.

. . .

When they get to the daycare, Maria and Silas are waiting by
the front gate. The little boy is excited at getting to see the
place after hours. It's an adventure. Donovan insists on using
the washroom. Maria protests, saying the place is closed, and
that the washrooms are for the kids only, but he ignores her.
He marches into the building and spends a minute trying to
locate the bathroom — he has only been here a few times. He
finally finds a room where there are four miniature toilets lined
up along the wall, side by side. Like at a prison, but for little
people. The smallness of them makes Donovan laugh. He un-
does his fly and snickers as he stands there, trying to get everything into one of the small bowls. When he is almost done, he
sways a little on purpose, letting a quick stream of piss hit the
side of the toilet and splash against the floor. After today he is
owed that much, at least.

X

CAT WAKES UP NAKED, SURROUNDED BY WHITE. Her body is held by sheets as crisp as new paper — she is a specimen in an envelope. On her, thick as a pillow, is a white comforter. Somewhere deep in the bed, her bare feet are fresh as new shoots. Her toes wriggle with life. She spreads her legs like clippers, then brings them back together. All this cleanliness sends jolts of joy through her sick skin.

The sheets are pinned under the mattress, which she usually hates. Whenever she and Donovan stay at hotels, she kicks and kicks at the sheets before she can settle, violently unmaking the bed from within. In this unfamiliar white bed, the forced confinement makes her feel secure. She has fallen, or jumped, and been caught.

"Oh *fuck*," she says with a sigh, then looks to see if anyone is in the room.

She is alone.

The walls of the room are almost bare, with just a few small frames that hold prints of abstract paintings. The night table near her head is made of wicker, stained white. On it is her purse, a small clock, an antique lamp with a string, and a glass of water that has been there long enough to acquire bubbles. Cat moans involuntarily at the sight of the water. She's been dreaming of long swims in the ocean, of running over and over into low walls of crashing foam and being pulled under by the strong, unyielding current.

She reaches out for the glass, and moans again. It is cold to the touch. When she drinks — greedily, desperately — she almost chokes. The water is unexpectedly carbonated.

The effort of coming into existence is exhausting. She is a new thing pulled freshly out of mud. She puts her head down on the white pillow, face first, and closes her eyes.

When she lifts her head again, the light has shifted in the room. There is a small patch of wet on her pillow where she has drooled. She has to pee. Bad thoughts hover, ready to pierce her limbs and pin her to the bed. She shifts sideways, as quietly as she can, away from their sharpened points.

Her clothes are missing, but there is a white robe lying across the foot of the bed that smells like a morning breeze off a temperate ocean. She presses her face into its softness, rubs it against her hot cheeks, slips it on, and steps out of bed. The floor silently accepts her weight.

She pauses at the door. Anything could be on the other side. Instead, there is only a hallway, at the far end of which is an empty vase beneath a painting of a naked woman who appears to have been boiled until she is barely recognizable as human. There is a small bathroom right next door. She quickly tiptoes in and closes the door behind her. On the walls are framed photos of very young women dancing — some nude, some partly so. The women look like children, their breasts like buttons. Only the tiny triangular tags of pubic hair indicate they are older. Cat has wandered into the lair of a tasteful pedophile.

A small digital clock next to the sink tells her it is after nine in the morning, which is shocking. When was the last time she slept until nine? Before she had kids. She sits and pees, then lingers, wishing there were a stall door she could close on herself.

She needs to think.

She knows she is somewhere in Meredith's house, but has no sense of where. "I've always got people landing here," Meredith told her the night before. Cat remembers laughing, imagining bodies falling from the sky, bouncing off the roof and slamming into the yard. She arrived at this house exactly like that — without warning, at high velocity, landing with a splat. Had she even called ahead to warn Meredith, or to see if she was home? Or had she believed her chances of being invited to stay would be improved with the element of surprise?

It was the latter. She simply showed up.

She remembers very little. Just flashes, short scenes. Getting home from the doctor's office, feeling numb and hollow, tired, scared, and ashamed. Lying on the couch, sliding in and out of consciousness. Trying to call her sister, but no answer. The doorbell, then Lena with that other woman, the one with the sunglasses. *Jesus Christ*, those sunglasses. She should have slapped them off.

What they told her, what Lena told her. *Jesus.* They carried that awful information all the way to her house, dragged it up the front steps and dumped it on her, smeared her with it. As if she needed more, as if she were running short of awfulness.

She has to stop herself from crying. She doesn't have enough water inside her at the moment to pull off such an operation — she might shrivel and shrink, drop into the toilet.

Cat remembers feeling strangely energized when she finally closed the door on Lena and her cousin. There was no more bad news coming. She was at her worst. She fought to convince herself that it wasn't true, that Lena, out of revenge or whatever, had made it all up. Or made some of it up. Maybe she walked in on him getting out the shower. Maybe he was doing what she said he was, but didn't actually ask her to watch. Guys masturbate. People masturbate. Maybe he didn't ask her to watch and maybe he didn't thank her. Maybe this young woman had come all that way to lie to her.

She poured out the last glass from a bottle of red wine, then went looking for more.

Drinking all afternoon she swam through the house. She found her phone and tried to call Claudia again, but accidentally called Silas's daycare, which had just called her. She hung up as soon as someone answered. Some texts came through, but she ignored them. All of that — daycare, school, children, and the obligations that come with them — was from another time in her life, an earlier time, another life. She came down the stairs on her bum, like a toddler, then climbed back up again on her hands and knees. Her ears were full of Lena's soft,

LUMP   177

deliberate voice, her mind filled with Lena's face, as the young woman told her that awful story.

She remembers sitting on the floor in the upstairs hallway, desperate for her children. She wanted to be covered by them, to use their bodies as blankets and be sheltered.

She crawled to the doorway of the bathroom and looked at the spot where it must have happened — where her husband humiliated himself, flung an axe into the centre of their marriage. Where there were probably still traces of his act on the floor and the cabinet. It all sounded so mechanical. And somehow inevitable, as if there were no possible reality in which her husband did not do what he did, and the young woman who'd just helped destroy her was not forced to witness what she did. All roads led to this. She was embarrassed for Donovan, embarrassed for herself. It made her sick.

But was it her fault, somehow? Not that he did it, but that he even thought he *could*?

It was a wild thing to do, and he is wild.

This is where she is to blame: she allowed his wildness into her life and her home. She let him loose, took off his collar. She called him *husband* and gave him the run of the place. He should've been out in the woods the whole time, fucking the rocks and trees, showing his cock to the moon.

Lesson learned. She is no longer anyone's wife.

But she has other titles, other roles. Mother lions hide their children from the males or else they will eat them, one by one. Sir David Attenborough has explained this to her. And yet, she can't protect them. She can't protect anyone, not even herself. The animal got her again. Climbed up on her and made another baby. A little reward for being such a faithful moron, a dumb sucker.

At some point she discovered a bottle of expensive vodka that must have belonged to Donovan. It was way in the back of the freezer. She'd been rooting around in there, looking for ice, and found a new friend.

"Cold," she said when she had her first sip. "Nice and cold." She couldn't stop giggling, and almost choked.

She remembers summoning an Uber while tears fell onto the screen of her phone. She waited on the porch, and the driver helping her into the back seat of the car asked if she was okay, if she was sick.

"*No* to your first question and *no* to your second."

She had to fight the urge to vomit the whole way. People who walk through blizzards to find shelter or swim to shore after boats go down tell themselves *just a little more, just a little more.* They rescue themselves in tiny increments. Cat did the same thing in the back of the car: *just a little more, don't puke.* She remembers yelling at the driver to stop in front of the liquor store, and him looking at her as though she were a crazy old drunk who might grab something cheap and run off. The joke was on him; she wanted nothing more than to stay in the back seat of his car forever, to sleep and eat there, day after day. But she needed something to douse the smoldering flames spreading throughout her insides. In the store she winced at all the light reflecting on glass, afraid she might topple sideways and take down a display with a wet crash. She made herself walk in the centre of each aisle, as far away as she could from the vulnerable bottles on either side. One of the store workers was taking things out of a box and lining them up on a shelf. A

young man who was shorter than her, and whose sleeves were
rolled up close to the prominent balls of his shoulders to show
off his tattoos and the fleshy dunes of his muscles.

She lingered in his aisle, openly staring at his shoulders
until he asked if he could help her find anything.

"Wine coolers."

He smiled and gestured at the bottles on the shelves, which
were all the colours of the sugar rainbow. "Nothing but," he
said.

She bought a bottle of sparkling white wine and opened
it in the back of the Uber. It tasted like sour apples and fizzed
her back to life from within. Delicious. Like candy after all
that sour Russian vodka. There was too much Tolstoy in her
life, already; she was a Harlequin girl now. Bring her a bare-
chested farmhand, firefighter, lawyer — she will flirt with him
and fight with him and grow to love him and, when the time
is right, she will free his engorged member from his crisp new
jeans and place it in the willing centre of her womanhood.

"You can't drink in my car."

"I just did."

She wants to see her Uber driver again, wants to talk to him,
to explain why she was in the state she was in. She wants to tell
him that she is heartbroken. That she is scared. She is alone.

"I was at the doctor's."

"I hear you."

Amazingly, he will be telling the truth: he *does* hear her, he
is listening.

"I got some very bad news. I'm pregnant."

"You don't want kids?"

"I already have two. I don't think I want three."

"I see."

"No, you don't, not yet. Because what they also told me, what the doctor told me — and it wasn't even my doctor, just some guy, some pretty gay guy ..."

"I'm sorry?"

"The point is, he tells me I have breast cancer. Just like that."

"I am very sorry."

"Thank you. They left me on my own — can you believe that they would leave someone on their own after telling them something like that? But they left me on my own and I think I lost it a little. I made a mess."

"Okay."

"*Not* okay. Not okay at all. And here's the most fucked-up part: after I get home and I've got all this *shit* to deal with, my old cleaning lady, this girl from wherever, shows up to tell me a whole bunch of shit about my husband. Tells me, then leaves. So I got really, really drunk."

"You're okay now."

"I don't think so, actually."

The imagined conversation seems so real in her mind. Slowly, she realizes she actually *did* say all of this to the poor driver. And then repeated most of it to Meredith not long after. She finally starts to cry for real, quietly, into the soft folds of her borrowed bathrobe.

Meredith had been surprised by Cat's arrival — surprised but not shocked. The older woman sized up the situation in an instant, right there at her front door, and brought her inside. She didn't try to hug Cat or comfort her in any way, just opened the door to her like she would for a wounded pet. This, Cat thinks, must have been partly why she went there in the first place: she knew instinctively that she would either be instantly rejected or accepted the moment the door was opened. There'd be no feelings of awkwardness or obligation. Meredith would say *yes* or *no* to her. That decision would be final, and rendered without further judgment.

Cat told her everything right away, spilling it all out to the poor woman. When she was done, or when she finally ran out of anger and exasperation, Meredith asked how much she'd had to drink. Cat told her, and Meredith nodded, saying that what she needed was something to calm the waters. She produced a well-rolled joint from somewhere — for a moment, Cat thought she'd had it hidden in her hair — and insisted they step outside to smoke it.

"Smoking inside is foul. My father smoked like a sailor."

Cat must have choked on the joint. It had been a while. She remembers Meredith telling her to calm her chest, to breathe.

"Nobody knows where I am."

"You only just got here."

Cat wanted to explain that it's different when you are a parent, when there are little people who expect continuity, and who have a tendency to lose their minds when that continuity is broken without prior warning or explanation.

She shook her head when the joint was offered again.

"I can't. I'm pregnant."

Meredith laughed. "We're well past worrying about *that*, I think."

Feeling embarrassed, Cat said, "I have cancer. Right here." She reached up to touch her left breast, then realized she could not remember where, exactly, the tumour was hiding, and so brought both her hands up to her face, which crumpled into tears.

"Oh no, is that true?"

Cat nodded behind her hands.

The lit joint, which was not yet even half gone, disappeared just as swiftly and magically as it had appeared, and Meredith stepped forward to take Cat into an embrace. She held on as Cat shuddered and wept. When the worst was over, she stepped back and discreetly wiped some of the tears and other sad residue from the front of her jacket. She was zipped up tight inside a black yoga outfit.

Meredith put her hands against her own chest, which was smooth.

"They took both of mine more than thirty years ago now. First one, then the other. My mother and my aunt died from it, and so did my sister Grace. They figured it was only a matter of time for me."

"Oh my God, I'm so sorry."

"Thank you, but I have no idea what you are apologizing for."

The joint reappeared. Meredith finished it on her own.

She doesn't remember asking Meredith if she could stay. At some point in the evening, it became understood that she would sleep there. Meredith told her to text Donovan to let him know where she was, which was something Cat had no interest in doing.

"I think I left a note."

"You *think* you did."

She could remember *telling* herself to leave a note. There was a paper, there was a Sharpie — did the two ever connect?

Meredith insisted again that she text him. Men like her husband have a tendency to bring out the police when they can't reach their wives.

"Men like him how? What is Donovan like?" What had she spotted that Cat missed?

Meredith said only that *most* men were like that. Young mothers were like that about their children, and men were like that about their wives. It is part of a whole history of control. A few hours gone and they call the police to come drag them back home, to restore order. The police were, among other things, a tool to enforce control over women. Meredith did *not* want police in her house.

Cat remembers nodding along to all of this, unable to resist Meredith's firm logic. She tapped out a quick message to Donovan: *Am at a friends house. Am okay.* She noticed the time as she typed; it was later than she'd thought. Meredith insisted on seeing the text before she sent it, which made Cat feel even more like a teenager trying to outfox her parents.

"*Friend's house* is good. Don't say anything about the children, don't tell him to kiss them or hug them for you or he'll think you're about to jump off a bridge. Believe me."

Cat laughed, but Meredith's face stayed grim.

After a minute of distracted searching, Cat finds her clothes inside the bed, pushed down to the bottom in a dense mound. The silence of her phone is puzzling. It should be leaping off the table trying to get her attention by now. Isn't the entire world out looking for her? She lifts it and sees that the device is turned off. She wants no one to know where she is, so she drops it in her purse.

Back in the hallway, she can hear music coming from some-where. A piano. She goes in search of the sound, trying to step as quietly as she can, carrying her shoes. There are multiple doors, all of them closed, and she wonders for a moment if behind each of them is another sick, unhappy woman sleeping off a night of wine and vodka. In less than twenty-four hours, Cat's life has become so disordered that she is back to sharing joints with relative strangers like a dirtbag. She grew up being told, over and over by Ron and Sue-Ann, that she was better than the people who slept in doorways or on hard chairs at the bus station or the hospital emergency room, that the fact she lived in the same small city as them barely rose to the level of coincidence. She no longer believes it.

She descends a staircase that curves down to the first floor. She goes down slowly, holding on to the railing. As if he has been waiting for her, along comes Louis the dog, hobbling along on meaty paws, his dense toenails clicking on the bare floor. He looks even less healthy than he did the first time she saw him, though it has been only a few weeks. There is a new bulge on his left hip that could be anything: a hernia, a cancer-ous tumour, a sac filled with spider eggs. She wonders why he does not bark. Perhaps the effort required is too much. She has to step around him.

"Pardon me, guy."

He gives a small canine huff that could be a bark or a sneeze.

The music is coming from deeper in the house. Cat rec-ognizes the sound of something by Erik Satie, performed so slowly and deliberately the player is either on the verge of fall-ing asleep or is still learning the piece. It is the same piece she attempted a few times when she took piano lessons as a teen-ager. She moves toward the sound, with Louis limping behind her like a discreet, aging butler. She comes to a set of large glass doors, and can see through them a pair of thin legs on a small sofa, contained within a maroon yoga outfit. Meredith is lying on her back, her hands resting on her belly, her eyes closed, and her expression utterly vacant, as if her soul has lifted away to roam free in the house somewhere, while her corporeal form lies here, kept alive by the sound of a solo piano coming from hidden speakers. On her head she is wearing what looks like a kind of white turban, into which her hair has been tucked.

As Cat stares through the glass, her mouth opens involuntarily. The turban is, in fact, a diaper. Meredith is lying on the couch with a diaper wrapped tightly around her head. Cat can see the tabs holding it tight.

Cat looks down at Louis, hoping for an explanation, but the poor animal looks even more baffled than her. His nose touches the glass, making a ghostly smudge.

During an uncharacteristically violent moment in the music, when the piano begins clattering and charging, Cat steps away from the glass doors and moves as quietly as she can back to the front hallway. Louis, entranced by the sight of his beloved owner, does not follow. Cat passes the portrait in the front hallway and, after reassuring herself that she has her purse and her phone, carefully opens the front door and slips outside. Almost right away she can feel the first patches of dampness appear in her armpits and on her back. She wishes she'd been able to find more water before leaving. It is as bright as a bare bulb out, and when she reaches the street, she stops to fumble in her purse for her sunglasses.

. . .

The coffee shop at the top of the street is all wood inside. There are newspapers and old magazines in a loose pile on the window ledge. She sees the same cartoon cats lining up for the same food truck on the cover of a *New Yorker*. She waits at the counter until a man appears. He is tall, with an enormous chest wrapped tight in a plaid flannel shirt. His head is shaved and his beard is whittled to a point, but he is friendly. She can imagine him working on a very stylish fishing boat. She orders a large black coffee, then changes her mind and asks for a large cappuccino; she wants foam and sugar. The trappings of pleasure, even if the real thing is unavailable to her. The large man only nods at her order, then turns to make it.

"Thank you."

"No worries."

She wants to challenge him on that. *None whatsoever?*

There are only two other people in the place, a man and a woman in their fifties with matching salt-and-pepper hair, who are sharing a copy of the *Globe and Mail*, silently and seriously stripping every bit of meat off its bones. A half-eaten biscotti sits on a plate between them. Focused on the task at hand, they pay no attention to Cat. She has a brief thought that maybe *they* spent the morning with diapers on their heads, too. Maybe it's a thing around here. She takes her creamy bowl of sweet coffee to the table farthest away from the couple.

Her head is spinning; there is still alcohol in her system. It might be there forever.

Cat has always believed, though she has no idea if the science backs her up — she guesses not — that some nights of drinking imprint themselves permanently on the body, while others get flushed away the next day. She believes that her body retains the memory and the damage from certain parties, certain wedding receptions, certain backyard barbecues where things got out of hand, and not others. It isn't dependent on *what* she drinks, or the sheer amount — more important is the *how*, the level of aggression, the extent to which she is drinking to destroy something, to poison a part of herself she can no longer stand.

With drinking, as with gifts, it's the thought that counts.

What she did to herself the day before, that was more than just damage. She drank enough to poison herself, and yet she never vomited, at least as far as she can remember. Oh God, she hopes she didn't. Maybe her body absorbed it all. Maybe she is so medically toxic that flooding her system with alcohol has little effect now. Like throwing dog shit into a cesspool.

And yet, somewhere within all that toxicity and poison, something else is growing. Something else is eating her alive from within. Two things, in fact.

It will be a race to see which completes its mission first.

She looks for one solid thing, one thing that did not crack and shatter in the storm that has fallen on her, and can only think of Meredith herself. That old woman standing, wrapped tight in her yoga outfit, on the edge of a rocky shore. The whole world wiped away, but this one woman standing straight, knowing exactly how much damage she can withstand, knowing storms like this have come before, and will come again.

When Cat turns on her phone to summon an Uber, it starts buzzing right away: Meredith is calling.

"Hello?"

She can hear the piano music in the background.

"Don't tell me you're on your way home," Meredith says.

"I'm in a coffee shop. I think it's called The Good Ship. I'm having a coffee, a cappuccino. It's huge. Listen, I am so sorry. I feel so stupid. What a stupid thing to do. I don't know what I was thinking. I wasn't thinking at all, actually. You must think I'm completely crazy. I must be. I am. Sorry."

Cat goes on like this for a while. When she loses momentum, Meredith says only, "I appreciate the apology, but it's not necessary."

"I couldn't think of anywhere else to go. If I'd thought about it for *two seconds* ... but I wasn't really thinking straight."

"Of course not. You were traumatized."

Cat smiles at such a grand and dramatic term being applied to the stupid mess of her own life. She has been *traumatized*. She is a victim of *trauma*. It makes her think of hospital rooms and clean sheets and clear fluid dripping silently in rubber tubes.

"I don't know what to do."

This time the tears do come, loudly enough that both husband and wife look around their paper at her. Any moment, the gentle fisherman who owns the place will come around the counter to throw her back in the sea.

Meredith tells her to come back to the house.

"What?"

Cat wonders for a moment if she forgot something.

"I would come to get you, but I am trying to conserve my energy for my next session. I was up quite late last night, as you know."

"I'm sorry."

"I have already said that you don't need to apologize. If you decide to go home to your family, I will understand completely. You don't even have to let me know. But if you do decide to come here, remember: that is *your* decision, so I don't want you feeling guilty or embarrassed. Just do one or the other and stick with it. Understood?"

Cat nods, stupidly, and says she understands. Though she doesn't. Her mind is only functioning at a level that allows her to remain upright. She is tempted to cry again. She remembers how she sat in her upstairs hallway, wanting her children with her. It feels like months ago, years ago. She can barely access that need now, which had been like a shock from a wire at the time. She can see her children, feel them pulling at her arms, but the shock is gone. She is seeing them through a Plexiglas screen.

She sits up straight in her seat when she realizes what has happened inside her: she doesn't want to see her kids. She had assumed the need was there, like it always is, dragging her through the dirt like a dead cow on a hook. Nothing she could do about it. But now it's gone; the hook has fallen out. She worries that, were Silas and Isabelle to run up to her right now, in this coffee shop, she might smack them both across the face. She can't be with them. They are both part of a whole tangle of mistakes she's been making since the moment she was old enough to make decisions about the direction of her life. Every year she pulled more vines down around herself, twisted them together and knotted them up until she was held fast. Until the sunlight could barely get at her. Deep in the twisted green, she knit together a family to wrap around her. Now that the vines have let her go, scratched and raw, she doesn't want to climb back in.

She has to go home, but she can't. That home isn't hers.

"I will come," she tells Meredith.

"Good."

"I just ... was there a diaper?"

"Excuse me?"

"Were you wearing a diaper before? On your head?"

Meredith doesn't hesitate. "Yes, for migraines. I freeze them for whenever I feel one coming on. A writer friend taught me that trick. I'm wearing it right now. Okay?"

"Okay."

Cat gets up, having hardly touched her giant cappuccino, and grabs her bag. She turns to say goodbye to the older couple with the newspaper, but they are gone. They have vanished — the paper is open on the table, and the biscotti is still on the plate. The man who made her coffee and took her money is gone, too.

Hours later, the sun has shifted and there are patches of shade throughout Meredith's backyard. Two figures sit out there on canvas recliners. Butterflies skitter around, and a red cardinal keeps returning to the same corner of the yard as if it has lost something. The older of the two women wears light-coloured yoga wear. The younger is wrapped in a light sheet. She is naked underneath. Her clothes are inside, spinning happily in a dryer.

Meredith's eyes are closed. Cat's eyes are closed, too. She is floating over the grass. Next to her, curled in a messy heap, is Louis the dog.

Cat's phone, on the table beside her, lights up but emits no noise. After a moment, it grows dark again. Cat doesn't notice. She has begun to slide into the warm tar of a nap. Wrapped around her head is a diaper — white and glowing, cold as a new moon.

XI

BIANCA IS LATE. SHE HAS ALREADY SHAKEN HER-
self into a dress, downed a smoothie the colour of new grass,
poured two hot shots of espresso onto her willing tongue.
Makeup applied, hair dealt with, phone in her bag. Also in
there: a small container of salad and quinoa, plus an apple.
All in a stylish bag that preserves cold and repels heat. She is
bringing her own lunch these days, part of a new approach in
which she makes small improvements on the margins rather
than wait for large-scale windfalls like a raise, a new job, or a
relationship with someone with the resources to spoil her. She
is tired of being spoiled, anyway. Her last two relationships —
one mercilessly long, the other mercifully short — were based
on the economy of spoiling, and she is sick of it. Spoiling has
been spoiled for her.

Before the end of the most recent relationship, the short one, she began demanding to pay her own way in restaurants and bars. The new laptop he bought for her as a surprise gift — slim, powerful, as black as his car — was refused and returned. She could've run a small country, airports and military included, using only that device. It was a beautiful item, but it was too much: in price, in power, and in terms of what it represented in their relationship.

"Mine's still good, I'm used to it. Sorry. That's really nice of you."

He was astonished, and so was she. Bianca had never refused a gift before. Especially not for the reason she'd given. For her, getting used to anything is normally the sign that a revolution is required, that she ought to start wrecking things. Becoming comfortable is an evil to avoid, routine is a sin. If more than two weekends in a row are spent in the same way, she will demand novelty, a trip to somewhere unexpected, a stay in a hotel where the sheets are like cream. If whatever man she is with begins to show signs that he has figured her body out, that he has cracked her sexual algorithms, she will react with instant fury. What has made her squirm with delight suddenly makes her impatient, forcing him to prod and lick at her with desperation, while she offers little help. She will happily sacrifice immediate pleasures for the more long-term satisfaction of never being taken for granted. How dare people presume to know her so well? Ravi — he of the gifted black laptop — was a foot-rubber. He would spend hours working her bare feet while they watched shows. He was good at it — he relieved hidden tensions and unwound muscles, sending sparks of pleasure up her legs. She lay there like a cat, and would sometimes doze off while this operation was going on. He never objected when she asked for a few minutes more.

And then one night, while they were binge-watching something about a female detective investigating crimes being committed by genetically engineered clones, she told him to stop. He'd been kneading her bare soles for nearly half an episode when she suddenly jerked her feet away.

"Let me finish," he said. "You like it."

He reached for her feet again. She kicked him.

Lately, however, she has been more welcoming of routine, even relishing it. She fears this is a sign of growing older. The past two weekends have been almost mirror images of each other. Friday night: out with her friends. Saturday: an hour or two in her building's tiny gym, a quick trip to the grocery store for a few basics and the makings of a solo dinner, then out again with her friends. Both Sundays: a little hungover, with her sister and brother-in-law in Etobicoke, playing the *fun aunt* to her niece Lily.

Bianca checks again that her lunch is packed. All ready to go. Her phone reassures her that she has well over an hour before she has to be in the office, yet there is already an email from her manager, Lydia: *We need to have a quick chat when you get in. Come to my office when you get in please.*

Bianca is used to these early morning messages. Lydia sends out a round of emails before she even has coffee, before the day and the sun have firmly established themselves. Work is her life. Lydia's partner, Lise, has confirmed this. Lise is a photographer — and a good one, as far as Bianca can tell. Her photos get shown in galleries. Bianca went to one of these gallery showings once with Mani, the boyfriend before Ravi. Lise chatted with them, and out of nowhere, asked if they could ever see themselves getting married.

"Sorry," she said quickly, reading the panic on their faces. "I just mean you look good together."

She told them she wants to get married, but that Lydia never will.

"Sorry, I should correct that, that's not fair. Ly would totally get married if I ask her to, but only to make me happy. Lydia is all about work. *You're* more married to her than me, Bianca. Oh, I'm drunk."

Mani's eyes were popping out of his skull. He couldn't believe he was standing there in an *art gallery*, drinking *wine* and listening to a giant *lesbian* talk about getting *married*.

Bianca can't imagine ever feeling that way about a job. By the time the streetcar crosses back over the broad river of Spadina at the end of each day, shaking itself free of Chinatown and heading west, she stops thinking about work entirely. She is often praised for her efficiency and speed with various tasks, though nobody guesses that this speed is a product of fear — fear that, if not completed during work hours, one or more of these tasks might easily infect her condo, her building, her life.

She finally has a pee that feels definitive and gets herself out the door. In the hallway, locking up, she hears one sharp bark coming from somewhere in the building. Every few days she will hear it: just one bark, with never a second or third to follow. In a building that is strictly pet-free. She waits for another one. When it doesn't come, she takes out her phone, holds it out at arm's length, and takes a photo of herself looking adorably perplexed.

Heard it again. Just one bark. #ghostdog #condolife

She waits a moment, and is gratified by the hearts that begin to accumulate almost immediately. She had to lock her account a while ago, and was worried that doing so would leave her images to die lonely and unloved, but the crowd of friends and colleagues and former schoolmates she has given access to is nothing if not generous.

Alone in the elevator, facing the mirrored wall, she tries a new expression: *intrepid female detective*. Fingers and thumb on the chin, a look of youthful determination.

What is the mystery she needs to solve?

A disappearance. Something has gone missing or been taken from her.

Follow the trail of clues. The biggest: it's been more than seven weeks since her last period. She's been late before, but never this late.

An easy case to solve. There would be lots of DNA evidence. A trail of blood.

She crinkles her nose. *Gross.*

On the streetcar she thinks about Ravi. He of the good hair and the good clothes and the good car. He of the chest shaved smooth like a little boy's, the well-formed but not obtrusive muscles, the small burps and farts while he sleeps.

The last time they had sex was shortly after they'd already broken up, though at the time only she knew this was the case. He'd taken her to a new place that made amazing tacos; they ordered a whole platter of them, plus Mexican beer. When they had sex, a few hours later, it was not as a parting gift to him, but one she gave herself. She knew — though he didn't — that she was about to enter into a sexual dry spell, and wanted one last hour of intimate attention before hiding her body away again. She even wore new underwear that night, blood-red things that were hardly there. He couldn't believe his luck. When he saw her bra and her panties, he looked like he'd be just as happy to have sex with *them*.

She asked him to go slow — Ravi had a tendency to rush things, a habit she worked hard to break him out of. After she came twice in rapid succession — both times, like bright, hot lights turning on and off quickly inside her — she grabbed at his tiny ass and called him *huge*, called him a *man*. That was the signal to let himself go. She felt the shiver of excitement go through him.

Afterward, as she lay there, she felt even more content than usual. Everything had worked out fine, all the strands of this relationship had come together in a satisfying way, like the end of a long binge-watch. She could almost imagine credits beginning to scroll above the bed. The next morning she told him it was over.

But was he wearing a condom that last time? Sometimes they moved too fast and forgot. Sometimes alcohol and the smell of each other bewitched them both.

"Ah, *fuck*," she says out loud.

There is a big drugstore across the street from her building. She can go there on her way home that night to get a test. She needs almond milk and frozen fruit, anyway. She'll do the test, it will say nothing, and she will get on with her life. Being late is nothing. This is nothing.

Good light comes in through the streetcar window. She checks how she looks with her phone, takes a photo, but declines to post it. Some pleasures ought to be hers alone.

Ranya is already at the front desk. Bianca hates Ranya's hair, which is so black and straight it's as if part of reality is missing and you can see through it to the void beyond. She hates Ranya's clothes, which are all variations on tight black dresses. She must get help putting them on and taking them off. Bianca used to be able to eat anything, drink anything, avoid the gym for weeks, and it didn't make a difference, but she's twenty-nine now, so those days are over. Ranya is barely twenty-one, so she can gobble birthday cake in the boardroom and drink weird cocktails full of Gatorade and vodka and do exactly nothing about it, and it will not show at all. Carbs glide through her, leaving no trace. Ranya runs every evening, though Bianca suspects it is not for exercise, but to burn off all the excess happy energy she stores up during the day. Like a puppy.

"Morning, Bianca!"

Ranya wears glasses with thick, black frames that are too big for her face, as if she has just taken them off the face of an older, richer boyfriend. Bianca used to wear glasses like these, with plain glass in the frames. She got rid of them years ago when she started to worry that people would think she needed them.

"Oh! Bianca! Lydia wants to see you. Can I let her know you're here?"

Bianca toys with the idea of saying no and slipping back out of the office.

"Morning, Douglas! Morning, Kim!" Ranya says.

Kim, the graphic design intern whom everyone assumes is a lesbian, appears on one side of Bianca, gives a quick *hi*, then hurries off to claim the better of the two intern workspaces.

Douglas, the company's head designer, appears on her other side, and lingers at the front desk. He's in his late forties, in good shape, with a full head of hair and a new beard that is just starting to show some silver.

"A beautiful day in the neighbourhood," he says, then points at Ranya and Bianca in turn: "*Would you be mine? Would you be mine?*"

"Oh, I love that guy," Ranya says.

"Is Lydia in her office?" Bianca asks. "I just need to drop my stuff and I'll go see her."

"Okay," Ranya says. "But she said she wants to talk to you right away. Like, first thing."

"Speedy delivery!" Douglas shouts.

Bianca moves quickly into the office, slipping into the warren of desks and workspaces. She has to pee again. She regrets not calling in sick.

In the boardroom Lydia is wearing a white button-down shirt and a thick scarf — she always complains about feeling cold in the office, even in the summer. There is a folder on the pill-shaped table. She puts her hand on it significantly. For a moment, Bianca has a surge of cold fear that she is about to be fired.

"Everything good? Your weekend was good?"

Bianca answers *yes* to both questions, knowing instinctively that further detail would not be welcome. Her boss is Making Conversation.

"Okay, good. We've got — there is a bit of a situation."

Lydia starts off by telling her that, although the situation involves Bianca, at least indirectly, she shouldn't worry; the company supports her 100 percent, and they will do their best to make this whole thing as painless as possible for her. In fact, if it was her choice, Lydia says, they would not involve her at all. Having said that, she has discussed the situation with Christina, the HR manager, and with the company's lawyers, and it was made clear there is no way to proceed with this without Bianca's involvement. No way at all.

"Christina is not here, but this can't really wait."

"Okay," Bianca says. The fear of being fired has been replaced with entirely new fears. Lawyers have been mentioned. That alone is enough to make her feel as though machinery is turning and grinding somewhere far above her, out of sight but almost audible.

"Am I in trouble?"

"No. Absolutely not. I don't want to give you that impression at all." For a moment Lydia looks uncharacteristically panicked. She opens the folder in front of her and touches the page on the top. "Christina should really be here for this. Okay, well anyway — here's the situation: last week we got contacted by a lawyer, who sent the company a letter that — well, the point it is we are being threatened with a wrongful dismissal suit. Just a threat so far, but we have to assume it's serious and that there will be action further down the line."

None of this is from the universe of possibilities Bianca had been expecting.

"Someone who got fired? From here?"

"Unfortunately, yes," Lydia says. "Not *unfortunately*. I mean, it was someone who deserved to be let go, whatever they're saying now. It's such a pain."

She looks at Bianca, waiting for her to work it out for herself.

Bianca thinks of Glenn, the design intern before Kim. Or
was there was someone else in between? The interns are mostly
a benign scramble in her memory. Glenn was only memorable
because he would not leave Ranya alone and because he spent
most of his work time creating web ads for his DJ business.
Douglas called him DJ Glassy, due to the state of his eyeballs
most mornings.

"It's Donovan," Lydia says. "He's threatening to sue the
company."

Bianca has to stop herself from laughing. "You're kidding."

"I'm sorry. I don't think there is any basis here for anything,
and neither does Christina."

"Can't you just tell him to fuck off? Sorry."

Lydia smiles quickly again, then resets her face. "I would
love to. I would love to tell him to … to *eff off*. But according
to Jason, this lawyer he's using is well known. Jason says that,
upon that basis alone, we have to take the threat seriously."

"Who's Jason?"

"Jason is, oh, he's one of the company's lawyers. We took
this to him as soon as we got it, and what he told us was that,
regardless of whether we think this is based on anything or not,
we absolutely have to take it seriously, because failure to do so
could be seen as more evidence that our policies around these
kinds of issues are lax, and because this is coming from a lawyer
who apparently works for some big people. I've never heard of
the person, but apparently this is someone with a reputation."
Lydia closes the folder. "I'm really sorry, Bianca. I am. Like I
said, I didn't want you involved at all."

"What am I supposed to do? Say it didn't happen?"

"No, absolutely not. No, no. You're not at fault in any way.
I think it … do you want me to see if I can get Christina on the

phone? We can get her on speaker. Having Jason here would help, too, actually. The problem is that you are named in the letter."

Bianca is stunned. She sits back in her chair and tries to absorb this.

Lydia unpacks the legal infrastructure upon which the complaint is based, and tells her that the company's lawyer, Jason, is already dealing with the situation.

"He is drafting a counter-letter. I guess with these kinds of things you start out by sending letters back and forth to see if any of it is serious. It's not impossible that this is all just an empty threat, and he won't go forward with it — especially if he sees we're ready with our own lawyer. That's my hope: that this is just a threat."

Bianca suddenly feels the thinness of the boardroom walls — she is vulnerable to attack. Anything might crash through these walls at any moment. A chair, a desk, a brick.

"Why is he doing this?"

"I honestly don't know, Bianca. He might be getting some bad advice, or maybe he thinks he can get more money out of us."

Bianca sits forward. "*More* money? He got money before? When you fired him?"

For a moment Lydia is at a loss.

"So, it's a very difficult situation when you have a long-time employee. Donovan was here for more than ten years. It was decided — Christina and I decided, and Jason advised this, too — the best thing to do, because he'd been here so long, would be to put together a package. It was actually to help avoid a situation exactly like this, to be honest. That was our thinking."

"I don't understand — he pretty much assaults me, I come and tell you, and you give him money? I thought he was fired."

"He *was* fired, or he was let go. As far as we are concerned, he was fired, even if that's not the technical … we took your complaint very seriously, Bianca."

"But I don't understand why you gave him money."

What she wants to say is: *you didn't give me any money.* She was the one who had to fight to get away from that asshole. She was the one who was jumpy for days afterward. Ravi noticed, but she didn't tell him what it was about. It was a long time later that she remembered how she'd bit Donovan on the hand, actually bit him. Somehow, she'd forgotten. The memory had made her a little happier. She wishes she had bit down harder, though the thought of having that guy's blood in her mouth makes her sick.

Ranya taps discreetly on the glass door, which prompts Lydia to tell Bianca she has a conference call happening with some clients, and needs to go over a few notes. Their meeting is over. She tells Bianca again that she has the full support of the company, and that they will all do everything they can to make sure this whole situation does not escalate.

"Speaking of which, more lawyer stuff, sorry." Lydia forces a nervous laugh. She's not used to having to deal with a work situation so tight with emotions and sex. "It's preferable if all of this is kept strictly confidential. I should have mentioned that right at the start — this is why I need Christina here."

"You don't want me to tell anyone," Bianca says.

"Obviously, if there is someone in your family you want to tell, or a loved one, a partner, that's fine. I'd only ask that you suggest they keep it as confidential as possible."

"What about a lawyer?"

"Oh, of course — like I said, Jason is already working on a counter-letter that we all hope will end things right there. Jason is very committed to protecting us here, and to protecting you. He'd be very happy to talk to you."

"I mean a lawyer for *me*."

"That's …" Lydia is at a loss. "That's fine, obviously. You could do that. That might be — we should maybe talk to Jason first, maybe, and to Christina, just so we have all of the details straight and we know exactly where we're going with this."

Bianca grows more certain that she's on the right track with the lawyer thing.

"I want to get my own lawyer. Just for me."

Lydia's face softens and she tugs at the layers of scarves around her neck.

"Of course, I'm sorry — I've never had this happen before. If you feel more comfortable doing that, of course. I'll let Jason and Christina know. Jason may even be able to recommend someone. Do you want me to ask him?"

"No, thank you. I have someone."

An hour later, having been told to take the day, Bianca is sitting on the broad, blue couch in her sister's living room, holding the coffee Nicola has made for her. A mild case of toddler sniffles has forced a cancellation of all planned activities. The child in question is sleeping. As soon as she is up, the little girl will demand that her Aunt Bianca explain, yet again, that horses and cows cannot marry each other, and that only grown-up boys like her father can grow beards, and that the planet they are on is completely round, despite all appearances.

"We're supposed to be at the library right now for storytime," Nicola tells her. Her voice is faintly manic, as if the opportunity to sit on the floor of a library for an hour with a dozen or so other young mothers and nannies was something she'd been counting on to keep herself from slipping into a dark place. There is a bamboo plate on the coffee table with a few purple grapes on it, cut carefully in half. Nicola grabs this plate and quickly eats the last few grape halves, holding the baby monitor in her other hand. She's wearing a loose-fitting pair of yoga pants and a T-shirt with no bra. She has her old glasses on. Bianca wonders yet again if stay-at-home moms are basically asexual.

Bianca tells her everything about the meeting that morning.

"What lawyer do you know?" Nicola asks.

Bianca is annoyed that this is the part of her story her sister has fixated upon. She'd told her at the time about Donovan getting fired for acting like a creep, but she hadn't gone into so much detail before, hadn't even told her his name. Nicola had pretty much dismissed the whole incident as *work drama* — the very kind of thing she had renounced when her baby was born.

"Do I even need a lawyer? They're saying this is just him trying get more money."

"That's probably what will happen, but you told me he might push this. I don't know the guy."

"I don't either. Not really. Don't say anything about this to Mom."

"Obviously not. But do you think he'll go ahead with it? Is he the type?"

Bianca says again that she doesn't know. She left the meeting with Lydia convinced that any reply he got from the company that tried to dissuade him would only cause him to dig in and fight harder. Or at least ask that his lawyer do so. On the trip to Nicola's, this belief got reversed, then restored, then reversed again at least a half-dozen times.

"I saw him," she says.

"Saw who?"

"The creep. Donovan. I saw him not that long ago."

"You *saw* the guy? Recently? The guy who's doing this shit?"

"It was so weird. I haven't seen him at all since he got fired, obviously, and then all of a sudden, I'm at a Starbucks and he's right outside, just standing outside the window with a big fucking smile on his face, looking right at me. And eating, like, a hamburger."

Nicola sits forward, holding the baby monitor close.

"He's a stalker? Oh my God, Bianca — did you tell your boss that?"

Bianca realizes that she probably should have. "I didn't even remember until just now."

"A stalker," Nicola says, impressed.

"It's probably just about money. What else would he even want at this point?"

"If he's showing up when you're getting coffee? Bianca, that's dangerous! Isn't he rich? You told me he's rich. Does he even need the money?"

"I don't know. I mean, I know his family is rich, but maybe they're not helping him?"

"That's not likely. People with money take care of their kids, no matter what. You'd have to be, like, a child molester and a murderer to get cut off. And even then ..."

Nicola puts the monitor on the table between them, with the red eye pointing at Bianca, as though it is listening to *her*, rather than the little girl asleep upstairs.

"Remember my friend Jackie?" Nicola asks. "From high school? She had the red hair and the huge eyes."

"Wasn't she fat?"

Nicola makes a face. "She wasn't *fat*, she just wasn't super-skinny like all *your* friends. God, Bianca, you're like the least feminist woman I know. Anyways, you don't know this because nobody knew it at the time, but she got pregnant and had to get an abortion when she was, like, nineteen. Her family *fur-reaked* out. I thought she was going to be disowned."

"For having an abortion? Wasn't it legal back then?"

Nicola rolls her eyes. "*Jesus*, Bianca. My point is, they had a complete freak-out on her, but guess who got a condo when she graduated? Listen, what lawyer do you know?"

"I was thinking I'd ask Ravi. Ravi's a lawyer. You met him on my birthday last year. Short black hair. Indian guy."

Nicola laughs. "*That* Ravi? Didn't you just dump him? What did he say?"

"I haven't asked him. I don't know anyone else."

"Have you even talked to him at all since?"

Bianca tells her that Ravi has tried texting her a couple of times in the past few weeks, once to say hello — just that: *hello* — and once to call her a *fucking liar whore*. She didn't respond to either text, and currently has his number blocked on her phone.

"So maybe he's not exactly available as an option," Nicola says.

"He has to talk to me."

"Why does he have to talk to you? He called you a fuck-ing ..." She lowers her voice. "A fucking *whore*."

"He has to talk to me," Bianca says again. "I might be preg-nant, and it's his, probably, so ..."

At that moment a howl fills the room, coming from the baby monitor. Nicola stares at her little sister, her hands still on her face. Then comes the summons that cannot be ignored: "*Ma-ma! Ma-ma!*"

Nicola stands up. "Holy shit," she says, then shakes her head and leaves the room.

Bianca finishes her cold coffee in one gulp. She hears the door of the little girl's room open and Nicola saying soothing words: *"It's okay, it's okay, it's okay."*

XII

IT'S GOING GREAT, DONOVAN TELLS HIMSELF.

"Going great," he says out loud, and reaches for a high five from his youngest child, his only son, his little buddy Silas, who is mounted on a plastic potty with toddler-size jogging pants around his ankles and a dry diaper unfurled on the floor behind him. The boy has been on the potty for a while; his expression is all adult. He has forgotten himself, which is exactly what Donovan has been hoping for. His goal is to have Silas potty-trained before the end of the summer. Something to drop casually with the ladies at the new daycare, who already think he is a hero for doing this all on his own. There are books splayed out on the ground around them. He has shown Silas pictures of bats and tigers, argued out the difference between a tyrannosaur and an allosaur, and read four whole stories about a frog and a toad who act like an older gay couple. Donovan is bored out of his mind, but he does this because his little guy needs him. He does this because he is a *father*. He's a *dad*. Weeks of solo parenting have brought this reality home.

"Proud of you," he says to Silas, meaning both of them, father and son.

Silas mutters something that sounds resentful.

"What's that, buddy?"

"I don't like the elves."

"Which elves, buddy?"

"Santa elves."

Having confessed this, Silas slumps a little. He has been carrying the burden of these troubled thoughts with him for a while, maybe even the whole day, which is forever.

Donovan is used to these random gusts of toddler emotion. It's exactly like being around a very old person, with disconnected thoughts and opinions and memories dropping like sparks. Donovan's mother used to make him sit with his grandfather in the years before he died. He wasn't expected to do anything, just to be there, a comforting presence while the old man babbled. It turned out to be worth it: when he died, a shitload of money came Donovan's way that later helped him buy this very house.

"You don't have to worry about Santa's elves, buddy. They're all way up at the North Pole, which is a long, long way away."

The boy considers this for a moment, then perks up. "Macaroni!" he shouts happily, as much for the sheer joy of feeling one of his favourite words leave his mouth as to request that this wonderful substance be made for him.

Then he asks the same question he does every day: "Mama coming?"

"I don't think so, buddy. Maybe soon, okay?"

Donovan skims through his phone, looking for something. He has no idea what is going on in the world. All day long, his phone pushes news items at him that he swipes away, unread. He has forced himself away from all social media, which even at his loneliest he recognizes as a wise move. He doesn't want to say anything about Cat publicly, doesn't want people to know how angry he is with her. Not yet.

He goes to Google Street View, plugs in his own address for the hundredth time, and zooms in on the front porch, where he can make out a smear of sidewalk chalk creeping up the brick walls like rainbow-coloured foliage. He imagines the whole house covered in plants and smooth, curving wood, like that building in the Philippines, the one that doesn't exist yet. The dream building. The front door of his house is propped open — perhaps Cat was in the process bringing the stroller in or out when the Google car passed by. No people are visible. He wishes the car had caught them all, the whole unbroken family, out on the porch or the front walk.

He holds up his phone out to Silas.

"Look, buddy, it's our house."

"Wanna show."

Silas knows that phones are magic and can do wonderful things like bring you cartoons and videos of cats tumbling around. All you have to do is ask.

"Not now, buddy."

It's been more than a month since Cat left, an unimaginable gap. More than a month since he got home with two unhappy kids to find the front door unlocked, the house a mess. The dishes not done from that morning, the cupboard doors all open. On the counter were two empty bottles of white wine and a glass. There was a bottle of vodka, too — expensive stuff that Donovan brought back from a work trip and had been saving. The more he saw, the more he was filled with dark satisfaction: he'd been right all along. It was not *him* who had fucked things up.

Donovan had walked through the entire house, looking into each room. He'd been hoping to find her passed out on top of one of the kid's beds, overtaken by a dark wave of boozy sleep. On the counter in the upstairs bathroom, he found a note written in Sharpie on a torn scrap of printer paper: *I'm Out — C*

He assumed Cat and her sister, or maybe a friend, were at a nearby bar, talking shit about their husbands and flirting with the bearded servers. Even in his angry state, Donovan felt as though he ought to leave her to it. Letting her have fun now would allow him to claim a cleaner victory later.

Hours later, long after he managed to get the two unsettled children into their beds — he didn't even bother with Silas's bath, and Isabelle fell asleep on top of her blankets with her witch costume still on — he got a text from her about staying at a friend's house. Which made no sense. He texted her back a few times, demanding clarity, but got no reply.

The next day, he got a long text from her that began with *I'm sorry.* He has it saved in his phone, and has read it over dozens of times, looking for clues, for some kind of explanation of what happened. The only facts that he can glean from the message are that she is staying with some older woman whom he doesn't know, and that she is not planning to come back any time soon. For a while after getting it, he was afraid that Cat was having a lesbian affair. He's still not totally sure she's not.

He has shown others the text.

"It's unacceptable," his mother said. "Who is this woman she's with?"

"I have no idea."

"Why is she there?"

"She says she needs to do this. She needs time."

He wants his mother to object to the idea.

"What *she* needs ..." Ruth begins. She doesn't finish her thought.

His father has no interest in reading the text, which would be like examining his daughter-in-law's soiled underwear. Too intimate. He only wants to know one thing: when is she coming back?

At first Donovan thought the kids were his ace in the hole. The sounds of their voices. He got them to leave her voice mails in which they told her they missed her, asked her to come home. Silas mostly yelled and sang. Donovan always coached them a little before he called. He sent Cat photos of the kids — not crying or looking pathetic, but doing day-to-day things: brushing teeth, reading, walking in the park.

He could tell from his phone that Cat was seeing the photos, and she never asked him to stop, but she would not comment on them or thank him for sending them. He helped Isabelle craft a message for her, which he typed out and sent:

Hi Mom. This is Isabelle. I really miss you and hope you will come home soon when you feel better. I ride my bike a lot and I want to go to Niagara Falls soon. Please come home.

That elicited a one-word reply: *Don't*. He was tempted to share this with their daughter.

Days later, Isabelle came to him to ask about the text. Did he remember which one?

Of course.

Did he already send it?

Yes, absolutely.

"I didn't want you to!" she yelled, rage going through her like flame through paper.

"What the fuck?" he yelled back, and was immediately sorry. In a gentler tone, he asked her why.

The girl wouldn't answer him. Later, he asked again, sounding as though he was only curious.

"I'm not talking to Mom now," she told him.

"You have to, though."

"No, I don't. She's not here. Spirit doesn't talk to her dad."

"Spirit's dad is dead, isn't he?"

She looked at him like he was an idiot, her face all screwed up. "No. He's working in America and never calls her."

Isabelle sleeps over at friends' houses a lot. When the parents text him to ask if she can stay, the messages come up as being from *Amy Mom* or *Heather Mom* or *Spirit Mom*, which is how he put their numbers in his phone. He can never remember their names. When he picks her up the next day — or a few days later — the parents make a big show of telling him how easy it is to have Isabelle around, and say that she can come back any time and stay for as long as she likes.

"Was fun?" he asks her on the way back across the park.

She shrugs. There is always a spark of happiness in her when he picks her up, but then it vanishes, and she folds her body around the space where it had been, to protect and preserve it.

Silas went through some things early on, too. There were a few days when the little guy decided he was done with walking, so he started crawling everywhere in the house, no matter what his father said. He got over it. Bedtime is still an issue, though. Silas insists that Donovan lie on the floor next to his small bed until he is totally asleep, which can take forever. Donovan will lie there, silent, for nearly an hour, but the moment he shifts his body to leave, the boy will wake up, wanting to know where he's going.

It's Daisy, a friend of Cat's from university, who solves the bedtime problem. She calls because the site Cat has been making for her was supposed to have gone live by then and she hasn't heard anything.

"Is this for the real estate stuff?"

For a while Daisy sold houses, until she finally admitted that it made her scared to walk through empty homes with strangers. She has a new business: homemade popsicles.

"Popsicles."

"Yes!" Daisy says, her voice flush with pride. Made from pure juices she presses out of various soft fruits and vegetables with her own hands, and filled with natural ingredients, no sugar allowed — not counting the "adult" category, which contains things like rum, vodka, and beer.

Donovan tells Daisy a little about what was going on. When he mentions Silas's sleep troubles, she recommends a YouTube video that she plays for her son every night while they lie together in his bed.

"The video was supposed to be for *me*, but he just loves it."

She sends him a link to the video, which is about pelvic floor relaxation. Montages of artfully photographed flowers and sunlight coming through trees like honey dust while a young woman murmurs things like *we're going to go on a journey to really root our bodies down into the earth.* The video works like a sleeping potion on Silas — he is out after less than three minutes. Donovan, on the floor next to Silas's bed, watches the rest in the darkness with the volume turned down.

There is no right or wrong with this, the narrator purrs. *You're doing it absolutely perfectly.*

By the end of the video, he's in tears.

There are things Donovan did after Cat left that he is not proud of. For example: walking into the back bedroom where Cat has her office, looking around for something on which to vent his anger and frustration, and yanking at the special keyboard she uses, expecting the whole assembly to come crashing forward with it. The keyboard was wireless. Without a second thought, he rammed it into the wall like a rifle with a bayonet. He thrust it into the wall over and over again until he heard a crack.

He isn't proud of calling Cat a *crazy fucking bitch* on one of the rare times when he was able to get her on the phone. He asked her flat out when she was coming back and was told — for the third or fourth time — that she didn't know, but that it wouldn't be soon. He told her he was sorry for whatever he did. Would she please just come back and help him work things out. The kids miss her. They're scared.

"Don't," she said finally.

There was no fear or sadness in her voice, no tears. She was firm.

"Don't what — don't tell you the kids miss you? They don't know what's going on, Cat. What am I supposed to tell them?

That their mother just fucked off and left them? I'm getting these calls from your doctor. What happened there?"

"Just tell them I'm fine and that I love them."

"Oh, *okay*. So, it's about *you*? As long as *you* are fine, nobody else matters."

"Don't," Cat said again, and again she was firm, not angry. His words weren't hurting her, they were not shaking her will. He was only exhausting himself.

"Do you even know what you're doing?"

"I think I do."

He was thrown by her quiet certainty.

"What are you doing, then? Tell me."

"I can't."

He laughed. "You can't tell me. Oh, okay. Do you know why you can't tell me? You can't tell me because you don't actually know. You have no fucking idea what you're doing because you're acting like a *crazy fucking bitch* and —"

Donovan hissed into his phone for another few seconds before realizing she was gone.

She didn't reply to any of the messages he sent for a while after that, not until he was pretty much grovelling in text after text, begging her to at least tell him she was okay.

After almost a day of it, she replied: *I'm okay. Just stop please.*

That's when he went into her bedroom office and broke her fancy keyboard. He also swept one of her big computer monitors off the desk with his hand and stomped on it like a crazy person. He isn't proud of that now — he enjoyed doing it, but wishes he hadn't. The kids aren't allowed in that room, and he won't let Jaslene, the new cleaner, go in there, either. He wants to preserve it all exactly as it is for when Cat returns. However that return goes, with tears or laughter or whatever, she must at some point go into that room and see what she made him do. She must know how he was feeling, and how she hurt him. Then he will clean it up, or ask Jaslene to, and will pay to replace everything that is broken. But truth must come before reconciliation.

He at least has help. The house — which, admittedly, went sideways in those first weeks — is looking and smelling better these days, now that he finally has someone coming in to clean the place again. Jaslene was a gift from his parents. It turned out she was already cleaning two houses on the same street, one of them just a few doors down.

"Right under your nose!" Ruth told him when they first hired her.

Jaslene is much older than Lena. If Donovan had to guess, he'd say around fifty, though he knows that a life like hers can add a decade to a person's face. At the same time, he thought Lena was sixteen the first time he met her, and was baffled to discover she was already in her twenties. And Lena was so quiet. She had a way of slipping in and out of the place. So many times, he'd walk into a room, fully expecting to find her there, and she'd be gone. He always knows exactly where Jaslene is in the house. She shouts "Hello!" when she comes in the front door, and she hums while she works. She talks, too: to friends, to relatives, to her grown-up children. She sticks a little earbud in her ear and yaks away while she tidies their house and wipes down the counters. Donovan has thought about asking her not to have these long conversations while she's working, but both kids say they like the sound of someone else's voice in the house.

Claudia has been helping, too. Which is a surprise. At first, after Cat disappeared, her sister would not talk to him, would not answer the phone or reply to his texts. He talked to Dale, his brother-in-law, who made it clear he didn't want to get involved. After a couple of weeks, when it became obvious that Cat was serious about staying away, Claudia got in touch. She asked if he needed anything. She even offered to take Isabelle and Silas for the night, which Donovan gratefully accepted, though Isabelle came back saying her aunt and uncle spent the whole time telling her what she was not allowed to do or touch, and that for dinner they ate some awful rubbery thing called *calamari*.

A couple of times a week, Claudia will show up, usually alone, carrying bags of fruit and flowers from the farmer's market and things like doodle pads and fancy colouring pencils for the kids. She occasionally comes late in the day, without Baby Jessica, to help with bedtime. Then she and Donovan will sit in the backyard — her with wine, him with bourbon or beer or both. Claudia always wants to talk about his family or his childhood or places he's gone to, but he only wants to talk about Cat. She tells him what she knows, which is that Cat is staying with some rich lady who owns a yoga studio — Cat told her that much, but would not say where it is. She is reluctant at first to pass on even that information, but at some point, it's as if she cannot sustain her sense of sisterly obligation to this crazy person who took off on her own family, so her loyalties shift. Donovan can tell that she is a little resentful of her sister for having supplanted her as the more interesting and unpredictable one in the family. By rights, a devastating stunt like this ought to be hers.

When Claudia leaves to go home, she always gives him a quick hug and a chaste kiss on the cheek. A few times, alone in the sleeping house, Donovan has expanded upon that kiss and blown it up into a full-on fantasy where the two fall into each other and fuck on the couch, maybe after a few drinks too many.

Cat's father calls almost every other day. He calls early, before Donovan is fully awake. The buzz comes through the mattress — Donovan has been stashing his phone under Cat's pillow when he sleeps. Ron doesn't ask if he is bothering his son-in-law by calling so early. The thought doesn't occur to him, having never fully relinquished his right as a father to control through disruption even those not directly related to him. Each of his calls is a progress report. He has taken it upon himself — again, with the open-ended mandate of a dad — to treat his daughter's strange behaviour as a kind of personal project.

"I spoke to a buddy of mine. A police officer up here, retired."

It takes Donovan a moment to work out that *up here* means Peterborough, not up in Ron's head.

"I asked him if there's anything we can do with that yoga person. He says there is definitely a case to be made for kidnapping, or something close to that. There are cases where a person can be removed."

"*Removed*? Like grabbing her and dragging her out? It sounds like you're talking about a raccoon, Ron."

Cat's father does not laugh. "Well, something like it, maybe. He says it's usually a thing that happens with teenagers, but he's seen one or two cases with adults. People get mixed up with things."

Donovan knows that for Cat's parents, there is nothing so worrying, so sinister, so worthy of concern, than the seemingly infinite category of *things*. *Things* are always being done that ought not to be, or being done in a way that is ignorant, thoughtless, destructive, and possibly even criminal. He has heard a lot about these *things* and been warned about them. Big shifts in culture that require the use of new terms and the ejection of perfectly useful attitudes and social categories, those are a *thing*. Most non-Christian spiritual practices, especially those that demand anything of their adherents beyond regular, passive attendance at a place of worship and the stashing of a holy book somewhere in the house like a set of emergency candles: very much a *thing*. Toronto itself is definitely a *thing*, and one they are often embarrassed to admit that their two daughters have become mixed up with. Look where it's got them.

"I don't think we can go there, Ron. Grabbing her?"

"Okay, but it's an option."

Which is only accurate. There are lots of options. Donovan does not say that they should probably focus their time and effort on exploring the *good* options. He convinces Ron to hold off on calling in ex-police officers from Peterborough to locate his wife and carry her away, kicking and screaming, from whatever *thing* has her in its evil grip.

Cat's mother calls regularly, too, though later in the day, after she has completed her gardening or is home from her volunteer shift at the church-run thrift store. She repeatedly offers to come help with the kids, to take them to the park or to one of the splash pads in their neighbourhood.

"You can have the whole afternoon. We'd be fine."

She is diplomatically vague about how Donovan might make use of the free time.

No matter what he tells them, Cat's parents continue to press him with opportunities to help. They are unnerved by Donovan's inability to provide them with information that makes any sense. This is the worst *thing* of all. Their daughter is gone.

What is he doing about it?

With the kids finally in bed, Donovan calls Cat for the thousandth time. He intends to leave her yet another voice mail, though he isn't yet sure what tone to take. Empathetic. Loving. Conciliatory. Apologetic. Neutral. Angry. Sarcastic. He has tried all of these. His plan is to tell her that Silas has mastered the alphabet, except for the *P* and *R*, which look too much the same, and for the tangle of *L M N O*, which the boy still thinks of as one letter called *ellamenno*. Isabelle has declared some interest in becoming a vegan chef like the mother of one of her friends, and made Donovan a salad for dinner, a heaping bowl of hand-shredded iceberg lettuce and half a tomato with the sticker still on it. He thanked her and made a point of crunching through some of it before quietly dumping the rest in the compost bin.

He is thrown when someone who is not Cat answers.

"Yes?"

It's a woman, someone older. The tone is not friendly.

"Oh ... I was looking for Cat. Who is this?"

"Who is calling?"

He feels like a kid who has walked into a room full of stern adults doing things he has no business witnessing.

"This is Donovan."

No reply.

"Her husband," he adds.

"I know that. She's not available."

"Sorry, who is this?"

"Cat will call you when she is ready."

"Why are you answering her phone?"

"She's resting right now. She left her phone with me."

None of this makes sense.

"Why are you not letting me talk to my wife?"

Her tone grows instantly colder. "I'm not preventing you from speaking to Cat. She will call you when she is ready."

"Oh, okay. And when will that be exactly? You have an ETA on when she might be ready to talk to her own fucking husband?"

The woman says nothing in reply. She declines to accept receipt of his anger.

"Hello?"

"I'm still here. Is there a message you want me to pass on?"

He forces himself to stay calm.

"Look, I don't know what's going on with Cat — I assume she's mad at me for whatever, I have no idea. But she has two little kids who are really missing her. I need to know that she is okay, and I need to speak with her. It's been weeks, and we're all worried. Please. Just tell her I'm not mad, the kids aren't mad. We want to see her — that's it. We want her to be okay."

"That's your message? That you are not mad at her?"

"Sure, yes. Fine. Tell her I'm not mad and that she can come back any time."

"She isn't waiting for your *permission*."

Donovan closes his eyes. "No, I know. I didn't mean ..."

"You may think you have that kind of control over her, but you do not."

"I fucking KNOW that! I just want to *talk* to her, you fucking ..."

The line goes dead.

He stares at the phone in the darkness of the quiet living room and has to stop himself from calling back right away. The hand holding the phone cramps, and he nearly flings the device against the wall as hard as he can. He wants to hurt somebody.

"Fuck!" he shouts. "Fuck, fuck, FUCK!"

After a minute he goes upstairs to see if his yelling has woken the kids.

Donovan's mother calls, too. When she does she isn't looking for updates, isn't interested in checking in, or in hearing what the kids are up to, or even finding out how her only child is surviving what is self-evidently the most stressful time of his life. She is looking for reassurance that the *obviously disturbed person* who is his wife — when she says it, it sounds like *crazy fucking bitch* — has not suddenly reappeared on their doorstep, acting like nothing happened. She wants to know that Cat will not simply slip back into her son's home just like that. She knows her son is weak enough to allow that to happen.

Ruth calls him while he is pouring a bath for Silas, who is naked on the bathroom floor, crawling in tight circles like a dog chasing its tail.

"What's that noise?" she asks.

"The bath. I'm running the water."

His mother makes an unhappy noise, as if she has caught him pouring a bath for himself.

"You're all there, then?" she asks. She has started referring to the three of them without Cat as a full unit, without any gaps, likely in the hope that Donovan will begin to see it that way.

"Isabelle is staying over at a friend's place."

As casually as he can, Donovan mentions a few unavoidable expenses that are sliding his way. Isabelle needs new clothes for school, a few shingles have come loose from the roof at the back, and he wants to put a big freezer in the basement to save money on groceries.

"I have to bring the car in this week, too. It's making weird noises again."

"You should be leasing."

"I should be, you're right." He grabs at Silas in a moment when the boy is a preoccupied by his toes and lowers him into the water.

"I'm talking to my guy about maybe moving some more money out of the RSPs. The penalties are a real bitch, though."

"Donovan."

"Sorry."

He waits. He has been hoping for another installment on his inheritance, which would be a godsend. He has to be careful, though, an outright request for assistance would be a sign of weakness, and he knows his mother responds only to strength.

"As soon as the kids are both in school and I can get working again, it'll be a lot better. And I'm still waiting to hear back from Andy about all the lawsuit stuff."

There is a noise downstairs. The front door closing. Someone calls out *hello*.

"Your father got a call from Andy, actually," Ruth tells him.
"He called Dad? What did he say?"

"I didn't speak to him, Donovan. He only spoke to your father."

"Okay, what did he say to Dad?"

"He said that we need to talk to you. About what happened."

"About what happened when?"

"Andy thinks we should talk to you about what happened at the agency."

"*Fuck's sake*," Donovan says quietly, with his mouth away from the phone.

Silas, his head haloed with bubbles, whimpers a little at the sound of his father's anger.

"You *know* what happened at the agency. They got mixed up about something and they fired me. That's why I have Andy to fight them. Fucking hell."

"Please don't swear at me."

"Sorry."

The bathroom door swings open. Claudia is there with a bag from the liquor store. When she sees Donovan is on the phone, she mimes putting bottles away. Donovan nods at her, smiles, and points to Silas, who is adding more bubbles to his hair.

"Cute," Claudia says, and disappears back downstairs with the bag.

Silas looks around at the empty doorway. "Who that?"

"What else did Andy say?"

"He said there might be more to the story than what you've told us."

"Who that, Dada?" Silas asks, trying to twist his body so he can see more of the hallway beyond the bathroom door.

"More to the story what? I told you what happened."

"So why are they saying you acted inappropriately? What do they mean by that?"

"How would I know? Look, one of the junior staffers complained about me, for whatever reason, and instead of actually finding out what happened, they let me go. Companies are being cowards about all this right now. There was nothing, nothing. Zero. They fucked up."

"Don't swear at me, Donovan."

"Sorry. I just don't know what is going on here. I honestly don't know what Andy is talking about, and I'm annoyed that he is calling you and getting you both all upset over something we've already gone over and over. It's nothing. Andy is my lawyer in this, isn't he? He's supposed to be working this out, not stirring more shit."

"I asked you not to swear at me."

Ruth's tone makes clear this is the last time she will make this request. When she speaks again, her voice is softer. "So what do I tell your father?"

Claudia appears in the doorway with two glasses — white wine for her, a bourbon and ice for him. Donovan is so happy to see the drinks he wants to strip down, climb into the water with Silas, and invite his sister-in-law to join them.

"Tell him it's all fine. Because it fucking well *is*."

While Claudia reads bedtime stories upstairs, Donovan drops onto the living room couch and opens his phone. He goes to Google Street View and navigates his way to his old office building, still intact and unharmed by the flames and destruction he has wished on it. With the tip of his finger, he slips down the street and stops at the corner. Standing there on the screen, waiting to cross the street or to hail a cab, is Bianca. He is sure it is her, though her face is digitally smeared, the way every human's face is in this virtual world, and when he tries to move the scene to get a clearer view, her body appears and disappears. She is only there in that one moment when the Google car paused to take a photo. In the next moment, she is gone. The date at the top of the screen tells him the photo was taken last summer, before any of the trouble happened. Before the Christmas party. She appears to be looking out from the photo, directly at Donovan.

He has spent a lot of time on this virtual corner, looking at her. Her smeared image stares out at him, daring him. This is the Bianca who still speaks to him, still laughs when he tells her things, still invites him out when she goes up on the roof for a smoke. This is the Bianca who doesn't hate him. Somewhere in this vanished world is the old Donovan, too. The one he wants to bring back.

He scans around the neighbourhood, wondering if she pops up anywhere else nearby. He finds his own car, parked in a spot around the corner. It occurs to him that the scene he is looking at is not just in the past, but from an entirely different existence. This whole world has been eliminated, as if destroyed by a bomb or a pandemic. He is looking at a dead city, an entire reality wiped out by a stupid misunderstanding, by one person deciding to create drama where there was none. The Donovan who drove his car to work that day no longer exists, either.

Claudia comes downstairs quietly.

"Your ice melted."

"Oh shit — I forgot about it, actually. Thanks for this."

She asks about the call from Ruth. Donovan tells her it's just a business thing he has going. An opportunity. It's all good.

"I might go up to their place this weekend, let the kids use the pool. They're going out of town. Feel like coming?"

"I would love that, actually. I am *so* in need of a pool."

"Silas has a little life jacket. We might have one that fits Jessica."

Without a pause, Claudia says she would probably come on her own. She slips farther down in the chair until her feet are hanging over the arm. They both finish their drinks.

"Where's Isabelle?"

"Another sleepover."

He tells her about the parents of the friend she's staying with: the mom a social worker, the dad something at the CBC. "I think they're into tantric sex," he says. Cat told him that last year. She had coffee with the mom and somehow the topic came up.

"Like sex for hours and hours and hours?" Claudia asks. "No *thank you*. Get to the point, already. How do you even *do* that with kids around?"

Donovan laughs.

They drink some more, and at some point, Donovan realizes he is on the verge of crying. He can feel a dark sob moving up through him like a belch. He tries to resist it. Right away, Claudia is on the couch beside him, holding his shoulder.

"I can't do this," he tells her, meaning everything — the kids, the house. But also Andy, the letter, Bianca. "It's too fucking hard."

The sob breaks open within him, and he coughs from the violence of it.

When he calms down, he tells Claudia his new plan: he will move out. He will send Cat a note, a total surrender, saying she can have the house and the kids. He will find an apartment or a condo somewhere close by. Or far away, if that's what she wants. She has won, and he has lost. It's over, whatever it was.

"It's what she wants, clearly. I can't fight like this anymore. It's not even fighting, it's just —" He struggles for an analogy. "I'm so tired."

Claudia brings her knees up to her chin and wraps her arms around her legs.

Donovan slowly becomes aware that he is no longer being actively comforted.

"What?"

In a single swift, unbroken movement, Claudia uncoils herself, stands up to retrieve her wine, and sits back down hard on the far end of the couch. Without looking at Donovan, she tells him that Cat is pregnant. Or that she *was*, the day she took off — who knows what's happening now. That's why she was at the doctor, she tells him. She didn't want him to know. Nobody else knows. Their mom and dad don't even know.

"Holy shit," he says after a while.

"I'm sorry I didn't tell you. I'm not telling you so you can be mad at her — it's just, if you're talking about leaving, you should know."

He asks her to tell him everything she knows — when Cat told her, how far along she was. Claudia tells him as much as she can about Cat's appointments and about the rich woman with the red hair, and apologizes again for not telling him sooner — she was respecting her sister's wishes. He gets that, doesn't he?

Donovan says that he does.

"Her doctor's office keeps calling," he says. "But they won't tell me what it's about."

He wants to get up and run around the room, his mind is spinning so fast. All this time, he has been operating under completely false assumptions. Every move he's made, every decision, was all done on the basis of incomplete data. He's been a complete fucking dupe. He sees himself as an older man, with three kids. He sees himself as a younger man, free and unburdened.

Claudia tiptoes back into the room. He didn't even notice her leave.

"I checked on Silas. Out like a rock."

She tells him she's going to stay over. She'll sleep in Isabelle's bed. She sits close to him on the couch. She puts her hand on his shoulder again.

"I'm sorry," she says. "I should've told you. It was totally unfair."

The pressure of her hand on his shoulder is warm and inviting. He wants to cover her hand with his own, pull her down toward him. To see what happens. Instead, he reaches up to his own face with both hands and rubs at it.

"This is so fucked up. *Jesus.*"

He stays there with his hands on his face, as if shielding himself from the sight of his sister-in-law. He hides from her behind his own hands, like a little kid.

After a while Claudia gets up. She leans over and kisses him lightly on his knuckles, then heads upstairs, whispering *good night* as she goes. He stays on the couch, wishing he could fall asleep there. His body is filled with wet sand. He finally gets himself upstairs and makes an effort to brush his teeth. In the hallway he sees a light on in Isabelle's room, the door ajar. Claudia is still up. He pauses for a moment, wondering if he should go in and see what is waiting there for him, but instead he goes quickly into his own room and closes the door, rolls into bed without getting undressed. The ceiling of the room presses down. He reaches for his phone. With a few clicks he finds the video.

Imagine the soft white light in your pelvis slowly transforming into a beautiful white rose in full bloom.

XIII

A MOUSE IS BELOW THE FLOOR. IT SCRABBLES along, sniffing for food and opportunities. It is small enough to disappear through any aperture, any crack; its tiny bones fold like wings. It investigates smells, dodges around the cinder blocks that support the whole structure and cannot be gnawed through. There is a sound from outside. Something drops softly onto the endless carpet of pumpkin-coloured pine needles. Most likely a pine cone, still fresh and heavy and full of sap. The mouse keeps moving, searching.

Cat listens to the creature as it goes. She follows it as it moves just beneath her, beneath the wood floor of the cottage. She hears it pause to assess the threat from another noise in the surrounding woods then continue searching for ways up into the place where humans drop food.

It's still very early. She has the curtains on the lake-facing window open so she can see the water. The low flare of light in the sky is a hopeful blue. There are no boats out yet, and the birds have not yet started celebrating having survived the night. Cat is alive in the centre of a V-shaped dip in the day, when all of the night-hustling creatures have stalked back into their holes and hollow tree trunks, and the more whole-some daytime animals are not yet awake. It's just her and the mouse.

At the northeast corner of the cottage, the sound of the mouse is lost, but the creature is still there somewhere, search-ing. It wants to get inside the cottage, but there is a problem: all of its favourite transit holes have been stuffed with an awful metallic hair.

Cat smiles. The steel wool was her idea. She was puzzled that Meredith had never tried it before, never heard of the prac-tice. She had to explain to her what the stuff even is. They drove to a hardware store in town and bought bags of it. Cat also bought sandpaper to fix the squeak on the front door and tools for the kitchen tap, which releases a tiny bead of water every ten minutes that pings against the sink. She is happy that she has been able to help Meredith in this way. For so long she has been helpless, folded under Meredith's wing. This woman, whom she didn't even know before the summer began, has kept her alive and kept her strong and said nothing about it except to dismiss any attempt to apologize or to thank her — she reacts to both as if Cat is being crass. Meredith wants Cat to shake off the empty politeness and false modesty she has wrapped herself in all her life.

We are here to be true beings, Meredith tells her day after day — not just in words, but by example.

They have spent a lot of time talking about Cat's cancer, about what is known and what is not known about the disease. For a while Cat felt as though she were hiding from the need to make a decision. She knew she didn't want to be sucked through the doors of a hospital and ground down by machines and people and treatments. She saw what happened to her friend Laura's mother. A couple of times, she and Laura sat with the woman while the clear bag, filled with stuff so toxic the nurses wore heavy gloves and aprons while handling it, emptied itself slowly into her arm. Laura's mom always said she was fine when it was over. But the next day, she'd be a wreck. And she would stay a wreck for a whole week. The moment she started to get her strength back, she'd have to return, get hooked back up to the clear bag and thrown back into illness.

Meredith talks about her own double mastectomy like a prank she fell for out of ignorance and naïveté. Had she known then what she knows now, she would not have let a doctor within ten feet of her body.

"But mine were no loss. You have two wonderful breasts."

Cat laughs in embarrassment.

Meredith gets up and leaves the room without a word. She doesn't speak to Cat for the rest of the day. At first Cat is confused and ashamed, but she soon learns the lesson: stop dropping to the floor and rolling like a subservient pup every time she comes up against truth. Meredith never shirks from truth, never grasps for answers or struggles to work things out; the answers are always right there in her grip. Meredith says she realizes now that illness is not something that happens *to* you, like a foreign invasion, but is a part of you asserting itself in ways that modern medicine cannot possibly understand. Because doctors only understand *cure* and *cut* — which is the same as *escape* and *destroy*. How can you escape yourself?

"Cancer cells are cells that grow too quickly for our bodies. You know that, don't you? They multiply too fast for us. That tells me the problem is not cancer, but *us*. Instead of attacking these cells as if they were the enemy, we need to calm them, bring them back into harmony with the rest of our being. We need to find their rhythms and move *with* them, not against them."

Cat nods along to this. Laura's mother was cut in half by the surgery and all the treatment. Months later, she told her daughter that if, years from now, they find more tumours inside her, she will refuse treatment. She'd rather die than go through it again.

When Cat tells Meredith this, she says only, "Of course, of course." She knows so many brave women who rejected chemotherapy and radiation and all the rest of it, who chose to try to *understand* the cancer within them, not fight it. Who were not willing to turn their bodies into a battlefield.

"Every advance in modern medicine has come through war, through violence. The same with cars, planes, computers — all of it is a byproduct of violence and harm."

Cat asks her about these women, the ones who rejected traditional treatment. Did any of them die?

Meredith says that yes, some were not strong enough. Or they discovered the truth too late. Or there was some deeper truth at work that none of them could perceive.

Cat knows she should be thrown by these odds. Just a few weeks ago she would have been saying *what the fuck?* But that's not her anymore. Shock is not the appropriate response to anything. Meredith is never shocked. Cat decides she wants to be strong for this woman.

. . .

Every morning, Cat sits and meditates on the floor in the cottage's main room, her back straight and her legs crossed, silent
and attentive. She pushes back the heavy coffee table made
from the wood of a barn that fell sideways decades ago. She
sits cross-legged on a rug that once hung in a bazaar. Meredith
tells her that Louis soils this rug out of nervousness whenever
bears come too close to the cottage, brushing up against the
outer wall. The bears huff or sneeze, and Louis, trembling, pees
on the floor.

The cottage originally belonged to Meredith's grandparents.
It was pretty much all they had in the world. When she first became the owner, Meredith didn't want it, but didn't want to sell
it, either. Something made her keep it. For years it just sat out
there, uncared for and slowly falling apart. She fell in love with
the place after her husband died. After the funeral she wanted
to be away from the city and her home. She wanted to be somewhere where nobody could see her. She came out here for a
month — not speaking, not seeing anyone, not accomplishing
anything other than the difficult work of putting her soul back
together, stick by stick. When she talks about her first weeks as
a widow, she makes clear that a transformation happened here.
So much of her previous self fell away and was lost in the lake.
She came back to the city with new clarity and in the grip of a
belief that she had been living for so long lost in illusion. Cat
knows without being told that this is what Meredith wants for
her: to free herself of the dense fog she's been stumbling around
in her entire life.

There is no TV here and no Wi-Fi, and she burns through
the data on her phone watching the videos of the kids that

Donovan sends her. She has been reading *Emotion Capture: Unlocking Art's Lessons on Life, Love, and Success* by Theo Hendra. She laughed when she first found it on the shelf; Claudia gave her the very same book as a birthday gift a few years ago, telling her it had completely changed her thinking about a lot of things — about art, life, love, and success, to name four. The key to living a more authentic life, Hendra tells her over and over, lies in the biographies of dead painters and writers. When she gets up each morning, just after dawn, to meditate in view of the lake, she is Jo, the wife of Edward Hopper, in *Morning Sun*, sitting in her room, drenched in light. Cat used to find that painting sad and cold. Now she knows that it is not, as she used to believe, a painting of a woman staring numbly out at an emptiness that mirrors her own, but rather a powerful portrait of someone strengthening her immune system and lessening her anxiety by drinking in the nutritious light of our friendly star.

Mostly, she reads paperback novels about a divorced alcoholic Scottish detective whose only prized possessions are his Rolling Stones records. He listens to them after a full day of sleuthing, as if they are powerful transmissions from a distant planet. Cat wonders how the books got here — she can't picture Meredith reading them. Cat has never liked detective novels, but it feels good to be pulled into the gears of a plot. One thing happens, then another thing happens, then another thing happens, until finally a big thing happens, and order is mostly restored. All events follow a strict chain of cause and effect. In the afternoon she sits near the water with one of the paperbacks, wishing she could match the Scottish detective drink for drink. There is no wine out here, no alcohol of any kind. There's no rule about it, no explicit prohibition — Cat could, at any time she liked, call a cab to bring her into town, where she could fill a bag with bottles. She doesn't. Meredith has made clear the importance of avoiding alcohol, so alcohol gets avoided.

When she is bored with reading, she swims. The lake is deep and cold. She pushes herself out until she loses the bottom and can drop down into cold blackness and feel only the pressure on her ears. She likes to stay down as long as she can, until her bruised lungs start clanging away inside her and she wonders if she can get back to the surface in time.

As she steps out of the water one morning, her left foot comes down on something unnatural: a rubber duck. It must have floated over from God knows where. It is pale from years of exposure and is leaking sand from a hole in its belly. Cat's weight pushes its blunt bill down into its body.

She wears nothing when she swims, because there are no other cottages in sight. Swimming naked is the norm here. Meredith always walks down from the cottage and drops her robe on the rocks like a queen. Cat has to stop herself from staring. The older woman's body is all muscle. She has no curves whatsoever, no soft points, no excess, except for the dyed hair on her head — her only concession to wildness, to extravagance — and all of that gets pushed into a tight rubber cap when she swims. Even the furry, ginger-grey grizzle of her pubic hair is pale and trim, almost invisible. Her breasts and nipples are gone, taken by surgeons who left only tough skin criss-crossed with deep white lines. Cat watches as Meredith towels herself off, watches as she swipes the towel across her chest just once, without lingering there. One quick stroke of the towel and she is done. There is no sense of loss in her movement.

Maybe it could be that easy, Cat thought. Just let the doctors hack away at her, give them their prize, and she'd be free of it all.

· · ·

Sometimes Cat is at the cottage for days at a time on her own.
Meredith tells her that, while she is here, the place is as much
hers as anyone's. Ownership means nothing, and Cat must
clear her mind of any notion of being a *guest*. Meredith tells her
to use this time to clarify herself, ready herself for the changes
that are coming, whether they be good or bad — not that those
categories mean anything.

A few times, Cat is choked by thoughts of her kids. Isabelle
loves to swim, and Silas, though he can't quite keep his face up
above the surface, will always push out beyond where it is safe
for him. Once, watching the sun burn the edge of the trees at
the end of the day, she catches herself missing Donovan, too.
He would sit with her and watch the sunset. They would smoke
a joint or share a bottle of wine. He would hold her and talk to
her and make her laugh. He is a beast, an animal, but he *knows*
her. He has seen her at her worst — or, at least, her worst prior
to her more recent breakdown. She doesn't dare tell Meredith
about missing him.

Meredith brought Cat out here for the first time a week or so
after that awful hour at the clinic, after a lump of potential
being was pulled from deep within her and discarded.

"I won't tell you to rebuild, and I won't tell you to grieve,"
Meredith said. "You are not broken, and there is no one to
mourn."

Cat had made one hard decision. There are more to come.

"I feel sick. I feel like a murderer."

"You are not a murderer, because you have not killed anyone."

Cat, floating on painkillers and sadness, held her head in her hands.

Someone who should have been born is gone.

"I need to see Silas and Isabelle. I need to go home."

"It's normal. You're looking for familiar comforts, familiar patterns. But if you go back to your family like this, you'll get pulled right back into the things you've been working so hard to fight your way out of."

"It hurts."

She was in constant pain; it hurt to not see her children.

"I want to see them. I know that means I'm weak, but I don't know what to do."

"You are *not* weak. Look at you: you are strong. Look at what you've accomplished in such a short time. You love your family, you miss them, and it hurts, but you are passing beyond the need of them. You need time."

"I want to go home."

"You don't. Not now."

Cat got angry at Meredith and wouldn't speak to her. She stayed in her clean, white room, hating everything she saw. *Who is this person to tell her what she wants? Who the fuck is she anyway? She doesn't know me.* She looked at the photos her husband sent her, wanting to be among them, to beg their forgiveness.

She went as far as to call a cab in the night, to slip out of the house and into the car and let it pull her partway across the city. She was dizzy and nauseous; she'd snuck a bottle of wine into her bedroom. As the car crossed the overlit swirl of Yonge Street, she called out for the driver to pull over and let her out.

It was almost three in the morning. He was amused, but didn't stop her. She was alone on the sidewalk, the towers slid up around her, humming and blinking. She walked part of a block before waving frantically at a taxi she could see parked across the road. When she got in, she realized it was the same car, the same driver. He'd been watching her from down the street the whole time. He smiled when she told him to take her back to the same address. The whole drive back, he chuckled deeply at the bottomless joke of crazy, drunk white women.

Shortly after her aborted attempt at escape, Cat attended one of the morning yoga sessions in the studio, at Meredith's insistence. She hadn't been inside the building since the day she passed out, the day she did the pregnancy test. She assumed she wasn't allowed. Dressed in the outfit Meredith provided her with, she walked up the stone pathway to the studio. Unrolling a mat in the back row, she almost toppled forward from dizziness and pain.

Meredith was beside her in a second.

"I don't want you to do the class. I just want you to sit here and be."

Cat felt ashamed, like a little kid being punished. The class began with organ music. Wendy and the other women put their foreheads on their mats, their palms flat down. Meredith walked to the front, next to Wendy, and unrolled her own mat dramatically. She bent down to the ground, flattening herself, and right away Cat could see there was something different about the way she did it. All these other women, Wendy included, were struggling to lie flat, to connect themselves with the floor and the earth beneath it, but Meredith slid into the floor like a ghost. Her mat vanished; the wood vanished. She *was* the floor. When she stretched her arms forward or curled her legs up behind her, she wasn't imitating practised moves, she was following the invisible patterns of the air and light. She was curving herself into the air, finding its seams and curling herself into them.

Cat watched this magic occur, this work that wasn't work at all. This wasn't exercise or stretching or breathing; this was connecting yourself to existence. Maybe another existence, an existence beyond her own. Meredith never said anything about Cat trying to escape in the taxi. This session, this magic, was an act of forgiveness.

When Meredith proposed the cottage idea, Cat said yes right away. She needed to be away, to be out of reach of the powerful gravitational forces trying to yank her back into her old life, which didn't even exist anymore. She needed to be far enough from her family that it could not reach her. In the city she was being pulled back into a body that was already starting to decompose, to fall away in shreds. Meredith drove her out, spent the day swimming and eating, then left early the next morning. She comes out for the weekends, bringing the fresh garlic, turmeric, oranges, and lemons that comprise most of Cat's healing diet. Cat's fingertips are stained from the turmeric, and there is a steady rumble in her stomach from all the citrus. She sniffs at herself, worried she might stink of garlic. She drinks the distilled water that sits in glass jugs in the fridge. She has not tasted milk or cheese in weeks. She sits on the floor in the lotus position, and is proud of herself for maintaining it for so long without pain. Her spine and muscles do not resist the position. When she lies in the spare bed, with its thin mattress, she wakes up with her back and her ribs on fire. She sometimes sleeps out here on the couch, though she knows she will wake up anointed with dog hair. But she can sit like this, cross-legged on the rug, for nearly an hour without any pain, her back straight and her palms together the way Meredith has shown her. She sits out here every morning for nearly an hour, willing the pain and illness to shatter and crumble. To fall away from her like an old barn.

Meredith comes out and brings Louis with her. She carries the dog down from the car, and it is in such a floppy, sweaty state that Cat worries that it has died, that Meredith is here to perform a funeral. Meredith has already said that when Louis passes on, his ashes will be scattered over the water from the end of the dock.

Meredith brings food and water, a few necessary things like toilet paper, and a canvas bag full of candles. Wendy has come, too, as she does every other week or so. She does not carry anything down from the car and walks past Cat without saying hello, straight down to the water, where she brings her trembling hands together and bows her head.

"She does this each time," Meredith tells Cat. "Asks for a healing blessing from the lake."

Cat makes them a salad for dinner, and is a little embarrassed at how much joy she gets out of putting it all together in the big bowl. She is desperate to prepare and serve food for other people. She has not spoken a word or seen anyone for days, has barely looked at her phone, has eaten only the foods that Meredith has instructed her to, and has done little more than stretch and read and rest and stare at the water. Throwing leaves and cucumber and seeds together, she thinks about Isabelle making birthday pancakes with her, about Silas forming wet balls of dough and chocolate chips that will soon transform into cookies. It doesn't hurt as much to think about things like this now. She is going farther and farther out into the lake, dropping down into weeds and silence. She can look at the photos Donovan sends and not feel as though someone is clamping their hands around her rib cage and squeezing. She can look at the water without feeling like a deranged, danger-ous criminal in hiding.

She makes iced lemon water in a big jug and grabs three glasses. Bringing the food outside, she is excited about what is coming.

Cat doesn't eat with the other two women, though she is rav-enous. Meredith wants her to have an empty stomach. Early on, almost on a dare, she allowed Meredith to talk her into under-going a coffee enema. That was in the first weeks of her escape from her life, when every moment it felt like she was a fraud, a liar. The young woman who performed the operation was young, which made Cat feel old. An old fraud and a liar. The brown wreckage that sluiced from her ass contained glass and plastic and wrecked furniture and old bicycles and shelves full of books. She won't allow herself to be drained like that again, but agrees to milder fasts. She consumes nothing but lemon water on the days Meredith and Wendy come out together to the cottage.

After dinner Wendy lies down in the cottage. Cat and Meredith sit together in canvas chairs, watching the water.

"Did you get in at all today?" Meredith asks. It's another of her instructions that Cat swim every single day out here, what-ever the weather. Something about maintaining contact with the element of water. Finding peace while fully immersed. She has multiple stories of miraculous recoveries made by people who'd been given up on by doctors, and who made themselves whole via swimming. Cat pictures her cancer dissolving in the lake like paper. She wants to believe it.

"It's still weird to swim on my own so much," she says.

"You only ever swim in pools?"

"No, I mean without my kids."

Cat was shocked, the first time she tried to go any distance on her own, at how little stamina she had. Years of standing waist-deep while kids played around her had made her weak.

"Your husband didn't let you swim?"

Cat, embarrassed, realizes she'd never asked.

A single boat cuts quietly through the sheen of the water. Meredith's eyes are closed, and Cat wonders if she's asleep.

"You want them to come out here," Meredith says, her eyes still closed.

"Who, Isabelle and Silas? Would you be okay with that?"

"That's not the question." Meredith turns to look at her, an owl staring down its prey. Cat has to stop herself from flinching. "I've been very clear about this: I am not preventing you from doing anything. I'm not making you *do* anything, either. I'm showing you a path toward healing, and I hope that you take it, but that choice is entirely yours. Don't make me responsible for your decisions. I'm not."

She turns back to face the lake.

"I want to see them," Cat says. She wants to say that she *needs* to see them, but can't make herself admit it.

"I know you do."

"They would love it here. But it wouldn't be ideal, would it. It wouldn't really work."

She waits again for Meredith to reply, then asks, "Would it make sense to have them here?"

"You're trying to make me responsible for your decisions again. I refuse to be responsible for another person's choices — you have to be strong enough to find your way. If you're not, that's not my problem to solve."

"It wouldn't work," Cat says finally. Meredith does not react to this, but Cat can sense that she is pleased with where the issue has been left.

Another boat crosses the lake going fast and pulling kids behind on a stylized inner tube.

"I don't understand why people do this," Meredith says, nodding at the boat. "They come all this way to be around water, and what do they do when they get here? They plop themselves into a thing that keeps them out of the water and completely spoil it for everyone. People have been so conditioned to be afraid of just being alone with the quiet. I feel sorry for those children, being raised to be so helpless."

As dusk stains the sky, Wendy reappears. She and Meredith spread a blanket on a soft patch of ground in the shade of a pine tree. In a circle around the blanket, they place candles, jabbing them into the dirt so they will stay upright. With all the candles in place, Meredith moves around the circle, lighting each with a long, wooden match. The two women kneel facing each other on the edges of the blanket, the little flames at their backs.

Cat undresses, then wraps herself in a towel. She moves to where Wendy and Meredith are kneeling, both of them silent, and drops the towel on the ground. She steps carefully over the candles and onto the blanket, then lies down with her bare belly against the fabric, like she is awaiting a massage. She lies flat, and right away the other women begin to hum. They hold their hands over her naked body without touching her, their eyes closed, both of them focused on transferring life and health from their fingertips to her skin, on being pure conduits for the light from the candles, the life force from the trees and water. They are trying to bring her into harmony with those rogue cells, with those overachievers. They are trying to make her body *see*. To heal itself. To correct itself. Cat doesn't feel hungry anymore. There is no self-consciousness as she lies there, no shame — feelings like these have a weaker grip on her the longer she stays out here alone, just as Meredith said would happen.

Cat will sometimes drift off as they are humming over her, as the warm waves of healing energy move across her and penetrate her naked skin. Louis is always nearby, watching and whimpering. The flames from the candles scare him.

Early the next morning, they leave. Sometimes they are gone even before she wakes up. Cat gets up alone to do her stretches. She sits, straight as a houseplant, and tries to stay within a place of deep focus. Soon, she gets up to pee and make coffee. There are no mouse turds among the coffee beans; the steel wool is a success. She hears the sound of a boat crossing the lake and is able to get through all the steps of getting her breakfast together without crying. She is not hurting too much. If she closes her eyes, she sees the flame of a single candle inside her, flickering but still burning.

XIV

WAVE AFTER WAVE OF BOREDOM CRASHES OVER
the young man slung low in the driver's seat of the parked car.
His boredom is ugly and grey, but the car is beautiful: ink-
black with red trim. He has the engine on, and a beat throbs
quietly through the stereo system. Red running lights glow
along the bottom edge of the car like it is leaking molten rock.
Silver rims spin endlessly, little universes unto themselves. The
car is fast and furious, low to the ground. Low enough that he
has to be careful with railway crossings and potholes. Speed
bumps are fucking evil — he almost scraped over one on the
way here. He forced his car, this powerful black machine, to
creep over the bump in fear.

   Ravi always drives with two hands on the wheel. Adeel and
Rishit make fun of him for it, call him a pussy. But Ravi likes

the feel of driving that way. It makes the car feel more like something in his full possession. When he's on the highway, it's like he's piloting a plane. Out over oceans or mountains, silent and sleek and fast, threading the clouds. Ravi the pilot. His black sunglasses reflect the red glow of the dashboard.

Now look at him: parked on the tarmac. Grounded.

He looks at the homes that line this quiet street. The whole neighbourhood looks like something from the kind of movie his mother and his aunt like, with white people taking forever to fall in love. That Tom Hanks dude. The house he's parked across from is a big one with a rickety-looking front porch. But Ravi knows these places are rooted to the ground by gold. Most of them are worth two million at least. More, if they did anything significant to the interior, cleared out some walls and expanded the kitchen, modernized all the fixtures and improved the wiring and plumbing. His head used to swim at numbers like that. Now there are places in fucking *Brampton* going for more than a million. Not even *nice* places. His parents' place is probably worth that now.

He wants to be home, in his condo. The windows in Ravi's condo are huge and clean. The lake is spread out to the horizon. No trees, no other buildings. There was a cheaper unit on the other side of the building, but from there you look down on the Gardiner Expressway and across into the windows of condos like his. He waited until one of the lake-facing units became available and paid extra for it. He's finally making some money now.

His mother and father don't know he paid extra for his condo just so he could see the water. They'd lose their shit if they did. They already think he is crazy to live downtown at all. There are houses being built in Markham that are cheaper than any condo. A whole house. And don't forget, they tell

him, there is still room in their home, in the house he grew up
in, on the edge of what used to be the borders of Brampton, but
which is now just another subdivision. Their house is big and
detached, and they're proud of both of those facts. Big yard.
Every kid with his own room. Finished basement with a big-
screen TV and a room just for the boys' weights, pulleys, and
ropes. Wouldn't it make more sense to save more of his income
until he can afford a real house with a yard? Then he'd have
something for when he gets married, for when he starts having
children. They've put a new dehumidifier in the basement, they
tell him. It's dry down there now. No more sweaty walls. His
youngest brother Arjun has it all to himself.

"My building has a gym," he tells them.

There are women in the gym Ravi uses now. Women in
yoga pants who work out with their makeup on. You're supposed to act like you don't see them, but the walls are mirrors. You can see which pairs of yoga pants become translucent
when they catch the light, which of these grown-up women
have chosen to work out in a thong. Or — Ravi can hardly
believe his eyes — no underwear at all. If you encounter one of
these women at the water fountain or the bin where you throw
your dirty towels, you might get a smile. Ravi has thought a lot
about those smiles and those sweaty, friendly faces. Most of the
women are white and super thin, some are married or live with
boyfriends who tower over Ravi, but he still thinks his chances
are better than zero.

Bianca used to say the gym in his building was better than
the one in hers. Her condo, less than ten minutes' walk away, is
bigger than his, but the gym is shitty and small, the equipment
cheap. When they were still together, she used to come over all
the time. She'd buzz herself in, go straight to the gym, do all

her stretching and cycling, then come up to his place, flushed and wet. Once or twice, she let him watch her while she was in the shower.

That was the kind of witchy shit Bianca always pulled on him. She dragged him around and left him spinning so he didn't know what the fuck was what. But then she'd pull out something like that, like letting him watch her shower. Dark magic.

He has told Adeel about those showers. He embellished every soapy moment — not that he had to, not by much. Adeel was speechless. Big, clumsy Adeel lives with his parents, and has never been in a relationship that lasted more than a month. He asked for details. Did she do like a *sexy* shower? Sort of sliding around and a little smile on her face like it's a show? Or was it just like a normal shower, with her just standing there and cleaning herself up?

A bit of both, Ravi told him. She acted like he was invisible, though she always gave him a big smile when she stepped out, all on display, jutting at him, dripping. Asked him to wrap her in a towel. Like she was a puppy, a gift for him.

Ravi is on this boring street in this boring neighbourhood, sitting in his car on a Saturday night like a dummy because of — who else? — because of Bianca.

She had texted him out of nowhere, asking how he was doing. It took every bit of strength he had not to answer. Ravi was at work, neck-deep in the file of an investment firm that was looking to shift some of its operations overseas. He forced himself to delete the text. She sent another one right away, saying she was sorry for treating him so badly, for acting like a bitch. She didn't want him to hate her. Could they get a coffee and talk? He wanted to bury himself in contracts and spread-sheets for safety. She *did* act like a bitch. And yes, he hates her. Why should they talk? Bianca never wants to talk, except when she wants to tell him what to do.

Deleting the first text gave him the courage to reply to the second one. He said *sure*, they could meet for coffee. She could talk as long as she liked. He would be frost. A block of ice. A glacier.

They met on a Saturday morning at the Starbucks on the first floor of his building. She arrived late, which didn't surprise him at all.

Right away, she apologized, saying he deserved a lot better than the way she treated him. Got right into it. Said she hated herself for what she did. Said she was all fucked up and didn't know what she wanted, but that in the end, it was better for them to break up — she said *break up*, as if it were a mutual decision. She said again that she was sorry, and then told him she was going through all kinds of things, that there were all kinds of stress in her life right now. Her job was boring as shit. She felt stuck.

Ravi just sat there, sipping at his coffee. What was all this to him? He was ice.

Her biggest worry, she said, the craziest thing — and here Ravi has to smile at the memory of it; she was so *good* at this, she had him wriggling on the point of a knife — was that she was pregnant.

She knew what she was doing — he sees that now. She probably had it all planned out. The first thing he thought of when she told him she was pregnant — and it embarrasses him to remember it — is what Adeel would say. Adeel would *love* this, love to know how fucked Ravi is.

He did one thing right, at least: he didn't reply right away. He gave her a little shrug. She started crying a little, and put her hand over her eyes. She told him she got suspicious when her period was late. So she bought a test, and it came out positive.

Ravi looked around — how could she be saying shit like this in public? But no one was paying any attention. He should've known. Bianca is beautiful. That is all anyone there would notice. She could yell about driving over a dog or a baby, and everyone would look at her and stop thinking entirely. Magic.

She went on about how stupid she feels, how scared. She's not sure she can do what needs to be done. She has two friends who had abortions last year. They said it was so horrible. Everyone always says it's nothing, that it doesn't hurt and you get over it right away. But her friends are still a little fucked up about it. Or one of them is, anyway.

"I can't be a dad," he told her.

"I know you can't," Bianca said. Stating a fact.

That makes him angry. Maybe he could and maybe he couldn't. Maybe he'd be a good dad. Look at him and Arjun. Look how he helps his little brother. He could do it. Who says he couldn't? He has thought seriously about inviting Arjun to come live with him. His brother almost flunked his last year of high school, despite being smarter than anyone else there. Ravi pictures taking his brother out, introducing him to guys who make enough money to buy Teslas. Showing him there is life beyond the flat, house-choked neighbourhood they grew up in, beyond the malls and moms and temples.

Bianca said she had to make a decision. And soon.

"Everything is so fucked right now. I don't even know what to do."

Then she started telling him a messed-up story about a guy she used to work with, an older, married dude. Sometimes they hung out together at work things. She'd get bored, and hanging out with this guy helped kill time. They liked to joke about the other people they worked with.

For a moment Ravi wondered if she were about to tell him the baby belongs to this other guy. Such a strange feeling: anger and relief. He might get out of this after all, but at the price of knowing his ex-girlfriend fucked around on him with some old guy at work.

And then she told him the most messed-up thing about how this guy got her on her own at some work party and started grabbing at her.

"Why are you telling me this? Do you want me to fight him or something?"

Bianca actually laughed at this. No, she didn't want him to fight the guy. She wanted him to act as her lawyer. The dude wants his old job back and had hired a powerful lawyer to help him do it, so she wants Ravi to push back for her, to send a letter that stops all this bullshit in its tracks.

"I'm not that kind of lawyer."

Not a lawyer at all, in fact. A paralegal. He looks at contracts, vets documents, makes sure numbers add up. The basics. Even if he could, he would never get clearance from his bosses to take her on as a client. And asking one of the actual lawyers to help would be a disaster. *Hey, my ex-girlfriend is getting sued*

*by a creepy, rich, white guy. Can you make it go away? Oh, and
she's pregnant with my kid. Maybe.*

Bianca wouldn't listen. She kept saying she was all messed
up because of everything going on. What if she got sued, what
if they made her pay a crazy amount of money? She didn't have
money like that. And how was she supposed to figure out what
to do about a baby with all this going on? She let the fact hang
in the air. It was like she was holding up two pieces of paper,
one saying *Baby*, the other *Help Bianca*. Waiting for him to
make the connection.

Blackmail. That's the only word for it. The most basic scam
ever. She had him right on the tip of a knife. Dark fucking magic.

Ravi has never even seen this Donovan guy in person and has
no idea how big or small he is. Ravi is short, but he's also dark,
and believes he can use that to his advantage. A brown face
delivering a few words of warning. Around here, with the kind
of people who live in these houses, that might be enough. Look
strong, tell the dude he's on the wrong track with the lawsuit,
and go. All he needs is for Donovan to think twice. At work
he's seen how people will shit themselves the moment legal
waters go above their knees. Bianca said the lawyer at her work
was going to write his own letter, anyway, so Ravi's visit would
act as extra incentive to let it go.

It's stupid, but what choice does he have?

His bucket of coffee is mostly just ice cubes now. There are
a few inches of heavily diluted brown water at the bottom. He
abandons the jumbo straw and tips the whole bucket into his
mouth, nearly spilling the ice over himself.

There are lights on in the house. Bianca told him the guy has kids, a wife. Ravi doesn't want this to turn into a neighbourhood incident, with people yelling and screaming. Cops getting called. As it is, the longer he sits here, the more chances a police car will slide in behind him. Working at a law firm does not shield him from the endless curiousity cops have about brown people in nice-looking cars.

He kills the engine. They won't get him for idling, at least. His phone's battery is starting to fade, so he sets it into the charging stand. Two white SUVs go past slowly.

There is a rattling sound, and Ravi sees a shadow move in the gap between Donovan's house and the one next door. A man emerges, pushing a green bin. Taller than Ravi, with dark, curly hair. T-shirt, shorts, and sandals. Bit of a gut. Donovan. Ravi can tell right away. Donovan positions the green bin at the end of the walkway that runs between the two houses, right at the edge of the sidewalk. He looks over at the car briefly. Before Ravi can get the driver's side window down, Donovan turns and goes back into the shadow between the houses.

"Shit."

Missed his chance.

He starts the car. It's not yet eight o'clock. Lots of time to get back home, get a shower, get dressed, and head out somewhere that will burn off his frustration. If Bianca texts him to find out what's going on, he'll be purposefully vague. He did his best; that's all she can ask of him. If she pushes, he'll say *this isn't my fight.*

He is about to pull out from the curb when the front door of the house opens and Donovan comes out. A boy stumbles through the doorway behind him, and Donovan shouts something to stop the boy at the edge of the steps. From a corner of the porch, he produces a black stroller. The boy turns and goes down the steps carefully. When his feet touch the ground, he immediately starts sprinting for the street. Donovan shouts at him, swears, and comes running down the steps to catch the boy just as he is about to leap off the edge of the sidewalk. Ravi smiles, remembering how Arjun, when he was this age, would aim for the road the same way, almost begging to have his head peeled open by a chrome bumper. Ravi would have to grab him around the neck and pull him back onto their yard.

Donovan wrestles the little boy away from the road and into the stroller. It's like trying to settle an animal into place. He offers the boy a hunk of what looks like Lego, which the boy, suddenly calm, starts poking at like he's texting a friend.

Soft, Ravi thinks. This dude is soft. Ravi hasn't been in a fight in years and years, but he's hard, thanks to the gym. He's wearing a tight black golf shirt with the collar up. His jeans are black, too. Can't do this kind of thing in shorts. With his eyes still hidden by sunglasses, he stares directly at Donovan, who angles the stroller so they will cross in front of Ravi's car, which is blocking the most direct route.

"Yo," Ravi says. He doesn't shout.

Donovan pauses in the middle of the road.

"Yes?"

He continues to push the stroller, though more slowly than before.

"Yo," Ravi says again.

Donovan slows almost to a stop. The stroller is close enough to the front corner of the car that the boy reaches out to try and touch the metal.

"Can I help you?"

"Yeah, bro. No, I can help *you*."

Donovan waits for more. Ravi stares at him. He's in control; he's the pilot on this flight.

"Are you dropping something off?"

"Just a message."

"For me? From who?"

Ravi pauses, then says, in a voice heavier and deeper than his own, "You need to cut this lawsuit shit out. It won't work."

"Excuse me?"

"Your lawsuit. It's not going to work, bro."

"What are you talking about? Who are you?"

"Listen, I know what you're doing, okay bro? You pulled some shit with a friend of mine, and now you're trying to hide behind a lawyer. It's not going to work."

Ravi sees Donovan slide one hand to his pants pocket, searching for the comforting lump of his phone. But it's not there. He has left it behind somewhere. This realization blinks across the older man's face, and Ravi wants to laugh. *You've got nobody.*

Donovan tries to stand straighter, to embody the authority vested in him by virtue of being a homeowner and a father.

"I don't know what this is about or who you are, but I have to go. I've got my kid here. You think you can just threaten me?"

"I'm not threatening you, bro. I'm saying you need to cut it out. With Bianca. The lawsuit. It's bullshit."

Donovan actually lets go of the stroller for a moment.

"Bianca? What the fuck — you're a friend of hers?" There's a tremor in his voice. "This is just ... I should call the cops right now."

Ravi has to fight to look unbothered, but he's sweating under his shirt, and his legs have gone cold. "I'm not doing anything, yo! I haven't said anything." He'd imagined this whole scene going down a lot quicker — roll up, deliver the message, roll off. Job done. "I'm just saying you should stop with the lawsuit. That's all. Not doing anything."

"What the fuck is this?"

"Free advice. Legal advice." He can feel his voice rising in pitch. The last thing he wants is to look like he's begging. "I know about this shit."

"Who *are* you?"

"It doesn't matter. I know this shit, okay?"

"Who *the fuck* are you?"

To cover up his own nervousness, Ravi points at Silas, who is straining at the straps holding him in place. The boy wants to know who's talking, but can't see into the car.

"You shouldn't swear in front of your kid like that."

Donovan looks baffled. "What?"

"Your kid."

"What about him?"

"You want him to start talking like that?"

"Okay, buddy," Donovan says, "that's enough. Get out of here. *Now*." He reaches over and slaps the hood of the car as if slapping a horse into running. Ravi, sipping at the ice cubes in his cup at the same moment Donovan's hand makes contact, feels the slap in his bones. It jabs at his heart.

"Hey, yo!"

He chokes on his words — a fragment of ice has become lodged in his throat. He struggles for air and loses his grip on the giant cup in his hand. Cold, sugary liquid spills down his chest and slops into his lap. His belly and his crotch are instantly cold, and he can hear cubes landing on the floor and tumbling into the space between the seats. As he struggles he accidently hits the horn, which is loud and shrill. In his stroller Silas yells out as if in pain, then starts to wail.

Donovan, looking more confused than afraid, tries to push the stroller through the gap between the two cars.

Ravi can barely speak. "You *fucking*…" Still coughing hard, he guns the engine. The only way he can regain his dignity is to leave a streak on the surface of this boring fucking street, stain it with his tires. He grabs at the gears and presses down on the accelerator, hoping to scare Donovan with the speed with which he reverses. But his hand lodges the car in Drive, and it shoots forward before he can stop it.

Donovan leaps back as if touched by a power line. Ravi feels the front of the car connect with the stroller at the same moment he flattens the brake. He sees the thin black handles tip over and disappear.

XV

ISABELLE NEEDS TO WRITE A NOTE. SHE NEEDS
paper. She has some in a wooden crate full of craft supplies she
hasn't touched in years, but all of it is the colour of chewable
vitamins: pale orange and pale green and pale blue. This needs
to be a *real* note, an adult note. The messages Dad sent Mom
on her behalf were not hers, even if she helped write them and
said yes when Dad asked her if they were okay. They don't
say what she wants to say, because what she wants to say to
her mother she can never share with her father. She helped
write those other notes because it made Dad happy, though not
for long.

In the back bedroom upstairs, the room they're not supposed to go into, the room where Mom used to do her work,
there is paper in packages on a shelf in the closet. The packages

are covered in symbols that tell you if the paper is made from other paper. She learned all about this in kindergarten. Mom told her she went around the house grabbing every piece of paper she could find, new and old, and throwing it all in the blue bin. She was four, and wanted no more trees to die. Dad had to fish out letters and bills and perfectly good blank paper. There was money in there, too. Mom and Dad told her they liked that she was enthusiastic, but that she needed to ask for help from then on.

Isabelle doesn't need to ask. She learns quickly when she makes an embarrassing mistake, which often seems like the only way she ever learns anything. There are words she only learned to pronounce the right way after saying them the wrong way in front of the whole class: *mischievous, hyperbole, Louis Riel, Tecumseh.* She wishes there was a way to learn things like that without feeling so dumb about it.

The door to Mom's office is locked. This is enough to keep out Silas — who sometimes has a kind of fit where he runs around the house looking for Mom, opening all the doors — but Isabelle can get through it, no problem. All she needs is a penny, and there are lots of those around, despite the fact they don't make them anymore. She learned that in school, too. What a weird idea, that all pennies are dead or dying. At some point they'll all get spent or lost in the grass or down a gutter, and then there will be no more. She is witnessing the extinction of a whole species of coin. Dinosaurs got recycled as birds, but pennies will just disappear.

Everything that isn't recyclable ends up at a dump. They went to a dump one time when she was little, at the end of a weekend of camping. Dad drove the car into this place going crazy with seagulls, and a man who looked like he stunk told him to leave all the garbage in a certain area and get back in the car. The man said Dad was the only one who could get out of the car. Everyone else had to stay inside, even Mom, who said that was *okay with her*. They weren't allowed because of bears. Isabelle looked everywhere for bears — wanting to see one and not wanting to see one. She wanted to believe that, were she to take a single step out of the car, were even *one* of her feet to touch the ground, right away a black mass of fur and anger would come crashing out of the woods. All the men working at the dump were dirty from head to toe, as if they swam in the garbage. One man was missing an ear — his baseball cap flopped over on one side with nothing to rest on. Isabelle wanted to ask him if a bear had eaten it. Another man was wearing a child's cowboy hat with a red-and-white string hanging down under his chin. The hat was a little too small for him and sat way up on his head.

"Look at that," Dad said. "He found it in the garbage."

She'd already guessed that.

If a bear did attack the car, her job would be to get Silas out of his baby seat, to unbuckle him and get him to safety. No one gave her that job; she gave it to herself. She has the same job if their car goes into the water; she must get Silas through the window and up to the surface. First, of course, she will have to wait until the car is fully under before opening the window, because of the water pressure, which she learned about on a show on YouTube called *MythBusters*. Nobody else will think to wait for the car to sink, she's sure of it. Dad won't help — he couldn't even stop that evil car from breaking Silas's arm. And Mom won't help because she's not here and has other things to worry about. So it's up to her.

. . .

It's like a little stab in her belly when Isabelle thinks about the car hitting Silas. She was at Spirit's house for a sleepover. Dad was supposed to bring pajamas and a toothbrush across the park to her. Spirit was being super bossy and snobby and didn't want to talk about books or dump bears or drowning in cars or anything like that. She only wanted to play a game where they said which famous actor each of them looks like. Spirit kept saying that Isabelle looked like an actor who always plays a more beautiful actor's dumb friend, so Isabelle went to Spirit's mom to say her stomach was hurting, laying the groundwork for her escape.

Spirit's mom was talking on the phone. She stared at Isabelle while she spoke and had one hand in the air as if ready to pull an alarm.

"Okay … oh my God, okay … No, it's totally … I will tell her. Oh my God."

Isabelle has not forgiven Dad for the fact that it was Spirit's mom, not him, who told her about Silas getting hit by the car. She hasn't forgiven him, either, for not coming to get her right away. Instead, he stayed at the hospital with Silas, while she was forced to lie awake in Spirit's room, trying not to shake or cry. It was a little bit gratifying to see how Spirit suddenly became quiet and humble when she heard what happened. When Spirit's mother brought her home the next day, there was a police car outside the house and two police officers inside, a woman and a man. Aunt Claudia was there, too, and she looked as though she'd been crying. Dad looked like a vampire had drained all his blood. He kept saying he forgot to look at the licence plate; he wasn't thinking straight. He wasn't even sure what kind of car it was, only that it was black.

"Do you think the driver did this on purpose or as an accident?"

Dad looked sick. "I don't know."

The police officers didn't believe that Dad didn't know anything.

Silas was sleeping the whole time the police were there. Aunt Claudia said they gave him some medicine that would help him rest. Isabelle went straight upstairs without saying goodbye to Spirit and sat on the floor next to Silas's bed, listening to his breathing. His face was bruised up. She could see the fat lump of the cast on the sheet next to him where his thin little arm was supposed to be.

Isabelle always watches Silas now, especially while Dad is napping, which happens a lot, or while Aunt Claudia is cleaning up, which also happens a lot. Silas acts all sucky because his arm gets sore, entombed in its grey cast, and the scrape on his face is always itching. He scratches at it, pulling away at the big bandage hiding the bloody skin. He begs for snacks and treats, and because he got hurt, he gets whatever he wants. But then he says he's not hungry when it's time to really eat something. *So* annoying. Isabelle is tempted to tell him how bad his face looks. Like a monster or a zombie.

"Don't touch your face," she tells him.

"Itchy!"

"It won't get better if you do."

"NO!"

"Hey now," Aunt Claudia says from the kitchen. She's usually talking to someone on the phone. Usually Uncle Dale, who gets angry about her being at the house so much, leaving him alone with Cousin Jessica.

"Just don't touch your face," Isabelle says, more quietly.

"My arm hurts."

"Don't move it and it'll feel better."

"IT HURTS!"

Grampa Ron and Gramma Sue-Ann came over a lot at first, but they've stopped because there was some kind of fight. Dad won't talk to them on the phone. He doesn't talk to Grampa Don and Gramma Ruth much, either. There was an even bigger fight with them, after the accident with Silas. Dad spent a whole night yelling at them over the phone about money. He forgot to put Silas to bed, so Isabelle did it, brushing at his teeth as best she could, then helping him climb into bed. She read him a chapter from the new book she's reading, about a girl who keeps flying back in time without meaning to, ending up in King Arthur times or surrounded by dinosaurs. From downstairs she could hear Dad yelling, "I don't fucking care!"

Isabelle wonders if part of the reason Mom stays away is because Dad swears so much. He didn't do it as much before. Only every once in a while a *f—* or a *sh—*. Lately he's been saying words she doesn't even understand, but knows are bad just by how they're said. She has been mentally collecting them. One time, when Silas was complaining about having to put on pajamas, she called him a *c-u-n-t*. She'd looked that one up. She feels terrible about it.

Aunt Claudia mostly comes at the end of the day and makes them dinner, then cleans up the kitchen while Isabelle gets Silas in and out of the bath and into his pajamas and into bed. She reads to Silas, then shows him the video about pelvic relaxation he likes. (Isabelle looked up the meaning of the word *pelvic* and was grossed out by what she found.) Aunt Claudia will sometimes watch things on her phone with her after Silas finally falls asleep. They both like videos about animals doing stupid things like running into glass patio doors or chasing the light from a flashlight. They especially love the ones where kittens or puppies fall asleep very, very slowly. The puppies fight so hard, trying to keep their big eyes open, their heads dipping, until eventually their eyes stop opening up again and off they go. It's beyond adorable.

"That's what Silas looks like when I read to him at night," Isabelle says.

"Your cousin Jessica looks *exactly* like that when she falls asleep. It's so adorable."

"Do you miss her?"

"Who, Jessica? I'm with her literally every day. She's okay with her daddy sometimes."

One night, after they've watched a dozen puppies drift off to sleep, Aunt Claudia tells her that Mom has a new baby inside her. Isabelle just nods at this information, as if she knew all along, but inside she goes cold. She wants to slam the phone down hard and break it, but that would be a baby thing to do. She doesn't look at Aunt Claudia when she is told this. She keeps staring at a black-and-white puppy making one last effort to get its head up. Isabelle is doing the exact opposite, fighting as hard as she can to go to sleep, to not be awake in this new reality where her mother is not only not around, not talking to her and not seeing her, but also off somewhere with a baby in her stomach, an actual little girl or boy.

"Don't tell Silas yet. We'll tell him soon."

Isabelle asks her when the baby is coming. Aunt Claudia says she isn't sure. She's not even sure if Mom will be able to have the baby.

"Why not?" This sounds even crazier.

"Because sometimes grown-ups can't have a baby. It's nobody's fault. I don't want you to be sad, okay? Your mom is sad. We're all sad. But sometimes this happens."

Isabelle wonders if this inability to have a baby has anything to do with pelvic relaxation. She thinks about asking Aunt Claudia to send Mom the link to the video Silas likes. Maybe if she listens to it over and over, does what the woman in it says, then she can have the baby after all. She can relax herself down there so the baby just slides out.

Isabelle was surprised at first when Mom didn't call after what happened to Silas. There was a part of her that was hoping she might even come home right away when she heard. Isabelle would be in the living room doing crafts with Silas, monitoring his use of scissors and making sure he doesn't smear the floor with glue, and Mom would come in the front door, run down the hallway and grab them both, hug them both. All of them crying.

Isabelle kept waiting for Dad to tell her that Mom was on the phone. Or on her way.

One thing has become very clear to her: if Silas getting hurt has not brought Mom back, then she must have something very important to deal with right now, just like Aunt Claudia keeps saying. Whatever that baby is doing to her is not good. She starts hoping it won't come. It hasn't even been born and she's already mad at it.

She gets super sad each night and first thing in the morning when she remembers that she will not be seeing her mother
that day, but she at least knows it's a fact. Whereas Silas keeps
asking if Mom is coming. He asks while they are doing crafts
or playing. He asks every night in bed. He asks when he gets
up in the morning. He sees Mom's absence as a kind of cruel
prank, one he can end by screaming or crying really, really
loudly. Or by acting out and breaking things. Last week he
threw a full potty of pee across the room because he was angry
about something. He sat down in the middle of the room, peed
into the bowl until it was almost full, then picked it up with
his good arm and threw it as hard as he could, without even
pulling his stupid pants up first. The new lady who cleans their
house had to clean it up.

Aunt Claudia is there the second time Silas throws his potty
full of pee all over the place. He flings the potty hard across
the room, just like the first time. Isabelle screams because the
pee almost hits her. She is certain at first that it has. Maybe
a drop or two did, but she can't find anything. She screams
at Silas and screams for Dad, but Dad is out in the backyard
staring at things. If he's not sleeping, he's drinking a lot of beer
at night and staring at things. And looking at his phone. He's
always looking at his phone — and never at anything interesting, never at a funny video. He mostly looks at addresses,
at buildings and streets. Isabelle learned about Google Street
View in class. It's boring. Google Earth is *much* cooler. She'd
rather look down at things from above and pretend she's flying.

Aunt Claudia comes running out when she hears Isabelle
screaming. She looks like she's going to be sick, but doesn't yell
at Silas, doesn't get angry. She keeps saying *o-kay, o-kay* over
and over again as she gets wet cloths to wipe everything down.

"It's fine, it's okay. It's fine. Let's not do that again, though, okay? Wow."

She cleans it up herself because it's the weekend, the new lady isn't coming. When Aunt Claudia comes up later to say goodnight to Isabelle, she tells her she used to throw her potty when she was upset, too. It made Grampa Ron crazy. He thought *she* was crazy.

"I think I was mad because I had to use the same potty that your mother had when she was little. That *really* bothered me. It still does — it's gross and unfair. I should've had a new one, don't you think?"

Isabelle agrees with her that using someone else's potty is gross.

Aunt Claudia tells Isabelle that she only did it a few times, maybe only twice. She doesn't even remember doing it. Then she tells Isabelle that sometimes now she will sit on the toilet for a long time after she pees, not wanting to get up. Just wanting to be alone for a while. It's a crazy thing to hear from a grown-up, but Aunt Claudia isn't smiling when she says it. She is holding a wineglass with a little bit of wine in it, and Isabelle has to stop herself from asking if she can try some, just a sip.

Isabelle asks if maybe her mom has done something like that, found herself a little room she won't come out of. Not a bathroom, obviously, but something like that.

"Totally possible," Aunt Claudia says.

Right around then, the best thing happens — the absolute best, craziest thing: they get to see Mom. A total surprise.

Dad is out somewhere, so Aunt Claudia is watching them. She is nervous and keeps laughing at things that aren't funny. She lets Isabelle and Silas watch shows all morning, which is unusual, but then she walks in right in the middle of *Woof Rescue* and turns off the TV. Isabelle doesn't care — she's been looking at a book about extreme weather and isn't really watching — but Silas howls. It is almost time for his cast to come off and his face looks a lot better. Aunt Claudia tells them both they are going on a special trip, that she has a treat for them.

They go to a park, but not the park they usually go to. They have to walk a long time with Silas in the stroller. The park is small, just a big square between two houses, with one small slide and a little sandbox that looks dirty. Aunt Claudia tells them to play for a bit, that someone special is coming. Like it is Christmas. She also tells them it's a secret, one they can't tell *anyone* about. She makes Silas make a special promise not to tell.

They are there for almost an hour on their own. Aunt Claudia is on the phone a lot, getting more and more upset. She tries to play tag with Silas, but jumps every time he catches her, so Isabelle plays with him instead.

"Thank you, Isabelle," Aunt Claudia says, and she gets on her phone again.

Finally, a small car pulls up. Isabelle can see Mom's face through the passenger window. A total shock. She looks fake, her face is so small. Isabelle thinks she is a weird mirage. A skinny old woman with crazy red hair gets out, walks around to the passenger side, and helps Mom out. Aunt Claudia runs over to help, but the red-haired woman makes her stop a few feet away.

Isabelle isn't sure what is happening with her body. She is all liquid. She is worried she might pee herself or that she has diarrhea. Silas, running to hide, has not noticed Mom yet. When he does, he just stands in place and howls, tears and snot flying everywhere. Aunt Claudia has to calm him down.

The whole meeting is scrambled like that. Nobody knows what to do, so they all cry a lot. Everyone except the red-haired woman named Meredith, who, after helping Mom out of the car, goes and sits in a far corner of the small park, in a patch of sun. She sits on the grass with her legs crossed beneath her, pretending to be miles away, though Isabelle can tell she is listening. She is like one of the old ladies who work in the school office.

They cry and cry. Mom says *sorry* over and over. She touches Silas's cast, then looks at Aunt Claudia with a scared face. She hugs them both, but Isabelle has a hard time hugging her back. Until the second she saw her through the car window, this person was her mother, she is Mom. End of story. But looking at her, being held by her, getting her tears all over the front of her sweater, a shift happens. This person is Mom, but also *not*-Mom. She is more like an aunt. Aunt Mom. Or a friend of Mom's. Someone else. She is like someone who has gone through a time portal and come out the other side changed. Part of her is missing, and there are new parts Isabelle doesn't recognize.

"Are you sick?" Isabelle asks her.

"I am, but I'll get better. I love you so much."

Meredith opens her eyes and stands up from the grass. She doesn't have to clean herself off because nothing sticks to her.

Silas wails when Mom tells them she has to go. He'd thought she was back for good, though Isabelle has already figured out this is just a visit. He only calms down when Mom and Aunt Claudia say they will do it again soon. They will meet in a park, or maybe in a special restaurant next time. Very soon. Meredith has to help Mom back into the car. The rest of them stand back. Somehow, they all know they aren't allowed to touch her, not even Silas.

Aunt Claudia promises to get them whatever they want. Ice cream and hot dogs. Isabelle wants sushi and the flavoured sparkling water she likes. Her mouth is dry. With Mom gone again, she doesn't want to play anymore. A man comes into the park with an angry-looking dog.

On the walk home, Silas says that Mom looked hungry. Aunt Claudia agrees. She says again that they have to keep this visit secret. It is important.

"We're all in a special club now. A secret club."

"The Mom Club!" Silas yells.

The Mom Club meets two more times, and both times Mom looks hungrier than the last and needs more help. The meetings are shorter, too. It is cold out on the last one, and Meredith makes Mom stay in the car while they all crowd around the door. They aren't supposed to touch her because of germs. Mom has a cane. She blows a kiss at Silas's arm, which is free of its cast, and asks Isabelle about school, her new teacher. The whole thing is over quick. And Silas keeps the secret, amazingly.

Dad finally figures out where Mom is. He says he was telling someone about what is going on with Mom, and when he told this person about the yoga studio and the crazy rich woman with the red hair, the person yelled, "I know that place! I used to go there!"

Dad's friend told him the rich lady is *a real force of nature.*

In her mind Isabelle pictures a kind of witch, with hair like fire, making the wind go crazy and bringing lightning down on her enemies. This image fits perfectly with the woman she met in the park.

Right away things start happening. Grampa Ron and Gramma Sue-Ann come around again, both of them agitated. Everyone is in the kitchen, and there are a million people talking at once. Donovan tells them the thing about the rich woman being a force of nature. Grampa Ron gets mad: "I don't care if she's the goddamn Bride of Frankenstein."

Silas yells, "Frankenstein!"

Plans get made. Grampa Ron talks about calling the police, but Gramma Sue-Ann tells him not to be stupid, which would normally make Isabelle giggle, except she's bothered by the thought of the police. She doesn't like the idea of her mother having *anything* to do with police. She doesn't say anything about Mom Club, somehow knowing this is one of the moments when keeping a secret is most important.

Everyone is talking too much — Grampa Ron, Gramma Sue-Ann, Aunt Claudia. Silas is running around, yelling with delight at all the commotion. Isabelle and Dad are the only ones being quiet. She keeps looking at him, expecting him say something that will make sense of what's going on, but he sits in a kitchen chair looking half asleep. He has his phone out, and is staring at it as if he's alone. Isabelle leans over to see what he's looking at, and is not surprised that he is in Google Street View. She can see a big white house. While she's watching, he looks up something else, and ends up in something called the Dream Sack.

Grampa Ron walks around and around the kitchen and says he is going to do what should have been done a long time ago: drive across the city to where this woman lives and bring Mom home — in whatever state she's in. He announces this to everyone there.

"Let *me* go," Aunt Claudia says. "I can talk to her."

Grampa Ron says no. He's sick of waiting around. "You've all been sitting around on your arses ..."

"Ron," Gramma Sue-Ann says.

"She might not want to come," Aunt Claudia says. "She's not a little kid, Dad. You can't just order her around."

"She's *acting* like a goddamn baby. I'm sick of it."

Dad offers some mild objections to Grampa Ron's plan. Showing up out of the blue like this might make Mom angry, might cause her to do something crazy.

"Crazy like what?" Grampa Ron demands to know. "This whole thing is crazy."

"She might do something desperate. You back people into a corner ..."

"Kill herself? Is that what you're talking about? Why are you even saying that? She's not the type. Neither of my girls are the type."

"I don't mean that."

The very idea of Mom killing herself makes Isabelle feel cold. There is a girl in her new class whose older sister committed suicide. One night when the rest of the family went out for dinner at a restaurant, she tied a shirt around her neck and hung herself in her bedroom closet. Everyone at school knew the details. It was the worst thing that ever happened to anyone.

"She might refuse to come," Dad says. "She probably will, in fact."

Isabelle wonders if Grampa Ron will start yelling again, but instead he goes quiet and looks at the floor. He looks tired.

"Donovan," he says. "I know Cat's your wife and you've got two beautiful children here and a beautiful house. But she's my daughter. Whatever happened between you two, whatever it is that set her off on this — it has to end right *now*."

Dad doesn't say anything more about Mom refusing to come back, and nobody says anything more about suicide, which Isabelle is very grateful for. She doesn't want to think about that again for as long as she lives. Grampa Ron tells her father to get himself ready. The two of them are going to this Meredith person's house right away. He says he would go on his own, but Dad needs to be there, too. Dad doesn't say anything, doesn't say yes or no. When Grampa Ron gets his jacket and his car keys and starts heading out of the house, Dad follows him like a teenager in trouble.

Aunt Claudia stays awhile, but she can't stand still. She is agitated and scared. She looks like she is going to cry. Finally, she says she has to go home.

"Go see your baby," Gramma Sue-Ann tells her quietly.

More than two hours later — Isabelle has been watching the clock — Grampa Ron and Dad come back. Dad doesn't say anything. He walks up the stairs to his and Mom's bedroom and closes the door. Silas wants to chase after him, but Gramma Sue-Ann tells him no. She has been trying to teach Silas how to play checkers, but mostly he's been stacking the pieces as high as they will go, then knocking them over with a hard swipe of his hand and laughing.

Grampa Ron comes in, looking mad — but not the same kind of mad as when he left. A deeper mad. He is moving more slowly.

"He didn't even get out of the goddamn car. Sue-Ann, he sat there in the goddamn car and wouldn't get out."

"What did you say to him?"

Grampa Ron lets out a huff of breath. "I told him he had to get himself together and take care of this. The little ... he just sat there. Said he couldn't do it. I almost broke the goddamn steering wheel."

"Did you go see her?"

Grampa Ron doesn't say anything at first. When he speaks again, his voice sounds weird — choked and small.

"She wouldn't let me in."

"Who?"

Grampa Ron makes an exasperated noise. "That woman. That crazy woman. She said I couldn't see Cat until I calmed down. I was ready to strangle her."

"Ron ..."

The two of them go into the kitchen. Isabelle can hear Grampa Ron breathing heavily in short stabs that come quickly, like he's scared or he's been running. There is the sound of a chair scraping and someone sitting down heavily. Nobody talks for a while. Silas finally gets all the checker pieces stacked together, then takes an enormous swing at his tower.

"How was she?" Isabelle hears Gramma Sue-Ann ask.

There is a sound like someone grunting, like Grampa Ron is eating something hot. He can't catch his breath. Isabelle realizes, with a shock, that he is crying. She throws a red checker piece as hard as she can against the wall, which makes Silas laugh.

• • •

A few days later, on a morning that looks like it might rain, Aunt Claudia offers to take Silas for a walk through the park. Isabelle hears him asking her about Mom Club, and her telling him *not today*. Dad is in his room when they leave. He comes out as soon as they're gone, looking smelly and tired, and leans into Isabelle's room to tell her he's going to see Grampa Don and Gramma Ruth. He might even sleep over there. He says he'll call Aunt Claudia and let her know — she's already said she would stay the night, anyway.

"Can I come?" Isabelle asks.

She doesn't really want to see Grampa Don and Gramma Ruth — she's midway through a new book and enjoying it, and her room is extra comfortable today — but wants to see what her father will say to this request.

He runs his hand through his hair, which is getting long and scraggly. He's wearing a Blue Jays T-shirt that doesn't look like it fits. He burps a little without noticing he's doing it. She hates that he burps so much now. The boys in her new class have a whole competition about burping swear words.

"You'll be bored, Iz. We have to talk about some things. Boring money stuff. I won't really be able to do anything with you, and Gramma Ruth and Grampa Don won't be able to, either."

"They never do anything with me. Or with Silas."

Dad winces. "That's not true, come on." He burps again.

"Am I old enough to be home alone?"

Donovan has to think about this.

"It's fine," Isabelle says before he can reply. "You go. I'll stay here."

. . .

It smells dusty in the back bedroom, but otherwise it's not much different than any other room in the house, just a little emptier. She isn't sure why they are not allowed to go in it. The bed is messy, as if someone slept in it last night, though no one has slept in here for months and months, as far as she knows. There's nothing in here, just the bed and a night table and the desk and Mom's office chair.

Mom's computer is broken. The big TV part is on the floor. The keyboard is on the floor, too, and looks like it was driven over by a car. There is a big mark on the wall. This was either Mom, which would be crazy, or Silas. That's probably why they are not allowed in here. Isabelle is willing to bet her little brother came in during one of his wild fits and smashed the computer. She's sad to see it like this. Mom won't be happy.

Or maybe it was the new lady who did it. Maybe she was so mad about having to clean Silas's pee all over the place that she came in her and broke Mom's computer.

She should be fired, Isabelle decides. They don't need someone cleaning the house. She can do it. Her and Aunt Claudia.

Isabelle finds the paper she wants, the really good kind, and carefully slips a sheet of it from the package. She takes a few extra sheets, so she can practise writing the note. She wants it to be perfect. She wants the letters to be neat. In her own room, she moves everything off her desk and looks for a good pen. She finds one she has never used, from last summer's computer camp. The pen is a pen on one side, a laser pointer on the other. Her dad couldn't understand why a computer camp would give the kids lasers — it's just irresponsible, he said.

Her note will be short, she decides. She had all kinds of things she was planning to write in it, but now, with the laser pen in her hand and the paper in front of her, she decides that the best thing to do is keep it short and simple. *KISS* — she learned that idea in school this year. Her teacher says it stands for *Keep It Simple, Students*, but nobody believes him. They all know the last word is *Stupid*. Her friend Amanda says it all the time, even when they are doing something that has nothing to do with keeping things simple, just swinging on the swings or eating their lunch. *Keep it simple, stupid.* It's so dumb, but it makes Isabelle laugh. Which is probably why she's been hanging around with Amanda lately — she's the only girl who makes Isabelle laugh, even if it's not always clear that she's trying to.

She knows exactly what she wants to say, and can already see the letters in her head. She scratches the pen across a corner of the recycled paper a few times, just to make sure it's working, then writes her note:

> *Dear Mom,*
>> *How are you? I am good. Dont worry I am taking care of Silas. You dont have to come home if you dont want to.*
>> *Isabelle Greene xoxoxo*

XVI

IT'S HARD TO CLIMB STAIRS. HE'S NOT SURE HE CAN
still do it — much better to be carried. But Meredith is in the
big room on the main floor, stretched out on a couch, completely out of it, so Louis will have to climb them on his own,
the way he did when he was a puppy, and for years after that.
He is certain he *used* to be able to climb stairs, but everything
about the time before now is very unclear to him. This much
is clear, however: if he wants to go up to where the sick woman
is sleeping, he will have to pull himself up onto each and every
step, without any help.

Unless someone offers to carry him. Unless Meredith gets
up from the couch where she has spent most of the past week.
She's not sleeping, just lying flat out with her eyes open, staring at something unseen, with a white thing clamped over her

head. Whenever she sighs or shifts her body, he gets excited that she is about to sit up, speak to him. Perhaps even take him outside, where he can pee and explore and fall asleep in the shade.

He sits close to Meredith. He is not allowed in this clean room, but all the usual rules have been forgotten, maybe because of the sick woman upstairs. He whimpers to get her attention.

"Louis," she says, and nothing else.

He whimpers again.

He wants her to talk to him, to tell him he's good. To explain the nature of his goodness to him. She has explained his goodness to him so often and so well that he can go whole days without needing to be told. The knowledge of his own goodness gets lodged deep within his body. It glows and warms him while she is away or sleeping. But it has been weeks since she has given him any attention at all. The sick person upstairs drains away all of her attention and all of her energy and all of her happiness. The woman who cleans the house will fill his bowl and give him water, and then let him outside to run while she works, and he will gratefully poop and pee in each corner of the yard. But that woman never comes outside with him. Nobody comes outside with him. After a while he gets spooked by all the noises, by the absence of Meredith, and will whine to be let back in.

The house is quiet today, after so many days with so much noise. So many people coming through, talking and singing and chanting. Today there is only Meredith and the two women upstairs. He wants to see them, especially the sick person, Cat. He only gets a glimpse of her when Meredith carries him up to bed. They look in, but she is never awake.

Meredith makes a noise. She is sleeping.

. . .

As hard as it is to do so, Louis leaves Meredith's side and walks
to the bottom of the stairs. The whole way there, he fights to
keep one idea in his mind, to not become distracted: *climb,*
climb, climb. A rubber chew toy is on the floor in the hallway
near the stairs. The desire to grab it in his jaws, to twist and
pull at it, is nearly overwhelming, but he walks right past. He
gets distracted so easily now that he will sometimes find himself in a part of the house by himself, sniffing at a corner or
staring out the window, unable to remember how he got there
or what he was sniffing for.

At the bottom of the stairs, it is worse than he remembers;
the first step reaches almost to his snout. Impossible. And yet,
he did this before. He is sure of it. He puts one paw up on the
step, then drops it back down. A sound comes from above, the
scrape of a chair on the floor. He lets out a small whine, hoping
someone will appear to carry him. He puts both front paws on
the stairs, tenses himself, and tries to launch himself forward.
His back paws push as his front paws pull, and a charge of pain
goes through him. His back hips are filled with broken glass.
But he is on the first stair. He has made it this far. He stretches
forward and up with his front paws again, and pushes with
his rear, whimpering a little at the broken-glass pain. He does
this again and again. After a half-dozen stairs, he is barking
slightly each time he draws himself up to the next. The pain is
no longer just in his hips, but has spread out into the rest of his
body. Every joint is bright with hurt. His back legs don't feel
like they are his.

When he is far enough up that there are as many stairs
below him as there are above, he stops to rest. He is hot and

has to pant hard just to stay awake. He can't see the bottom of the stairs very well anymore, and the top of the stairs is a blur. The world goes grey and silent for a little while. When the greyness clears, it is darker in the house. He is still on the stairs. Someone is holding him too hard, squeezing him. He puts his front paws up on the next step and continues.

He has no sense of how long the sick person named Cat has been in the house. She appeared at some point, and didn't leave. He is sure she was not here when he was a puppy, when he was able to race up and down the stairs, to leap up onto beds, and to chase animals in the yard. She was bright and fast and loud when she first appeared. She moved things around, cleaned rooms, cried and cried, and took him for short walks down the street that were quickly abandoned when it became clear he could not go more than a few house lengths before needing to lie down and to sleep. She would stand there, saying his name over and over again and shaking her head, then carry him back — not as comfortably as Meredith does, but as if he were some-thing dead and discarded. She would hold his body away from her body, talking the whole time about his stink and his fur. When they got back home, she would wash her hands. But she would try again, a few days later, fixing a leash to his collar and coaxing him outside with a treat. The results would be the same: his breath flying out of him a few doors down, and her carrying him like a bag of garbage, swearing and telling him she would not try again.

Those moments were enough to make him love her. The minute or so when she held him, carried him back to the house — he could sense the goodness in her. She hurt him while she carried him, but he could tell she was not trying to, and he did not bark at her or bite her for it. Before she began to stay in bed all day, she would sometimes sit in the kitchen with him when Meredith was gone and hold out a toy for him. Sometimes she would throw it for him to retrieve, and sometimes he was able to do so, though more often he lost track of what he was looking for before he was able to locate it, and she would say his name and shake her head. Sometimes she would only hold the toy in her hands and look sad, and he would be forgotten. But he still loved her.

At the top of the stairs, he does not stop to rest, though his body is being pushed to the ground by fatigue. He can sense a tide of sleep sliding toward him, a darker sleep than he has ever known. The tide is black and cool. It touches the tips of his paws, tugs at them, but he keeps moving along the hallway. He doesn't worry about his goodness now, or about Meredith or the woman who cleans the house. He doesn't need to pee or poop. He only needs to stay ahead of the black tide, to step out of it each time it reaches him with its comfortable suck. His paws are immersed in it, they've gone numb. He can feel the movement of his tail behind him, but can't feel the tail itself. In one eye the hallway appears normal. The other eye is filled with dark fog. He tries to blink away the fog, but it only gets thicker. The floor doesn't feel flat anymore — it slopes upward like a ramp. If he stops moving, he will slide back, tumble down the stairs, get lost in the fog.

The door of the room with the sick person named Cat is open, and Louis is able to slip through it before the tipping of the floor slides him sideways. He is panting heavily, and each pant escapes him with a small squeak, as if his breath is scraping against something inside his throat. He waits to be scolded, for someone to tell him to leave. It is brighter and cooler in this room. There is a tall fan in the corner, moving its head back and forth in sadness. Things are burning in little bowls; lazy tails of smoke flick slowly above them. It smells like fire and flowers. The sick person is in the bed in the centre of the room. The woman Wendy is in a chair near the bed. She is asleep. Louis can't tell if Cat is also asleep. He can only see her arm, pale and thin along the edge of the bed.

He pulls himself past the fan and closer to the bed. He is sure he was once able to jump from the floor up to the bed. He can picture doing it in his mind, can imagine the act. In Meredith's room he has a large, deep purple cushion bed that is warmed and cooled by some unseen power. From the cushion bed, he can lie there and watch Meredith sleep, though he often falls asleep before she does. Meredith, despite knowing about his goodness, will not let him sleep with her in the big bed. She blames this on his fur and his smell and his tendency to fill the darkness with dog farts.

A fart — giving no warning, as usual — escapes him as he stands in the room with the sick woman. The numbness in his paws spreads up each leg. He is being lifted up, as if by invisible hands. He sits down hard, pressing his numb rump to the bare floor to avoid floating away. He barks to ward off whatever is attempting to whisk him out of his own life.

There is a rustle in the bed, and a weak voice: "Louis?"

The voice is strained and faint, full of dark bubbles. Meredith and the other people who were in the house have not been letting the sick woman eat. He has heard them say that she must not eat. If they make her as light as they can, as empty as they can, she will float out of her illness. Or perhaps her illness, seeing that its prey has become thin and unnourishing, will slip away of its own accord.

If he could, Louis would tell them this will not work. He can smell how deep the sickness goes in this woman. It has its teeth in her. It's in her bones.

He tries to bark again. It comes out like a sharp cough.

"Louis," the weak voice says again.

His ears twitch at the sound. There is a hum in them that he cannot shake.

Cat's pale hand moves, and the whole bed shifts and creaks with her attempt to sit up so she can see him. After a few moments, the shifting and creaking stop and the woman's body settles back.

"Fuck's sake ..."

He can hear breath going in and out of the sick woman, and can smell her. She smells like sweat and illness and lavender and lemons. His tail moves, though he no longer feels it. Something below him is wet; he has peed on the floor without meaning to. He is sorry about that. He moves toward Cat's hand, dragging his hind legs with him — the climb up the stairs has drained them. He can almost feel his bones and muscles fusing and going dark. The numbness has moved up into his body, and he must fight the urge to splay out where he is. The floor here has no carpet and is wonderfully cool.

He pulls himself forward until he is directly below her hand. If only he could straighten himself up, get his front paws up on the side of the bed and stretch forward, he could touch her fingers with his nose. He has forgotten about Meredith and his cushion bed. It's not clear to him how long it's been since he has eaten or had a drink of water, but it doesn't matter. He is being lifted out of his pain, the way he hopes the sick woman will soon be. He is floating into a realm of warmth and comfort. He pushes himself up, trying to get his paws onto the side of the bed, and manages to catch the edge of the sheets with his long toenails, which have not been cut in months. He is hanging there now, suspended between the bed and the floor.

Cat can sense him, can feel his weight pulling against the sheets, and she tries to sit up again.

He tries to bark to let her know that he is there, that he is attempting to reach her, to touch her hand, but his breath is gone. Still hooked to the sheets by his toenails, the dark tide overtakes him, engulfs him, and for a few seconds he is nothing but goodness.

XVII

ON THE DAY OF THE FUNERAL, LENA WAKES UP CRY-ing. As she always does, she falls out of sleep seconds before the alarm on her phone goes off. The side of her face is wet, and there is a damp patch on her pillow the size of a small hand. Her body could not wait to declare its sadness, to release it into the air. She checks the weather on her phone and sees that, after a week of springlike sun and warmth, it is supposed to snow again this weekend.

It's still early. The restaurant has only just started serving breakfast. Hotcakes and apple pies and lots of coffee, but also Big Macs and french fries and big milkshakes, because many of the people who come to eat at this time of the day have not yet gone to bed. Some come in to sleep sitting up on the hard chairs, or with their faces down on the tables.

She showered before bed the night before, so all she needs to do is eat something, slip on the black dress hanging carefully in the kitchen, and fix her hair, which won't take long. She's been growing her hair out. It's already touching her shoulders. Patricia says she still looks like a boy, but like a *pretty* boy, at least. Patricia's own hair is shorter now, so she might be feeling jealous. Patricia's boyfriend tells her he likes short hair better. His wife has short hair, as does the actress he has a huge crush on, and because he has finally left his wife and children for her, she feels obligated to keep it short. The first time Lena saw it, she laughed, and Patricia hit her hard on the arm. Short hair doesn't suit her.

Lena is not growing her hair for anyone. She's tired of hacking at it in the shower, of feeling the little clumps of hair cling and tickle her as they slip down her body, pushed into oblivion by the force of the water. Plus, she is ready for a change.

For someone to die is a kind of change, but obviously not the one she was hoping for.

Timothy from the Bible study group is gone. After more than a year of disappearing, of being deflated by an invisible illness, he finally dies in his sleep. Ria, one of the Trinidadian sisters from the group, calls Lena when she is on her way home from work. Lena wonders how the woman got her phone number, then remembers that, at some point early on, everyone was asked to add their contact info to a shared list to make cancellations easier.

"*Oooohhh*," Ria moans by way of hello.

"That's so sad," Lena says when she hears the news.

For the past few months, Timothy had been shrinking a little more in his old suit and spending more time in the bathroom. He still wasn't exactly nice to her, but he was milder and more willing to let her arrive and leave without comment. Lena only realizes this after she hears that he's dead. She wishes she'd realized it earlier, so she could've revised her feelings about him while he was alive. Is it selfish to appreciate an improvement in the way someone behaves if that improvement only occurs because they are dying? And should a newly dead person be judged in this way at all, or have they passed beyond such judgment? She assumes the answers to questions like this are in the Bible somewhere, though maybe not direct answers. More likely a story or a sermon or a psalm that suggests she ought to rethink the whole idea of judgment, open herself to the idea that asking such a question in the first place may be what is preventing her from finding the Truth. Which isn't much help. It would be easier to ask Patricia. Or look on YouTube.

Ria tells her Timothy was found in his bed by one of his neighbours. Somehow, Ria already knows all about it, every detail, which means her sister knows all about it, too. A story like this only comes around every once in a while, and the two sisters will not be denied their chance to feed on it from nose to tail, to chew and digest every scrap like hungry cats in the wild.

Ria lets out another moan.

"God bless him."

The neighbour entered Timothy's apartment because the front door was open and he wanted to make sure there hadn't been a robbery or a home invasion. Ria knows what happened: the Lord himself opened that door. Jesus reached out and undid the lock — what is a common door lock to the Son of God, the King of Kings? Slap on the biggest one you can find. He will push it open with his beautiful, damaged hands. Jesus was there in that bedroom, she tells Lena, standing beside Timothy as he crossed over, comforting him and waiting to take him home.

"That's so sad," Lena says again. She has never liked the idea of a hand-holding Jesus appearing at people's deathbeds. For Jesus to show up every time someone is dying makes Him look weak, even hypocritical. If anyone is in a position to do something about the whole issue of mortality and death, it is him. What would really be useful, she thinks, would be for Jesus to appear, not just in the rooms of those passing on to another plane of existence, when it's too late, but also of those feeling bored, restless, and unmotivated. That's when people *really* need him. He could show up for her when she is glued to her apartment, when she is thirsty and humming from all the weed in her system, when she is stopping herself from looking at other people having sex or sneaking down to the laundry room to steal clothes, just to have something to do.

He could provide a pep talk, as only he can. *Go out. Have fun. Be blessed.*

At the next meeting of the Bible study group, they do nothing but pray and pray for the safe passage of Timothy's soul to heaven as if trying to push his soul up through a tight celestial tube. Everyone comes, even some members who have drifted away or who are usually too busy with work to attend. Nobody mentions how Lena has hardly been there lately. They talk about how Timothy used to leave his jacket behind after the meetings all the time. And how he stopped using other people's

names, and would exclusively refer to other people in the group
as birds. One was Pigeon, another was Robin, another Finch.
Lena was Sparrow. She hated the name.

After the meeting, desperate to get the sound of prayer out
her head, Lena goes to Rabba's. Javed is busy with a young
woman buying bananas, so she wanders up and down each
aisle. She has become so familiar with the layout of the store
and the stock on the shelves that she is able to answer people
when they ask her where to find things. They always assume
she works there. One time a lady came in wearing pantyhose
over her jogging pants and asked to see the manager. To her
surprise, Javed agreed to talk to her, and when she left — there
wasn't a scene, though the lady's eyes were as huge and black as
buttons — he just shrugged, smiled, and said she lived in the
neighbourhood and came in every once in a while, looking for
a job. He said he always tells her to bring in her CV, then she
disappears for a long time. She's harmless.

"No McDonald's today, Fry Girl?"

"Day off."

"Lucky."

Javed asks how thing are going at work, and she admits to
him that, although the place is obviously awful and the money
is not good, she has been there long enough to have some seniority — people come and go fast — and the manager trusts her
now, so it is better than before. She doesn't have anything to do
with the big yellow bags of garbage anymore, and sometimes
the manager asks her to help with the work schedule. They have
a lot of students working there, some people in night classes,
too, so scheduling is a pain.

"I could just tell people when they have to come in and
let them figure it out," the manager tells her. "But I don't like

doing that. If people are going to school, that's good. We work around it if we can."

It's the first time she notices how large and sympathetic her manager's eyes are. Which is a shock.

She tells Javed this, and is pleased by his reaction. He looks jealous.

Timothy's funeral is attended by the other members of the Bible study group, plus the neighbour who found the body and one of Timothy's adult sons, who doesn't speak to anyone and leaves as soon as the brief ceremony is over. Lena is amazed at how little the son looks like Timothy. His skin is not even the same tint of brown. Timothy was pale, with dozens of irregular black freckles stirred in like raisins. This son is inky and dark. His mother must be even darker. Lena has to remind herself that she only knew Timothy in the last few years of his life, when all the best of him had already leeched out, leaving an empty space that the illness was eager to occupy. Lena guesses that the son is here because he paid for the funeral and wants to make sure it is conducted as per the terms he'd agreed on. He doesn't even go to the front to look inside the casket.

Lena does. She makes herself join the short line of sad people waiting for their turn to confirm that Timothy's soul has indeed left his body, that the only thing left is a well-groomed corpse. To get through the funeral, she swallowed two gummies. Her body feels exactly as snug and padded as the coffin. Timothy is wearing a new suit that fits him, which makes her happy. He looks thin, but not unhealthily so. His skin is pale, like his whole body has been brushed with powder.

His dark hands, which were always trembling slightly and fidgeting while he was alive, are at peace and folded together on his chest.

Later on, in the reception area, Lena is hugged hard by the sisters, Ria and Anya, who wet her hair with their tears. While she has Lena in a tight grip, Anya tells her all about how Timothy left the door to his apartment open, and how his neighbour — who at that moment is standing alone at the edge of the small group — found Timothy there on his bed. Lena doesn't say that she has already heard all this from Ria. She waits patiently to be told there was a third man in the apartment, a very *special* man, with very special wounds on his hands and feet.

In mid-squeeze Lena remembers what Timothy used to call Ria and Anya: the Turkeys.

Everyone is standing around drinking coffee and tea. A woman with shock-white hair comes at her with a hungry smile. Her name is Katrina. Lena has seen this woman moving around the room, from group to group. Her white hair is easy to track from a distance. When Katrina comes over, Lena assumes she will say something about how they are blessed to all be there, or that Timothy is with God now. People have been saying things like it to her ever since the formal part of the funeral ended.

Instead, she asks if Lena is still cleaning houses.

"I'm right about that? You clean houses?"

Lena is taken aback. She isn't sure the two of them have ever spoken before, and can't imagine how she would know about her housecleaning work.

"No, I stopped. A while ago. I got something else."

"Oh, that's good. Good for you. Something a little easier, I hope?"

"It's … different."

"And different is better?"

"It's better." Lena laughs out of self-consciousness.

The white-haired woman nods, satisfied, and offers to get her a coffee. She is planning to have another herself. Lena says no — she's drinking tea.

"Ooohh, that's smart. I *really* like your dress."

"Thank you."

Lena looks quickly at Katrina's dress, which is mostly hidden beneath a jumble of coloured scarves. She has a pair of thick-rimmed glasses on a chain around her neck.

"What makes your job better, your new one?" Katrina is standing very close, so close she could easily lean in for a bite. If she were a bird, she'd be some kind of vulture or crow. "The hours, the money, was your old boss a creep — what makes it better?"

"It's closer to my apartment. It's a restaurant."

"Oh interesting. I always wanted to work as a waiter. I think that would be fun for a while. Running around. New people every night."

She waits for Katrina to leave to get coffee, but instead the woman slumps a little and shakes her head dramatically. The scarves flutter around her.

"I didn't know if I was going to come today, I really didn't. Tell me if I'm a bad person for this, and be honest. It's embarrassing, but whatever. Last year, I loaned Timothy some money."

"That was nice of you."

"It was. But here's the thing, he never paid me back. Not a cent. Not that I was really expecting him to. But he promised. And he never said sorry. I thought, *if he didn't think enough of me to even apologize … am I a bad person?*"

Lena doesn't say what she is thinking, which is that everyone she meets is fundamentally a bad person. The hard part is
working out *how* bad.

"How much money?"

"Did I give him? Oh my God, it's not even important. A
lot."

She tells Lena anyway: more than two thousand dollars.
Lena's face betrays her surprise.

"That was very generous of you."

Katrina leans in closer. "I know Timothy didn't have a lot
of money — he couldn't have, if he was borrowing off me. But
here's the thing, he borrowed from other people in the group,
too, and he paid some of *them* back. Not all of them — I've
been asking around — but some, for sure. That's what's bothering me, that he was selective about it. And I didn't get selected. He didn't think I was important enough to pay back, so he
didn't. And that really burns. It was a lot of money."

"I think you should forget about it," Lena tells her.

Katrina laughs with a huff. "I'm trying to, I really am."

"You have to forget about the money. It was a gift.
Timothy's dead now, so he doesn't have your money anymore,
and he can't say he's sorry."

"I'm not looking for an apology." Katrina isn't smiling
anymore.

"Yes, you are. But you won't get it. Timothy is dead."

"I *know* that."

"Then forgive him. And then maybe *you* will be forgiven."

Lena turns and walks away, ashamed and exhilarated, her
face burning. She grabs her winter coat, which is hanging from
one of the chairs. As she puts it on, she looks through her pockets to see if she brought any more gummies. Her phone rings,

but the number comes up an *unknown*, so she ignores it. As she approaches the doors leading outside, a young man walking behind her says, "Nice." He is young, maybe nineteen or twenty, but dressed like an older man. He leers at her as they go through the glass doors together and glances down at her legs.

"*Very* nice."

Then he waggles his car keys at her.

On the bus Lena listens to piano music, something she has not done in a while. She has been loving Chopin, who makes her feel like she is lowering herself in a deep bathtub and letting warm, soapy water rise over her ears.

She doesn't want to go home right away. She doesn't want to lock herself in her apartment. She doesn't want to go looking for naked brown bodies. Not yet. She is not scheduled to work, which means that if she goes into her apartment now, she might not come out of it again until tomorrow. Which makes her think of Timothy leaving his door ajar for the coming of our Lord.

When the bus stops in front of the Rabba's, a few stops before her own, she steps off without thinking.

Has Javed ever seen her in a dress? Probably not — she only owns two, including this one, and would never wear either to the store. She's wearing makeup, too, which she knows he hasn't seen on her in any significant quantity. She wants to see if he will notice, what he will say. She smiles in anticipation of being teased.

Her phone rings again. Again, an unknown number. She answers, just in case it's someone from the funeral. Maybe she forgot something. Maybe Timothy sat up in the coffin.

"Hello?"

"Oh, uh, hello? Is this, uh, *Leena*?"

"This is Lena."

"Oh okay, *Lay-na*. Sorry. I just have your name here."

The voice is female and familiar, but she can't place it. There is a slight edge to it, as if this call has already stretched her patience. The voice has a strange echo, too. She sounds like she is calling from a large, open space.

"You're a housecleaner, right? You clean houses?"

How does this question keep following her?

"Sort of. I used to be."

"Good. Listen, are you super busy? We need to get a house cleaned. Pretty soon, if that's possible."

"I *am* busy," Lena says. The big doors of the Rabba's slide open, and a man comes out pushing a stroller. He has a pack of diapers balanced on its hood. Inside, swaddled in multiple blankets, a small, dark face peers out with a look of curiosity and fear.

"Okay, so, this wouldn't be like a regular cleaning job, like week to week," the woman tells her. "We just need a one-time job before we sell the house. A really thorough one, like all the windows and the bathrooms and everything. Can you do that? It would have to be early next week, if you can do it. Our regular person can't."

"I don't actually clean houses anymore."

There is a noise on the other end, and the woman's voice is lost for a moment.

"Sorry, what's that? Listen, my name is Claudia — I think you used to clean for my sister? Cat? Catherine Joseph? That's how I have your name. It's Cat's house that I need to get cleaned."

Lena freezes. A woman pulling a young girl out of the store makes a huffing noise and steps around her. The young girl, whose arm is in danger of being pulled out of its socket by her mother, looks around at Lena as they pass.

"Hello? *Lay-na*?"

"Yes."

"You knew Cat? You used to clean her house?"

"Yes."

"Okay!"

Lena recognizes the woman's tone: exasperated at how long it is taking to explain a simple matter.

"We have to sell the house, and the usual person is not available. I'm calling you because you know the place. That's right, right? You used to work for Cat and Donovan, right?"

Something stops Lena from agreeing to this, though it is only a statement of fact. She waits for the woman to continue. She is told the real estate agent wants to start showing the house the following week, so they need the place cleaned quickly. If she has time before then, that'd be great. They could pay extra.

"Why are they selling it?"

There is a snarl of glitchy sound. "What? Sorry?"

"Why are they selling the house?"

Lena can hear Claudia take a deep breath. In her mind Lena sees the crumpled version of Cat who answered the door to her and Patricia last summer. When she got home that night, Lena felt sick to her stomach. She actually ran to the bathroom a few times, thinking she was going to throw up. She kept thinking about how her cousin called her mean, and how the two of them laughed.

"Is she okay?"

Claudia's voice grows quiet. "So, I don't know how much you knew about what was going on."

She tells Lena that Cat was very sick, that she had breast cancer and died less than three months ago.

"Can you hold on a second?" Claudia says, and Lena hears the sound of a phone being smothered by a hand. The sidewalk shifts beneath her. Each time she sways forward, the store's automatic doors swish open. Javed appears to see what's going on. He's wearing a maroon-coloured golf shirt with one side of the collar trapped inside. He must not have noticed, and she imagines fixing it for him. He smiles when he sees her.

"Everything is out of the house," Claudia says when she comes back on the line. "All the furniture is gone, but it's a mess. Nobody's been taking care of it for a while. I'm sorry."

Lena tells Claudia she needs to call her back.

Javed is back behind the counter, dealing with a woman buying a dozen single-serving yogourts with half-price stickers on them. When he's done with her, he makes a big deal about Lena's dress and her makeup, but she isn't interested anymore. She picks the yogourts up off the counter — the woman decided she didn't want so many — and takes them back to the dairy section. She tells Javed about the call, and the request from Cat's sister. She doesn't tell him about Donovan, but says that she was treated badly.

"Not by both of them. Just the husband."

Javed tells her to ignore the request. These people, whoever they are, can deal with their own problems. She says she's not sure about that.

"She died, the wife. Her sister said she had cancer."

"So? Did *you* make her sick?"

Lena shakes her head, but she's not sure. By telling her what her husband did, by pouring all that poison in her ear, she may have allowed whatever illness to take hold and destroy the woman. Because that's what she was trying to do. Seeing Cat standing there in the front hallway, sweating and crying and on the verge of collapse in her big house, swearing at them for interrupting her day, distraught about having to have another baby with Donovan — it had enraged Lena. Not in a way that made her lose control, lose her temper. Exactly the opposite. She remembers becoming strangely calm the moment she realized what was going on, what had happened. She still can't explain it. All the anger and resentment and fear she'd been feeling left her body, slid up and out of her mouth like a sharpened stick that she aimed directly at the other woman's chest, at her heart. She slid that stick between Cat's ribs as slowly as she could. And then walked away, laughing.

"Is it money?" Javed asks. "Do you need some extra money? I can lend you some."

She smiles and reaches to fix his collar.

A few days later, Lena is on the porch. All the toys are gone, but the chalk marks are still on the brick wall. She wonders if they will want her to wash those away herself. The cat decoration is gone, too. There is no wind outside, but it's cold.

A woman opens the door, smiling. She says nothing. She is holding her phone near her face. Lena guesses this is Claudia. She has on a long black coat that holds her body like a wrap. Her black boots have enormous heels. Her blond hair is pinned back and shot through with dark streaks.

"That's fine, I can be here to give him the keys," she says into the phone.

Claudia silently mouths the word *Lena*. A question. When Lena nods, she motions for her to come inside, then walks quickly through the house to the kitchen, her boots resounding on the bare floors. The hallway is empty, except for a few small scraps of paper, some unopened junk mail, and magazines stacked neatly on the floor. There are square-shaped ghosts on the bare walls where mirrors and pictures hung. Lena takes a pair of running shoes out of her bag, slips her boots off, and puts the shoes on.

Claudia clops back in a rush, sighing loudly as she comes.

"Oh, don't worry about boots," she says.

Lena quietly ties her laces. She can't clean in boots, she explains. Claudia watches her take a bottle of water out of the bag, open it, and take a sip. "Okay," she says when Lena closes the bottle again. Her face is flushed, and she moves with the hurried impatience Lena remembers well from her first meetings with her old clients.

Claudia picks up the magazines, looks at a few of the covers, then holds them out to Lena.

"Do *you* want these?"

Lena shakes her head, so Claudia drops them back on the ground.

"Just recycle them, I guess. I don't need to show you around? The bedrooms are all empty, the kitchen is mostly empty. I wouldn't worry too much about the basement. It's really this floor and the upstairs we need done."

Claudia steps into the front room, where there used to be a dining table and a bookshelf. All of it is gone, even the gaudy, octopus-like light that hung low over the table. The wooden floor is scratched in some places, and there are scraps from cardboard boxes in the corners. A fat roll of packing tape is on the sill of the front window.

"It's not bad in here, actually," Claudia says. "Maybe just sweep and mop. The agent's going to bring in a ton of furniture later before they start showing it. It's a lot worse upstairs."

Lena follows her into the living room. There are wires and cables hanging from the walls. Someone has tried sweeping in here. More cardboard scraps, a few papers, a boy's sock.

Claudia picks up the sock, looks at it, then drops it back on the pile of scraps. She struggles with the side window, but can't get it open.

Lena sees a familiar toy among the scraps in the corner of the room: a green robot man who folds down into a sleek sports car. She steps over and picks it up. It takes her a few seconds to work out how the folding goes, but manages to get it all back into car form. She sets the toy on the windowsill so it won't get thrown out with the garbage.

"It's a nice house," Claudia is saying, "but it needs a ton of work. I would've opened up this whole first floor and put in some nicer lighting, bigger windows. Get more light and air. But anyway, it's great that you can do this on such short notice. There was this — *oh God* — there was a whole thing with the last person they had cleaning the place, so we were worried. Whatever. Thank you."

"What happened?"

Claudia goes back to looking at her phone.

"Sorry? Oh, with the other cleaner? It's not ... I actually don't know if she was even getting paid by the end. There was a lot going on. But you're here now, so we're all good."

"What happened to the family, I mean."

Claudia looks up at the ceiling, then back at Lena. "Oh God, well. We had some problems." She laughs, surprising herself. "Understatement of the century!"

"Please tell me. You said Cat was sick."

"Yeah, well, that and she took off for a long time. Did you know about that? She took off for, like, a long time. And when she came back, she needed a lot of help. But, you know, too late." She shakes her head. "It was really hard. I can't even think about it yet, to be honest."

"Did people help her?"

"Of course we did! That's *all* we fucking did! Sorry, that was rude. I was here all the time. So was my mom and dad. It was ridiculous. Even the kids helped."

"And her husband?"

Claudia lets out a bitter snort. "Oh, *sure*. I think I told you on the phone — did I tell you? Donovan is a bit of a ... well, he's fucking useless, sorry. Did you ever meet him?"

"Yes."

"Well, you probably saw some of that." She shakes her head again, then turns to Lena with a sudden look of panic on her face. "Oh, hey, so, did Donovan ... sorry, I have to ask you a weird question. There was all this shit with his job. It got weird, and he tried to sue them. Such an idiot. Anyway, it didn't work, and we all found out. Exactly what we needed just then."

"What was the question?"

"Oh God, right. You don't have to answer this if it makes you uncomfortable, but was he ever ... was Donovan ever *weird* with you? Like, with anything?"

Lena fights to keep her face as neutral as possible.

"No."

Claudia's shoulders drop, and her face slackens. For the first time, Lena can see the resemblance between the two sisters.

"Okay, good. That's good. Cat said some things, but I didn't know if it was real or just her being sick. Honestly, I don't think I can face any more shit about Donovan. Everyone is just starting to get better. We've all been in shock, I think. The kids are with my mom and dad for a while. Oh, and don't worry, there is a cheque for you on the kitchen counter. I don't want you to worry about that."

"Thank you."

"And *I'm* paying for this by the way. I didn't want to leave it up to anyone else, because who knows? I'm handling all the house stuff. Sort of helps me deal with everything. I like knowing it's being taken care of." She lets out a big breath before choking up. "It was really bad. I'm still ..."

Lena looks around at the room again. For a moment she imagines they are standing in the belly of a whale made of bricks and wood. "My mother died when I was little," she says quietly.

"Really? Of cancer?"

Lena shakes her head. "Something else. But I remember my father being sad, and everyone else being sad. I was two. I remember all that sadness more than I remember her."

"It's not fair. It's really not."

"Maybe. There should be more than just sadness when someone dies," Lena says. "Or else that's all you have left."

Claudia has to hide her faces as she cries. When she recovers, she tells Lena to not touch the medical equipment in the back bedroom.

"The bed is one of those hospital ones you can make go up or down. They're coming for it tomorrow. It's rented. Maybe just strip the sheets off the bed. Cat hated it, but she didn't want to be in a hospital. I get that. I should actually double-check that they're coming to get it."

"What happened to the baby?" Lena asks.

"Who, Silas? He's not really a baby anymore. He and Iz are at the school Cat and I used to go to in Peterborough. It looks totally different, though. My dad takes them every morning. Poor guy. Back at it."

"I mean Cat's baby. She was pregnant the last time I was here."

Claudia, perched in the middle of the empty living room on her grandiose boots, looks at Lena with shock. She struggles to say anything.

"It's okay," Lena says, stepping past her toward the kitchen. "I should get started."

It's a mess everywhere — bags open with garbage spilling out. Broken glasses and plates on the floor. Old pizza boxes with hard crusts. The cupboard doors are all open. Most still have food and cans in them. The fridge has been stripped of photos, but is still spotted with small magnets. Lena opens the door tentatively, takes a quick breath when the smell hits her, and pushes it shut before anything else can escape. The blinds are off the window, and Lena can see out to the back-yard, which is a tangle of brown and green. Muddy patches of frozen snow slouch in the shadows.

Claudia shows Lena the cleaning supplies. She says she got everything on the list Lena gave her, but asks her to make sure. Lena looks quickly through the bag of cleaning fluids and at the small stack of virgin cloths, the box of garbage bags, the bright mop still wrapped in plastic, the new bucket, the broom and dustpan. There is another bag with a few smaller things: gloves, masks, sponges. She tells Claudia she has everything she needs. She'll put all of it in the kitchen closet when she's done.

Claudia watches Lena fill the bucket with warm water and remove the plastic from the mop. Before she slips on the canary-yellow gloves, Lena hooks her hair behind her ears with her fingers.

"Did Cat *tell* you she was pregnant?" Claudia asks. "Did she tell you about the cancer, even?"

Lena lifts the bucket out of the sink and sets it gently on the floor without disturbing the sudsy water within.

"No. She didn't really tell me anything."

She dips the mop into the bucket to let it soak. She slips a garbage bag out of the box, hooks it in a belt loop at her waist, and grabs the broom by the neck.

"You don't have to be here while I'm doing this," she tells Claudia.

"Oh. You sure? Is it easier if I'm not here?"

"It is. You should go."

Claudia looks relieved by this, but is reluctant to move.

"It's fine," Lena says.

Claudia finally clomps back through the house in her boots. "I'll get rid of the magazines!" she shouts from the front hallway. A moment later the front door closes behind her.

Lena notices the bell still attached to the kitchen wall, next to the door. She carefully removes it, walks out into the living room, and places it near the toy car on the window ledge. She looks at it for moment, then picks it up again and walks over to her bag and drops it in.

She texts her cousin: *I have a gift for you.*

She takes the broom and starts up the stairs to the second floor, not worrying about being quiet. With each loud step, she takes possession of the house. By the time she reaches the top, the place is hers.

Acknowledgements

MANY THANKS TO:

Russell Smith, Kwame Scott Fraser, Erin Pinksen, Laura Boyle, and everyone at Dundurn Press. Shannon Whibbs. Zoe Whittall. Jen Sookfong Lee. Allison LaSorda. Jill Strimas. Carlo Javier. Kendra Marjerrison. Julie S. Lalonde. Andrew Pyper. Elyse Friedman. Rachel Matlow. Sarah-Jane Greenway. Guillermo Acosta. Vera Beletzan. Humber College. Martha Webb. Regan Leader. The Odette Cancer Centre at Sunnybrook Hospital. Paul and Mary Lou Strimas. Dr. Brianne Grogan. Theo Hendra.

I am grateful to the Woodcock Fund, administered by the Writers' Trust of Canada, and to the Ontario Arts Council, which helped fund the creation of this book through its Works for Publication program.

An earlier version of this book served as the thesis for a master of fine arts degree through the University of British Columbia and was assessed by Maureen Medved and Tariq Hussain.

Even more thanks (and love) to:

Meaghan, Lou, Olive, and Iago. (And Midge.)

About the Author

Photo by Kendra Marjerrison

NATHAN WHITLOCK is the author of the novels *A Week of This* and *Congratulations On Everything*. His work has appeared in the *New York Review of Books*, the *Walrus*, the *Globe and Mail*, *Best Canadian Essays*, and elsewhere. He lives with his family in Hamilton, Ontario.